SIGN WAVE

ANDREW VACHSS

Pantheon Books · New York

All rights reserved. Published in the United States by Pantheon Books, a division of Penguin Random House LLC, New York, and distributed in Canada by Random House of Canada, a division of Penguin Random House, Ltd., Toronto.

Pantheon Books and colophon are registered trademarks of Penguin Random House LLC.

Library of Congress Cataloging-in-Publication Data
Vachss, Andrew H.
SignWave : an Aftershock novel / Andrew Vachss.
pages ; cm
ISBN 978-1-101-87044-0 (hardcover).
ISBN 978-1-101-87045-7 (eBook).
I. Title.
PS3572.A33S54 2015   813'.54—dc23   2014043378

www.pantheonbooks.com
www.vachss.com

Jacket photograph: *Grave of Abelard* by Paul Thulin
Jacket design by Evan Gaffney Design

Printed in the United States of America
First Edition

9 8 7 6 5 4 3 2 1

Always an icy realist, Olaf knew he was too badly wounded to move, even if any of our team had remained behind to help. And the medic had been so panic-stricken that he'd forgotten to drop his kit before running for his life.

"Those who manage to return to base, each will have his own story to tell, but they all will match. Lying is the Esperanto of cowards."

Olaf spoke as he always did, in the confidently commanding tone of a surgeon ordering a nurse to hand him a scalpel. He never needed volume to get others to listen—if you had any sense, you just moved closer.

Even now, sprawled on the jungle floor with his life bleeding away, his voice was devoid of anger or bitterness. Assuring me he knew how to die quietly—it wouldn't be *his* screams that would bring the enemy closer.

All terrorists operate off the same premise: People can never find answers in the center of their own fear. Stampeding sheep will follow those ahead of them, even if it's into a waiting slaughterhouse.

But not all human minds are programmed the same way. An injection of terror will cause an instant response in us all, but that response runs full-spectrum. Some will run; some will freeze in place, closing their eyes as a child would: "You can't see me if I can't see you." It's not that people can't think when they're frightened, it's that they can't think *clearly*.

This knowledge is not useful unless a fear injection takes you beyond reasoning. Some of us respond as we've been trained to respond. *"Ne pensez pas!"* our instructors would scream at us, again and again, over and over. They knew fear was inevitable; their task was to make certain it would not control us— shooting a running man in the back is not much more difficult than shooting one too terrified to run at all. So they drilled the "correct" response into us until we became Pavlovian dogs of war.

"La peur, c'est votre alliée. C'est elle qui vous titille gentiment les nerfs pour vous signaler l'approche de l'ennemi. Elle ne cherche pas s'installer, mais si vous lui ouvrez la porte, alors c'en est fini de votre alliance."

I could translate that easily enough:

"Fear is your friend, lightly tapping on your nerves to warn you the enemy is approaching. It does not seek entrance. If you invite it in, it will no longer be your friend."

La Légion wasn't teaching us to protect ourselves; it was protecting its investment. We were none of us individuals. We were, all of us, disposable. But to create such disposables was time-consuming, labor-intensive work. The fewer of us they had to replace, the more value they got from their investment.

Their method was to program us as you would machines. To instill in us a sequence of reactions that left no room for thought. The better the soldier was programmed, the more reliable he would be considered. In a *légionnaire,* "reliable" and "valuable" were one and the same.

A distant sniper, a foamy-mouthed lunatic swinging a machete, the sound of an approaching vehicle . . . all the same. A trained soldier's response to danger is as instinctive as a mother's when her child is threatened.

Some mothers, anyway.

But the medic wasn't a former *légionnaire,* just another hired hand. Maybe he didn't drop his kit because he was too frightened to realize that the extra weight would slow his retreat. Or maybe he was thinking he might need it for himself if he wanted to *keep* running.

Whatever his reasons, the result was the same: there were no more morphine syrettes to ease the dying man's last minutes— he'd used all of his immediately after the first bullet dropped him. I'd waited until the pain became deadlier than any bullet before I'd plunged all of mine high on his arm, just past the collarbone.

"**W**e started with eight men," he said. "I don't know how many they had. It doesn't matter—each side will tell the same lies."

I didn't interrupt him; he was using his inner calm to open his receptors to the fading morphine, and I didn't know how much mileage was left on his life's odometer.

"Three of us survived. If the other two get back to base, they will report dozens of the guerrillas attacked us."

I didn't want to correct him, but I needed to make sure he wasn't already out of his head from the pain: if he lost control, he might scream, and then I'd have to finish him myself. "Four survivors," I reminded him. "Four dead. Two ran, leaving the two of us behind."

"There will be only one of us," he said, his tone telling me that he wasn't talking to himself. "Were I not so certain the enemy will report we had *them* trapped—perhaps three separate squads working a triangle kill—I would have told you to follow the cowards."

"I don't—"

"You understand perfectly." The blade of his quiet voice easily separated the tissue of the lie I was about to weave. "I will die here, right in this spot. No rescue team is coming. Our *actual* commanders are not back at base. To the men with the money, we are all the same. To risk an entire squad to save a pair of us—especially if one could not be moved without extra equipment—that would violate their basic rule."

He was an educated man, much older than me. Too old for this life.

"Then why am I still here?" I asked.

"That, I do not know. But for that gift, I am in your debt."

"Gift? I am only—"

"Stop! No man wants to die alone. You know this. To stay, that is your gift to me. I do not question your motives; do not question my logic. Just listen to the truth; it is all of value I have left. We are what the world calls 'mercenaries.' Professional soldiers. We fight not for country or cause—we fight for pay.

"For us, 'fight' and 'kill,' those are the same. Whatever you fail to kill will not fail to kill *you*. So we keep killing until the paymasters have achieved their objective—whatever that may be. Then we are discharged.

"You understand, yes? A rifle is discharged until its magazine is empty. Then another magazine is slapped into place. But when there are no more magazines, the rifle itself is discarded. When all you can do is flee, weight becomes still another enemy. As mine is now to you."

Olaf turned slightly away from me, to release some of the blood pooling inside his body.

"I speak English because I know you could not be an ex-*légionnaire* and a native Frenchman both. I know you are not following that fraudulent 'code' of theirs . . . that sworn oath to never abandon your dead, your wounded, or your weapons. You left them, so you must have learned why that 'code' was drilled into you. Who it was *really* meant to protect.

"We are hired killers, but to kill is nothing. It says nothing; it means nothing. No skill is required. Not even intent."

He twisted his body once again, a reaction to pain that never reached his face or changed his voice.

"To be paid for your work does not make you a professional. Amateurs are everywhere among us. They confuse the capability of their tools with capabilities of their own. They shoot their rifles, launch their missiles, drop their bombs. Their targets are some amorphous 'enemy.' They do not interview the dead, they count bodies. And one body's value is the same as another's."

I showed my palm, telling him to stop talking—every word would only shorten his time. Either he didn't see my gesture or he ignored it: his voice never changed tone, as inexorable as his forthcoming death.

"If the amateur survives enough of these little wars, others will regard him as a professional. And they take care to never call him what he is: another tool, manipulated by hands he will never see, the hands of men seated at a table where no chair is reserved for him."

There was something in his voice that told me I would not have wanted to be one of those who had manipulated the man dying next to me. Especially not *this* close to him—Olaf was a walking cobra, never without snap-out spikes taped to the underside of both wrists. The spikes were not much thicker than a pencil; they had a black-anodized sheath with a knurled handle, divided near the top so a thumbnail could send the venom-tipped fang on its mission. The fangs themselves were works of death-art: triangular to provide three cutting edges and a ripsaw effect when twisted, so no need for blood grooves. Why he called them his "scribes," I never knew.

"Outside these wars we are paid to fight, there are those who kill for other reasons. Some noble, some justified, some in self-defense. And some to quench their own repulsive needs. Such foul creatures are never satisfied, no matter what they do to the helpless. For them, a kill is a meal . . . some more satisfying than others.

"Those kind, they take trophies; they leave signatures. When captured—and they always are—they talk. Some are cowards, who fear pain as much as they loved inflicting it. In some countries—'civilized' countries," he said, hardening his voice to be sure I didn't miss the sarcasm—"they might trade what they know for less time in prison. Some talk because that is the only gratification left to them: they count their victims in their heads as others would count money in their hands."

"Not here."

"No, not here. We are soldiers. If you heed my words, you will remember this, always: A soldier is paid to take orders. An assassin is paid to take lives."

"What we are called—"

"Not the names we are *called,* no. Those are as false as the mythic reasons we are given to come to places like this. You know I am Norwegian—do you think I fight for the glory of Odin?"

Blood was bubbling around his mouth, but I knew that he wasn't really asking a question, so I let him go on.

"Soldiers and assassins. Both kill. Both are paid. But only the assassin—the *true* assassin—understands his place in the universe.

"You might think this jungle is a lawless place, but laws are only words on paper. The assassin understands that mathematics is the only true law . . . always present, no matter the situation. Physics and kinetics are intuitive to the assassin— the inverse relationship between certainty of success and certainty of escape. Not merely to escape the scene of the act itself, to escape its consequences."

I could see life ooze out through the field bandages I had pressed against his wounds.

I had acted quickly, with precision and skill . . . but without faith. I had been taught both sides of that lesson years ago, when I was still a boy. Still the property of La Légion.

"Escape is *always* a three-stage process," he said, still as soft-spoken as if he was using a microphone inside a lecture hall instead of lying in a blood-leeching jungle, awaiting his last visitor. "First, not to be caught in the act; second, not to be discovered by an analysis of evidence; third, not to be betrayed.

"Betrayal may be as focused as a sniper's bullet, or as blind as a bomb dropped in darkness—they are equally lethal.

"Evidence of assassination has no meaning. All this nonsense about disguising death—cutting a brake line so a car will crash, faking an accident—that is for the cinema. Worse, if it fails, it warns the target. And the payment for an assassin who fails is not money.

"In Asia, natives will come upon the torn body of one of their comrades. They may look closely enough to say with certainty, 'A tiger did this.' But they cannot say *which* tiger.

"So if a known tiger is missing a claw, or a tooth, they can analyze the evidence more closely. They may even name the killer: 'Old One-Fang did this.' But that knowledge brings them no closer to his capture.

"Why? Because tigers do not answer to names. And tigers always work alone. A tiger's motive is not to kill; it is to feed. A tiger will always be a tiger—any other belief is superstitious babble. The tiger is as indifferent to an analysis of what it has left behind as it is immune to betrayal. It can detect a target without being seen. It carries no weapons—it *is* a weapon.

"The assassin has learned from the tiger—all martial arts came from the study of animal behavior. So the assassin knows:

The closer to the target, the greater the possibility of success. But also the greater the chance of capture at the scene. And the greater the distance to safety. Polar opposites.

"Are you listening? *Bra!* The assassin need not be close to his target. He may leave no trace of his presence. But he always remains vulnerable until he reaches the highest evolution of his profession—the point where he has no comrades. The finest assassin always works alone. He works outside those deadly snares of emotion and personal need. Like the tiger, an assassin kills only to feed . . . not his belly, his bank account."

I shifted position slightly.

No tigers roamed this jungle, no assassins threatened us. But my habits were too deeply ingrained to be abandoned. Just as darkness could impair my vision, it would sharpen my hearing—only certain creatures moved in the night.

And I knew I would always *feel* the presence of others. So I knew we were still alone—what I couldn't know was for how long.

"The assassin's ranking is measured by his longevity. And the single factor most determinant of longevity is to be anonymous," the man said.

He did not reach for my hand, as some would have done. He used both of his to push against the bandages, as if he could prevent his life from escaping. Not to stay alive longer, to finish his lecture: Olaf was a man who paid his debts.

"The assassin understands misdirection. He knows that to use the same tools—or even the same method—will eventually attract the attention of those who hunt by pattern recognition.

"Does that mean the assassin should never use the same tools or repeat his methods? No. But both must be abandoned at some point. And best if at *different* points.

"Not buried, not hidden—*vanished.* Atomized into the same air we all breathe. The assassin may take intentionally what those who hunt for their own needs have a compulsion to take. Done several times, it will throw the hounds off the scent. Trophies may be taken, but never kept. This is a rule that cannot be violated.

"So 'clues' may be scattered as carelessly as seed, but only if the field beneath it is incapable of penetration—seeds that do not take root cannot yield blossoms. A symbol left at the scene may require a spray can, but that spray can must never be purchased, or even stolen from a nearby store. A sniper's bullet may yield a ballistic match only if the barrel continues to exist beyond the shot. An assassin may never have a 'relationship' with his tools—whatever is used must be as doomed as the target itself.

"You must never accept a contract where the death of the target would produce only a single beneficiary. The leader of a criminal organization is not the same as the wealthy husband of a much younger widow."

You? I thought to myself. *It feels as if Luc is still teaching me, through this dying man's mouth.*

"If the target is always surrounded by bodyguards, the assassin must regard them all equally—they are as much a danger to him as he himself is to the target. The perfect assassin would have no human contact.

"But that is only half the perfection. And the other half cannot be achieved . . . because the assassin must be paid. The elite assassin will have a receiver-dispenser, one whom neither he nor his employer ever meets. Once, it was mail drops. Today, it can be done electronically.

"Still, *some* degree of trust is required. The electronic middleman will know if information about him is being sought. So the assassin must never seek such information—he would be detected as easily as a scorpion on a white sheet, putting himself in danger. And if the assassin himself detects a probe for information coming *from* that unseen middleman, he must use his skills to protect himself."

I moved my head just enough to assure Olaf I was listening.

"There are, in all the world, perhaps less than a dozen such middlemen," he said. "They can minimize any risk to themselves, but not eliminate it entirely—those who wish to purchase the services of an assassin must have some way of making contact. Why less than a dozen? That is a dozen *left*. Their success is measured exactly as is the assassin's . . . in longevity."

"**W**hy do you tell me this?" I asked, my volume tuned to his—pitched as low as a whisper, but without the hiss.

"Because you have been taught nothing but lies. You still worship the samurai, those men tied so closely to their masters that they were required to take their own lives when their master lost his. Ah, great warriors, the samurai. Like the Vikings. But all they truly have in common is their enslavement."

"We are free to—"

"Serve *new* masters, yes. Ronin, then, if you like. But only the ninja is truly free. The despised ninja. The stealthy man-for-hire. Not some warrior with a 'code,' an assassin with none. Only the assassin has that ultimate freedom—to make his own choices, and to be his own judge.

"I know I am finished. Finally. I have no fear of what is to come. I know there is no Valhalla awaiting my entrance. That I *would* fear, if I believed, because I have long since forfeited any such possibility. But no religion will defeat the laws which govern all on this earth. I am quite ready to die. And I know it will happen well before the enemy returns to this spot."

"But . . ."

"Yes, I heard you. Why do I tell you all this? You could have left me to savages who would prolong my death for their own entertainment. You *should* have. Why you did not, I cannot know. I doubt *you* know. If I had money, it would be yours. I would tell you where it was . . . because you have made no attempt to learn that for yourself. But I have no money. So what I give you is everything I have left. This knowledge."

"*You* had all this knowledge, yet you ended up in this miserable jungle," I answered him, "fighting as a soldier with no flag. A man for hire. Why, then?"

"You were a *légionnaire.* So you have already heard this nonsense the French call *'philosophique.'* Proudhon says, 'Property is theft,' and spawns what? Anarchy? Any man who signs on as we did knows anarchy better than some café philosopher. Or perhaps we have all achieved existentialist perfection? We know the world is absurd, and all attempts to understand it are doomed. We are what we do, so we have chosen to invent and live by our own values, rather than slavishly follow those of another."

His throat spasmed as he fought back a cough. But he expelled flesh from his mouth, so I knew whatever had hit his midsection had finally reached a lung.

"There is no inherent truth in *any* philosophy. Everything is 'flexible'; all 'open to interpretation.' Your great Camus, he was an existentialist, but so was Nietzsche. Camus resisted fascism when his country was invaded by Nietzsche's 'supermen,' the Nazis. A contradiction? No. But what position did Camus take on the French campaign to keep Algeria in slavery?"

I didn't know, so I didn't answer. And I could feel Olaf was almost gone.

"Here is my only legacy. When you leave, take my scribes

with you. They will write the truth. And this electronic address"—he dropped his voice even lower—"it will allow you to contact one of the few middlemen still alive. You say you are selling special ice cubes from the best of refrigerators; he will then know I am gone, and that your message is genuine.

"What I have passed on to you was passed on to me," he said, very softly. "I listened with respect, but I failed to listen closely enough. The need for . . . I don't know what to call it, perhaps the need for another person to be in my life, that need is what has now cost me my own."

"You picked the wrong person to . . . ?"

I never finished the question I wanted to ask. When I glanced down, I saw that the man who had willed off his approaching death long enough to pass along his legacy had finally finished his journey.

A nd started mine.

The last man I killed for pay had wanted to die. Desperately, needfully wanted to die. The job had come to me from a cyber-person I would never meet. I say "cyber-person" because I never knew if communication was with a man or a woman— a machine has no gender.

But I didn't fear betrayal from that source. Long ago, I had told myself that, somehow, "he" was the grandson of a man Luc had served with in La Résistance. Luc was my father—in all ways but biological. Luca Adrian was the name he gave me, knowing that it would no longer exist the moment my *nom de guerre* was entered on the roster of La Légion Étrangère.

It had been so many years since the cyber-ghost had entered my life that betrayal was not a question in my mind.

Later, a woman—a girl, really; I believe she was too young to have served with Médecins Sans Frontières without having erased her past as I had mine—triggered something in me. She was everything the man who had once been an assassin had warned me against.

Maybe that started when she took my weapons: my pistol, the Vietnam tomahawk, and my garrote. No weapons inside their field hospital allowed. I never got them back.

It was years—and that blind tumble of the dice that fools call "destiny" or "karma"—before I saw that woman again. More accurately, our paths crossed for a second time. But from that moment, I knew she was real, not some angelic phantom my fevered brain had summoned up while I was close to dying. In another jungle, another war.

From that moment, I did everything I could think of to bring her to me. She'd told me her secret. I knew that her "it will never happen" dream was a place where she could live in peace, finally out of that unrelenting stream of dead, dying, and tortured human beings. The stream she'd been trying to stem with her own life—body and soul—since what seemed like forever to her. She knew if she didn't get out she'd be swept along, too. And what good would she be to anyone then?

I found that place, just as she'd envisioned it. I offered it to her. I offered myself, too. I knew I had not been part of her dream, so all I could do was ask to join her.

That meant telling her the truth.

I did that.

When she accepted me, I lived without fear of what Olaf had warned me against. If my Dolly were to betray me, I would not want such knowledge to precede my death.

Before Dolly, I had given up many things.

Some taken from me, before I learned. Some after, when I had to discard weight to move quickly.

Both my childhoods—the one that had been wiped from my memory before I ran from that "clinic" in Belgium, and the briefer but so much richer one that I'd had with Luc—gone forever.

To be a mercenary may not have been my fate, but it was the only option I had. When that first five years was up, I left La Légion. I'd served long enough to walk away . . . but to where? The five years gave me French citizenship, but I didn't want that any more than the French wanted me. No *gitan* could be truly French, and that part of my chromosomal chain was stamped across my face as clearly as the thickened slab of scar tissue on my wrist. And I couldn't cover my face with a sleeve.

Soldiering was all I knew. I went back to Darkville, and signed on with one of the mercenary outfits. Being a former *légionnaire* was all the credential I needed. They knew no man would make such a claim falsely—too many of us had later become soldiers-for-hire to take that much risk.

But waiting with Olaf as he stayed alive long enough to deliver his only legacy, that was when I decided. That was the moment I knew that the day would come when I would walk away from soldiering for paymasters, and never return.

Still, in a strange way, I have always followed his rules. Killing for money, that I did. But when Dolly accepted me, that part of me was gone—the man she wanted was no killer-for-money, and I *had* to be that man.

And now, so many years later, I was an impossible construct. A force mathematics could not rule; an assassin who once would kill anyone for money and now would forfeit his own life with equal lack of concern.

Worse, he would do that only for the one person who could really, truly betray him.

I spent half my life searching for what I would spend the rest of it defending.

That wasn't some random thought. It wasn't something I ever consciously considered—it was simply the way things were.

If others are trying to kill you, "Why?" is a question you get to speculate about only if they don't succeed.

"Simple" isn't the same as stupid. My world has been black-and-white ever since I could remember.

But my memory—my *actual* memory, a past I could look back on—that started much later than most. I'm not even sure how old I was—nine, ten, eleven, even?—when I escaped that "clinic." That's the word they used for it, but it wasn't healing anyone. Or curing them, or whatever clinics are supposed to be doing. It just kept us.

And there really was no "us." I didn't actually understand this until many years later. Not until I was a *légionnaire* did I learn that even POW camps aren't what they appear to be. The razor wire and the armed men walking the perimeter—some with shoulder-strapped machine pistols, some with dogs—you'd think that was just one side guarding its captives. But those captives weren't a single unit. They probably killed more of their own than any guards did; the only weapon they would need for that was betrayal.

None expected to be traded for their side's captives. Men awaiting execution are desperate. Men who would *welcome* execution instead of the daily "interrogations" are driven past the edge of sanity. Digging a tunnel is a madman's task. But the plotting, that never stopped. And was never shared.

When the guards learned of a plot, or even discovered a weapon, some captives died. Not just the ones the guards took away; those who had betrayed them, too. The most deadly thing in those camps was always their inhabitants—suspicion was God, and traitors were sacrificed on that altar all the time.

If any of the captives wondered if perhaps the man they killed hadn't actually been *proved* a traitor, they would keep such thoughts to themselves.

No barbed wire had surrounded my childhood. There were no patrols. The adults—doctors, nurses, orderlies—they were kind to us. The food was plentiful, and it was good food, not a prisoner's slop. The place was always the same temperature, and the inside air was clean.

But the children inside that place had nothing in common, not even whatever brought us there. Some kids were malformed, huge heads on stick bodies. Some drooled. Some never stopped talking, in a language I didn't understand. Some hardly moved.

All we had to share was the truth, and it wasn't a truth we *could* share. Only this one truth: It had to be very expensive to keep us there. All that equipment, even the buildings and the grounds, never mind the salaries. So, really, *two* truths: whoever put us there didn't lack for money . . . and didn't want us in their lives.

I knew what "retrograde amnesia" was. Not because I was so smart, but because the doctors explained it to me. That was why I had no memory of anything before that place, they said. They also said that, if the trauma that had wiped my mind had been powerful enough, those memories might never come back.

"You have to start from *now*," they would say. Kindly, but unyielding. They either didn't know what had erased any memory of my life before I woke up in that place, or wouldn't tell me. For me, those were the same.

They would say this "Start from *now*" as if it was a magic chant. But they never would say where I would be going once I started.

Somehow, I knew I could not "start" unless I stopped waiting. One night, I just dropped out the second-floor window of my room onto the soft, moist grass of the manicured lawn, and walked into the darkness.

How long it took, I couldn't be sure—time is more difficult to measure when you move only in darkness. I know I walked all the way to Paris. There, I became a gutter rat. I was sometimes very cold. I was always hungry. But it never occurred to me to try and return to that clinic.

Then Luc found me.

I was a boy then.

By the time I was big enough to lie to La Légion about my age, the time had come for Luc to leave. I think he probably stayed longer than he should have, but he wanted to be sure I had . . . a chance, is the best way to put it.

The same thing Olaf had done, many years after that.

English—"American," as it was called by some men I served with—was my native tongue. French I had learned: some in the clinic, more from Luc. He had warned me not to let anyone see I knew more than the few words La Légion required us all to learn.

I knew I must have a mother—a woman who gave birth to me—somewhere. A father, I never thought about. Luc was my father. I could reason that whoever had placed me inside that clinic must have been wealthy. But if they ever spent a sou looking for me after I'd fled, I never knew.

I never looked for them, either.

I had Luc. Then Patrice. Both long dead. One from age, one from bullets. But, really, from the same cancerous truth:

They could never go back to what they had lost. There was no "home" for them.

Olaf had been my friend, too. Not as I was with Patrice, but we were close enough to watch out for each other in that jungle.

All those I had once cared for were gone. After they left, I became a man very skilled in making people dead.

Making them dead in exchange for money, that is what I always told myself.

Had I not found Dolly—found she was a real woman, not an apparition—I would never have abandoned my life. Nor ever become part of hers.

Now none of that mattered. For the man I had become, killing wasn't about tools, or even skills—it was embedded, forever to be a part of me.

And *that* part, no amnesia would ever enter.

The Crown Jewel of the Coast is what they called it on the signs that welcomed tourists.

I couldn't really say if this little town was a strange place. It always seemed so to me, but I'd never lived in any one place before. I'd been many places, but I was always a stranger, passing through. Or an invader, with a job to do.

After La Légion, after I'd stopped working as a soldier for pay and followed Olaf's last advice, there was only one thing that mattered. All I'd ever looked at was how to get out . . . as soon as I'd done whatever I'd come there to do.

Maybe towns are no different from cities; it's just that the cities divide themselves into neighborhoods. Maybe every little spot has its own personality, because people who feel the same way always seem to clump together.

For me, it never mattered how people felt. I didn't go to those places to find a job; I went there to do one. I didn't need to make friends; I only needed to make myself a part of my surroundings. And never for very long.

I never wanted people to remember me. It would be best if they never saw me at all.

Now all I wanted was to be left alone.

But to be alone with my Dolly was impossible. I knew the truth of this village before I found the little cottage near the ocean, the place Dolly had dreamed of for so many years. Why would a tiny little town be any different from the biggest city?

I never said this aloud. To me, it meant nothing. There is a perimeter around our cottage, one several layers deeper than any fence that could be built. Inside it, my Dolly would always be safe.

That was my mistake—thinking the barrier built to protect her would also contain her. I may have wanted only to be left alone, but Dolly, she couldn't *leave* things alone. Once she got the scent of . . . I don't know what to call it, but it would turn her into a rat-hunting terrier. And once she clamped down, Satan himself couldn't make her drop the bite.

Dolly was immune to bribery or threats. Any fool would know that a former battlefield nurse who had worked the darkest parts of Africa with a Médecins Sans Frontières team wouldn't be tempted by money, and couldn't be scared off. Such attempts would only make her shake the rat by the back of its neck until she heard the *snap!* that confirmed the kill.

"What is *wrong* with these people?"

"What people, honey?"

"The people here, Dell. They can get into blood feuds over that stupid 'paper versus plastic' thing, but when you add *one* more layer to *any* fight, they won't even look at it."

"Paper is better because people throw the plastic away, and the seagulls could choke on it, right?"

"Dell . . ."

I just looked up at her. Once Dolly's hands went to her hips, I knew anything I said could set her off—silence was always my best course then.

"They need trees to make paper," Dolly said, quietly. "So where does a true-blue environmentalist stand?"

"I don't know."

"When you build a road through the other side of town so the logging trucks can reach the bay, the 'Buy American' crowd says you're helping the local economy. But when that garbage lumber is shipped to China, so they can make crappy furniture or whatever and sell it *here,* is that supposed to be helping the economy?"

"I guess both sides—"

"Don't even," she warned me. "The first step you take, in *either* direction, you've started walking in a circle. If the supermarkets have to use paper bags, they say it forces them to raise prices. And the people who have to clean up after their dogs, they want plastic, too. But don't tell them about jobs for the people who *make* those plastic bags—*those* jobs are all in China. And some of those fools actually think you can use dog droppings to make a compost heap. But paper bags are pulp—biodegradable, right?"

"Dolly . . ."

"Dolly *what*?"

"You're just doing what they do."

"You mean . . . just talking?"

"No. I'd never say that about you. But we both came from the same place, didn't we?"

"Us? The jungle, you mean? When we first . . . I guess 'met' doesn't exactly fit, but it *is* the jungle you are saying, yes?"

"Yes."

"What does that prove?"

"We weren't on opposite sides then."

"Dell! You were there to . . ."

"Kill people for money?" I said, watching that special shade of rose blossom on her cheeks, then turn dark.

"I don't care what you call it. I didn't care then; I don't care now. But whether you were a . . . soldier, or a mercenary, or . . . It doesn't matter. We—our team, I mean—we were there to *save* lives. You were there to *take* lives. How could that make us on the same side?"

"Because, for both of us, there was no 'right' or 'wrong.' You didn't care what uniform a man was wearing when you patched him up. Or took off a leg to save his life. You didn't judge. At least you—your people, I mean—you didn't judge *then*."

"We still don't," she said, in a tone that told me she wasn't going to be moved off her square. A voice I'd heard before. Many times. Dolly could out-mule anyone.

"It's not that way anymore, girl. Today, your comrades have to make certain deals just to be allowed to save lives. I don't mean take sides, but the only way any medical team can work in some of those places is to negotiate free passage. And when they don't, they're gone. Didn't Burma—or whatever it's calling itself today—didn't they just kick Médecins Sans Frontières out of the country because they didn't want anyone who wasn't Buddhist to have medical care?"

"That's not—"

"Yes, it is," I cut her off. "You want to drop fifty tons of food supplies into a starvation zone, you have to give the warlords their piece before they allow you the privilege of driving into the zone yourself."

"So?"

"So what's the difference between feeding an army and giving them weapons?"

"You're saying it's wrong to do that?"

"No. I'm saying what I've been trying to say. Just let me finish, okay?"

She didn't say anything, letting the tapping of one fingernail on the tabletop tell me to get on with it.

"For me, there was no 'right' or 'wrong.' If you're a working merc, you assume whoever's hiring you is *some* kind of liar. And once you hit the ground, it doesn't matter—the only way you collect your pay is to get through the fighting alive. And the only way to do *that* is to make some other people dead.

"See what I'm saying here? Sure, you can lie to yourself. But even that doesn't matter: the winners get to name the losers. We're 'liberators' or 'freedom fighters.' Or we're hired guns, with no loyalty to any cause . . . or, worse, a loyalty that's for sale.

"You don't have to hate a man wearing a certain uniform to shoot him, not if you know he's going to shoot you. And you don't have to care what a man's uniform is to *save* his life, either."

"Saving a life is always—"

"You don't believe that, Dolly. Not anymore. Not for a long time."

"I guess I don't," she said, the sorrow in her voice mourning the loss of True North in the compass she'd once carried inside herself. I still remember her telling me that everyone carried *some* kind of compass, but, until I atoned for the things I'd done, mine would just be a dial with no needle.

"You think it's like that . . . like *this,* everywhere?" she asked me in bed, late that same night.

"I'm not a philosopher," I told her, as if Olaf was speaking for me. "It's been like that everywhere *I've* ever been, that's all I could say."

"Corrupt?"

"The place itself doesn't have to be. I don't even think it's human nature to value . . . things. Yeah, 'things,' that fits. Everybody wants food and water, everyone wants to be safe. That's in all of us. But some people want . . . not things, exactly. Maybe, I don't know . . . power? Whatever you call it, some people want it. Want it bad enough to do anything to get it. Anything to keep it.

"And when they can actually *see* what they want, it's like a sniper acquiring a target—if you're in the way, your life means nothing. We, you and me, we could be the only two people on some tropical island, and we'd be fine. But if one of the people I'm talking about discovered that island held something they wanted, they'd do . . . anything."

"Maybe that's why I thought saving lives had a special value," Dolly said, propping herself on her elbow, like that could make her see me better in the dark. "How could someone whose life was saved, saved by people who asked nothing in return, how could they be the same person after that?"

"Why not? They might bless you, call you their savior, thank whatever god they worshipped for your existence on this earth. But they'd be back doing whatever they'd *been* doing soon enough."

What I didn't say is how I knew this was pure truth. I'd been one of those killers. When my life was spared only because I stumbled into a coven of mercy-dealing angels, I didn't bless anyone for that. Or even thank them. What I did was go back to work.

"What could be so damn valuable about *this* place, Dell? That stupid logging road, what difference is it going to make? Some people will make money; some people will lose money. It's just money."

"For a lot of people, there's no 'just' in there, honey. If you think money can buy you what you want, what you need . . . if you think money can transform you into someone else, then—"

"Dell, remember—just a few weeks ago?—that old man was walking by himself near the jetty on the other side of the bridge? And that gang of . . . I don't even know what to call them, but they beat him to death. Four of them, and what did they get? Seventy dollars and some change. How could that be worth a man's life?"

"You've been reading those press releases again."

"What is *that* supposed to mean?"

"Isn't that what it said in the papers? That the prosecutor said they killed an old man for a lousy seventy dollars?"

"So?"

"So they didn't kill him for seventy dollars, honey. They killed him because they've got lizard brains. When they threatened him, maybe the old man still wouldn't give them his money. So they figured he must have a *lot* of money to stand up to the four of them. Or maybe they just beat him to death for the fun of it, and the money was just a bonus."

"To you, there's no difference? I mean, whether they were just stupid robbers or blood-thirsty savages?"

"I wasn't there, little girl. But it sure didn't make any difference to the old man."

The next few days were quiet.

Early summer. Hummingbirds fighting over a fuchsia bush,

jays screaming at the chipmunks digging up acorns they'd stashed. Rascal patrolling, keeping the whole place a cat-free zone.

But that wasn't his job; it was just something he wanted to do. When Dolly was outside, humming a Piaf tune to herself as she groomed one of the lily hybrids she was trying to develop, Rascal went into a different mode.

Guard.

No barking, no threatening. If you walked back there and surprised Dolly, you wouldn't be walking out. Rascal was a self-launching torpedo in a tiny ocean he could navigate blind. And if you dove in, you were dead in the water.

Everything as it should be.

Peaceful. Precious. Protected.

Then a coalition of environmentalists showed up.

I don't mean they were outsiders. This town is home to dozens of Green Groups, each of them aimed at a different target. Lumber mills, toxic waste, endangered species . . .

Some of them were always "calling for" something. Boycotts were a favorite: eggs had to come from free-range chickens, beef from cattle that hadn't been dosed with antibiotics, salmon mustn't have been "ranched." Some also went international: whaling, dolphin capture, global warming . . . a long list.

"Green" had religious status, but some of its splinter groups were so small they only had one member. I know this because of a letter the newspaper printed. The writer proclaimed he'd "be well within my rights" if he were to go ahead with a lawsuit he was "contemplating." His next-door neighbor actually *smoked* in his own backyard! So, every time the wind shifted, the letter writer was exposed to secondhand smoke against his will.

I don't know if he expected some enviro-posse to form or what, but responders either took his letter as some kind of spoof or loudly distanced *their* group from him.

Me, I didn't think this nasty little man cared about anything but his "rights." Deep-rooted entitlement was like any other infection, except for one thing: whoever caught it didn't want it cured, he wanted it spread.

Normally, for the actual groups to join forces on *anything* was unheard of, but now they'd united for the common cause of blocking this logging road the government wanted to build.

It wasn't the road itself they had banded together to fight, it was the route that had been picked for it—a jagged Z-line through a few hundred acres of land nobody wanted. Nothing grew there except for some scrubby bush and stunted trees. No river, no lake, no access to the bayfront. Any road cut through there probably wouldn't even displace a raccoon. But it was state-owned land, so it belonged to "the people."

As at other places I'd been, everyone was claiming to speak for "the people." Harder to do in Oregon, since the Indians were the "original" people. At least, that's what those who had voted against building a casino on private land said . . . and they won. But when the local tribe wouldn't even take the land as a gift, the gates opened up.

That was when this coalition emerged to protect "virgin green space" from "government rape." Why chain yourself to a tree that was going to be cut down no matter what you did? Why not just *buy* the whole parcel outright, and legally bar any road? It couldn't cost *that* much.

But that wouldn't work, they said, shouting "Eminent domain!" like the threat of an approaching tsunami.

Then the "small government" crowd jumped in, forming common cause with the "enviros" for the first time. The state couldn't just *take* property--private property was no different from the right to privacy itself. If the Second Amendment was to have any meaning, it would have to apply to more than just fighting any ban against a citizen's right to own firearms, including those stupid background checks. The state wouldn't even know who to take the property *from,* except that all deeds had to be filed, and "Registration Is the First Step to Confiscation!"

Those posters were plastered all over town. That put the "all power belongs to the people" crowd on autopilot.

So many referendums were slated for the next ballot that the Voters' Pamphlet would be the size of a phone book. It's easy to get damn near anything on a ballot out here. I don't know how many signatures you need, but it's not a lot. There's no polling booths; you just mail your ballot in.

But even *that* was too much trouble for some.

One group had a Web site saying that they were united against paper voting. Dolly had insisted on showing it to me. "Can you believe it? It's not about the hassle of standing in line, or even 'hanging chads.' They're angry because they actually have to *mail* their ballots. They want to vote over the Internet, the same way they do their banking, pay their bills, and find their true love. They need to be 'connected' all the time. There's enough of them to actually get a referendum going. But a ballot initiative requires a certain number of signatures, and you can't gather those online . . . so they're not going to be bothered even doing *that* much!"

Their Web site's banner was "Passive Resistance." I guess that meant, if they couldn't vote online, they'd boycott every ballot.

I got the "passive" part easy enough, but I didn't think even Gandhi could find a trace of the other half.

"Get it, Tontay!"

I looked out the back window. Half a dozen teenage girls in cheerleader outfits, bouncing up and down in their eagerness to encourage Dolly. For years, our "kitchen" had been swarming with teenage girls, turning it into some kind of . . . clubhouse, I guess. Not a hangout for outcasts, but a place where they'd be welcomed—one of Dolly's rules.

Dolly's rules always had reasons. Her reasons. The school's princesses mixed with the untouchables in *her* house or else it was *la porte* for them. None of them wanted to be excluded from a place where they could learn things they all wanted to know . . . and be loved at the same time.

She'd been "Aunt Dolly" to them until she suddenly decided that made her sound too old. The minute she said, "That's *Tante* Dolly to you!" they all picked up on it. But my wife hadn't made the jump from English to French quick enough, so *"tante"* came out "tontay," and they'd converted that mess into *their* name for her.

Any kind of strict glance from Dolly when they used it just started them all giggling. I guess she finally gave up trying to stop them.

Those girls knew Dolly would rapid-fire French at me if she didn't want them to understand, so I think they were playing dumb with this "Tontay" nonsense. I kept that thought to myself.

"If I break something, you'd all better start running," Dolly mock-threatened, igniting another chorus of giggling. Then my wife—who had been a yoga practitioner since she was a child—jumped up, threw her hands toward the sky, and floated to the ground, landing in a perfect split.

"Wow!" one of the cheerleaders shouted. They all applauded, as happy as if it was raining beauty on them.

"Something else is going on, Dell," she said to me.

It was after midnight. We were in bed, and Rascal had planted himself at the threshold to our bedroom, like he'd trained himself to do.

"With what?"

"With that whole logging-road fight."

"Fight? It's like some kind of hobby for them. They have to show how 'green' they are, like a damn religion. But it's just talk. Like those anti-tax people. They always get stuck in their own glue."

"I know you don't think much of—"

"It's not that, honey. It's that circle thing. Uh . . . Okay, you remember when some of them started a campaign to ban the sale of cigarettes? Not to minors, to everyone. Statewide. But before they could even get it on the ballot, some of that *same* crowd said tobacco was sacred to Native Americans, and we couldn't disrespect their culture. They kept going round and round, but they never *got* around. To doing anything, I mean."

"I know," my wife said, a sad tone in her voice that I'd heard before. Not often, which is probably why I picked up on it so quickly. "But there's a different . . . intensity to this thing."

"Because . . . ?"

"I don't *know,* Dell. But it's not like usual. That piece of ground, it's, I don't know how to say this, but . . . vibrating. Like a big train is coming."

I didn't know what people in the village thought of me.

Most of them probably didn't even know I existed. But those who did knew if anyone tried to hurt Dolly it would be the worst kind of mistake. Nothing to do with my pride, my self-respect, or my ego. And it wasn't possessiveness, either. You don't own a woman like Dolly. But protect her, *that* I could do.

For me, Dolly was that *raison d'être* future-promised to all new legionnaires. A promise none of us ever expected would be kept, so we felt no disappointment when it turned out to be still another lie, part of our daily diet. To be disappointed, you must first be surprised.

Olaf had never been a legionnaire. To us, "survivor" had a different meaning. Those who survived the training could never lie about it. Who would we lie to? Our commanders watched the training. They could count the survivors easily enough—they knew exactly what those survivors would have proved.

The tests would get progressively more difficult. Not just physically—the assault on each man's will never stopped. They said this tested the ability to "adapt." To show fear, that was acceptable . . . so long as the fear did not alter your conduct. But to show despair, no. That was considered a sure sign of a man who would not succeed in the field.

Our ranks were culled as a breeder of dogs would destroy runts from each litter. Only the "best" got to prance around in shows, pampered like royalty throughout their lives. But such a life was reserved for dogs. For men like us, passing all the tests meant we would be awarded the privilege of war.

And *those* survivors could not lie, either. If you started out with eight men, you returned with eight men. Not necessarily alive, but all bodies had to be accounted for.

Never abandon your dead or your wounded. Never. But instead of some *esprit de corps,* our only code was that of the criminal: Whatever you see doesn't matter, not if you keep that information to yourself.

I was there when a tall, ink-black Senegalese we knew only as "Idrissa" locked eyes with my friend Patrice, forming an invisible bridge over the body of another man—a soldier so badly wounded he would never survive being carried back to our camp. I watched as both men nodded their silent agreement. Patrice shot the dying man in the top of his head. Idrissa swung his heavy blade in a short arc, cutting through flesh and bone as easily as a knife through brie. I picked up the dead man's rifle as Idrissa held the severed hand of the forearm he'd removed and slammed it against the brush to roughen the edges of his too-clean strike.

When we got back to base, Patrice explained that the enemy had launched an RPG round, and all that we could find of the dead man was what Idrissa was still holding. I handed over his rifle.

We were questioned, individually first, and then as a unit. Our accounts did not vary. Our commanders were not surprised at this.

Maybe that was why they reacted with such lavish praise years later, when I carried what was left of Patrice's machine-gunned body all the way back on my own. None of our unit had offered to help me with that insane task. I would have refused if they had. I knew they would still stay close enough to cover me. Even if they regarded me as a demented fool, they couldn't move much more quickly than I did. If they arrived ahead of me, they would have to explain why *two* bodies had not been returned.

I could never say why this mattered so much to me. I knew there would be no shipment home, no funeral mass held, no tombstone to honor him. Patrice would be buried in the dark earth that surrounded our camp.

The officers allowed me to dig the grave. It took me all through the night to make it deep enough to keep predators from digging up the body. Hyenas count on vultures to point out fresh kills, but those carrion eaters are pure sight-hunters. I rolled some heavy stones over the spot to discourage the jack-als even more.

I must have passed out at some point. When I awoke, another night was coming on.

I wished I knew some words, but I was empty.

How could I say aloud that my true friend's only dream would never become truth? Patrice had avenged his childhood mate so openly that even his comrades back in Ireland told him he could not hope to return for many years. Any revolutionary who dared take the life of a soldier in the Army of Occupation would be ruthlessly hunted. Or informed on. Patrice had to stay away until . . .

I knew there would never be another like him in my life.

Dolly wasn't the kind of woman who could content herself with sadness.

"Widow's weeds suit some," Patrice had told me, another life ago. "That's their role, to mourn. Ah, sure, after a proper period . . . a year or so . . . they could find another man. But some of them, they never do. It's not that they loved their man so deep that no other could measure up. That's their story, maybe, but a story it is, lad—one they keep on telling, because no one would dare tell them to stop."

I don't know what Dolly would do if I was gone, but I know what she *wouldn't* do.

Like I said, our kitchen wasn't just a place to cook.

Dolly had me take down a wall when we first moved in. I'm no expert with tools—not with the kind you use for carpentry, anyway. But I can tell if a wall is load-bearing, and the one that separated the kitchen from the living room wasn't.

When I was done, we didn't have a living room anymore, but the kitchen was big enough for a damn restaurant. It even kind of looked like one, with that long slab of butcher block, the chairs surrounding it, and the "half-bath" I'd built into a corner.

That's where Dolly's mob gathered. Every day, after school, it would be crammed with kids—mostly girls, speaking some foreign language. They used English words, but I couldn't decode their speech. What was I supposed to make of a bunch of girls gathered around a laptop screen, looking at a boy with blond-streaked red hair holding a pistol in one hand and a microphone in the other?

"Oh, *get* you some of that Wonder Bread cred!" one of them cracked.

Dolly was laughing, too.

Like I said, I couldn't understand any of it.

But I always knew when they had some kind of "project." The table would accumulate mounds of paper, more would be pushpinned to the cabinets, still more littered around the floor. Maybe they were having fun, but it looked like work to me— they didn't talk as much, and when they did, it was in short, clipped sentences.

"You got the plat map?" Dolly asked a girl wearing a camo tank top. That had become their private fashion statement, ever since Dolly had started wearing that same top over cargo pants.

The girl just nodded.

"Can you make some room for it, Cue?" I wouldn't have known how to spell that name. "Queue" would be pronounced the same, or even just "Q." But that was on a long list of things that were none of my business.

A very tall girl with long black hair that fell straight down her back, as flat as if she'd ironed it, stood up. She took some piece of paper from the other girl, got up on her toes, extended her arms, and managed to tack it up above some other stuff.

That was my Dolly. Making the other girls see that being a beanpole had value; it was nothing to snicker about.

There was no set of written rules, but they all seemed to know them. The little bathroom was always sparkling and fresh-smelling, the stainless-steel twin sinks immaculate: "You use it, you clean it" was as much a part of the climate as the ban on dope and booze. Dolly didn't care if any of her mob had a pack of cigarettes in her purse, so long as it *stayed* there.

Everybody got a second chance. Nobody got a third.

Rascal was making his rounds, circling the table, scoring treats from every girl. Dolly made sure those treats were healthy stuff, and all of them the same—there was always a big jar in the middle of the table, and the girls were limited to one each. The mutt acknowledged me with a look that said, "I'm on the job."

Meaning: his job was to protect Dolly, and he could handle that just fine without me.

I didn't know what they were all up to, and I didn't feel like trying to read in the room Dolly insisted on calling my "den." Sometimes, kids would wander in there, and I didn't feel like talking to any of them, either. They always asked questions. Some days, that was okay with me. Not now.

In my basement, there was no chance of unexpected visitors. The only entrance is down at the end of a hall, and there was no reason for anyone to enter the hallway. Even Rascal knew that.

The door was heavy steel, coated with a thin veneer of cheap-looking wood. It opened with a keypad. When I closed it behind me, I was in another world.

"Mercenary" has always been a synonym for "myth."

More today than ever, with so many viewing screens that are most people's only connection to what they think is "real."

Books, too, I guess. Some of them would have you believe that there were hundreds of martial artists with magical *chi* who'd once worked as secret agents before they turned into movie stars.

If those guys could only find a way to pull off some "death match" over bandwidth, the Internet would be swimming in blood.

None of that is dangerous, not by itself. But some mercenaries who learn distrust is their truest friend never learn to distrust *themselves.* That kind, they work jungle long enough, they're at risk for believing the worst myth of all—the one that says they've developed some "sixth sense." Not hyper-acute hearing or selective sense of smell—you work the field long enough, that comes naturally. No, some kind of special power—a magical alarm system that's theirs and theirs alone.

That only ends one of two ways: they let themselves nod off, trusting that "signal" to alert them in time, or that signal never stops beaming its message. If that happens, they start emptying every magazine blindly into the dark. That's the worst. Exposed and out of ammo at the same time.

Nobody stays that way for long.

What *does* keep you alive is pattern recognition. When that software finally downloads into *all* your senses, you'll lock onto any disruption in the patterns you expect.

I learned this slowly, over a long period of time. Each piece added to what I had before it. The only way to learn all that was by listening. And I was a good listener, always careful to sift. The only thing I knew for sure was that anyone could lie— *would* lie—if it got him something he wanted.

Surviving that "training" was . . . I'm not sure, exactly, but some part of it had to be blind luck. And maybe some part of what Luc had taught me before I ever opened the only door left open to me. The longer I soldiered, the better I got at learning who I should be listening to. Men like Patrice, men like Olaf. I say that as if there were so many. There were not. But each one made me even more cautious about the next.

Even when I quit—quit *forever*—I never forgot.

That's why I had to be down in my basement that day. Something was wrong. I knew it, even if I couldn't explain how I knew. Inside me, only this: to distrust that knowledge would be disrespectful of all those who had taught me.

"You think *this* is a jungle, lad, you should spend some time in Belfast when Her Royal Majesty's killers are on the hunt," Patrice had told me, a lifetime ago. "Some with maps drawn for them by the bloody grasses."

Yes. If "home" is a piece of surrounded, landlocked ground, you're out of options. Patrice knew the truth of things.

In their own way, they all had. All those I trusted enough to listen to, anyway.

But now, no matter how hard I concentrated, nothing came to me clearly enough to *do* something with it. Just that sense of disruption, too jagged for any image to emerge.

Hours passed. I stayed as still within myself as I knew how. Dialing down my heartbeat, slowing myself inside and out.

It wasn't until I felt Dolly at the core of my stillness that I knew. It wasn't me being hunted.

"It's me," I whispered to Rascal as I moved toward our bedroom late that night.

An unnecessary alert—his evolution to a sensory warning system was superior to anything humans had yet developed.

The marine fog lights planted all around the house would throw off a clear image of anything approaching and send it right to Dolly's tablet, making an audible *ping!* at the same time. We could carry the tablet around and set it up so that sound would wake us if we were asleep. Those weren't "security" lights, just information—they worked even in daylight.

After dark, they watched for bad intentions—intruders experienced enough to mask off security cameras, moving with their eyes aimed down, to watch for trip wires or dry twigs. Their eyes would be hit by wheel-spinning high-lumen LEDs, intense enough to induce an epileptic seizure. Unlike the marine lights, these were hidden behind carbon mesh, so the blast would come as a stun-level surprise.

I didn't know if the setup would work; there was nobody I could test it on. I'd learned about it from a man I served with. He told me he had the . . . disease, or whatever it is. He said flashing lights would set it off, but closing his eyes didn't stop them once they got inside his brain. Years later, Dolly told me that man had a specific form of the disease: "photosensitive epilepsy" is what she called it.

Still, I turned around and went outside, just to be sure they were all working.

When I got back, Rascal's snort had turned to outright sarcasm—*his* motion detectors never failed.

I slipped under the sheets without a ripple, but Dolly had her own detectors.

"What is it, Dell?"

"I don't know," I whispered. I wasn't going to try pretending around my woman, even if I'd thought there was one chance in a million I could get away with it.

"Someone from your . . . ?"

"No."

"From when you and Mack . . . ?"

"No."

"Dell . . ."

"It's you, Dolly. Someone, some people . . . something, I don't know. Tomorrow we'll talk, okay?"

She put her head against my chest, listening for my heartbeat. My woman knew me as no other—I was too calm inside for her to believe I wasn't waiting for the enemy to show itself.

The next morning, I tried to deflect what I knew would be coming.

Coming from Dolly, I mean. So I said, "Rascal's getting fat, huh?"

"What!?" my wife snapped, deeply offended on her dog's behalf. If I'd said that about her, she would have laughed. I remember hearing her answer one of the bolder girls, a while back. I hadn't heard the question, but Dolly's answer—"I don't know, probably sixty-three, sixty-four kilos"—was enough.

"Huh!" one of the other girls said, clearly surprised. Either at Dolly weighing somewhere around a hundred and forty pounds, or at her actually answering such a question, I couldn't tell. Dolly claimed to be five foot five, but that was really stretching it. I wondered how surprised they would have been if she told them she was the same size she'd been for decades, but I opted for silence; if my wife wanted her girls to know something, she'd tell them herself.

"Well, just look at him, honey," I said. "He snarfs treats all day long, polishes off his own food in the evening, then gets anything you leave on your plate."

"So what? He gets plenty of exercise. Anyway, every time he goes to the vet, they weigh him. Everything goes onto his chart.

They store it online, so I can log in anytime I want to check on something, like medications I might want to try. Dr. Jay set it up that way so if Rascal goes to a specialist they'll have instant access to his whole history."

Not his whole history, I thought. *They call a dog like Rascal a "rescue." That word would fit me just as well.* Aloud, I said, "So I could just dial up his weight chart, then?"

"You could," she said, grinning at me, "if you had the password."

I was out the door before she could start asking the questions I knew I'd have to answer sooner or later. If there was going to be a test, I wanted to do as much last-minute cramming as I could.

Or find a way to cheat.

Mack was waiting for me at the bottom of the gentle rise our property sits on.

I'd texted him while Dolly was taking a shower. With me walking out of the house like I had, Dolly would think I was close by, as long as she didn't hear her battered Subaru or our "licensed for farm use only" Jeep start up. She knew I could get my motorcycle out of its slot behind the wall of the garage without making a sound, but she also knew I only brought it out after dark. And started its engine only when I'd coasted down to near the bottom of the hill.

"What's up?" Mack asked, as I closed the door of his rust bucket, a battered compact something so not worth stealing that he'd never replaced a missing rear window. The sheet of heavy plastic duct-taped over it kept the rain out, and any potential thief could see there wasn't even a radio in the empty slot.

"I should be asking you that," I deflected his question. "How come this thing's so clean inside all of a sudden?"

"Bridgette and me, we're married now. So we only need one place to live."

That wasn't news to me. The only question I'd ever heard Dolly ask Mack was "Bridgette, as in Bardot?" And his answer, "That's kind of the way it's spelled, but you say it like 'Bridget.' She's Irish . . . some part of her, anyway."

Dolly was especially proud of helping him find their engagement ring, some big chunky thing, with a flat-topped amethyst held in place by gold clasps. The pale-lilac stone was inlaid with what she called a "Rose of Sharon," gold-leafed, with a tiny dot of diamond in its center. The first time I saw it, I had to take a deep breath. I knew, even if I couldn't say *how* I knew, that the woman who had been waiting for Patrice would still be wearing such a ring.

Dolly had flown out to Chicago for the wedding. I knew she greatly preferred Mack married—no more of his "distracting" her girls every time he came over. And she was crazy about Bridgette. What I didn't tell Mack: their mortgage bank *was* Dolly. Bridgette knew, and she handled the money for both of them, so she just transferred money into Dolly's account every month.

"You let her drive this thing?"

"She rides in it sometimes," he said, almost as defensive about his car as Dolly had been about Rascal's weight.

"I get it," I told him.

"So—where, then?"

"Down by the tanks."

"Where they're building that . . . ?"

"Yeah. But we're going past that spot, maybe a mile or so. I'll tell you where to pull over."

"**W**hy'd you want me to leave Minnie at home?"

"She's a fine dog for your work," I told Mack. "But, as well trained as she is, she's still a pit bull, and where we're going, people let their dogs run free all the time. One of them could get stupid."

"So it's *your* work, then?"

"Not like last time," I told the social worker whose caseload was the "homeless by choice" population the town's liberal majority tolerated . . . so long as they didn't interfere with business. And they were happy to pay Mack to cover the seriously disturbed, who sometimes didn't know what planet they were on—it was a hell of a lot cheaper than hospitalizing them. Plus, he was the one the jail called when a prisoner started talking suicide . . . or when they'd just finished cutting down a body and it was still breathing.

Mack's work was funded by the town—although I knew they got some federal money for the "services" he provided. Probably made a profit off it, too.

That "last time" ended with a few people dead, and a new client for Mack—a client I never asked about.

"Just want to take a look around a few spots."

"You're a million times better at . . . surveillance, or whatever you want to call it, than I'll ever be," the social worker asked. "What do you need me for, then?"

"Camouflage," I told him.

"**Y**ou're looking for a runaway," I said, explaining Mack's role to him.

"I wouldn't be called in on a—"

"Not a kid who ran from home. Or even from custody. This runaway, she's a girl. Been spotted in one of those homeless camps you already have on your rounds. She's your client, so you don't have to answer anyone's questions, right?"

"Nobody around here would even ask," he said. A hard mask dropped over his face, changing his voice from his usual social worker's neutral-flat to a lifelong outlaw's "I've got nothing to say." His right hand pulled a chain he wore around his neck. A trio of laminated badges came out, each one with his picture in the corner. I'd seen them before. Even the most suspicious cop could call any of the numbers on them, and the answer would back him off. Far off.

"You'll be coming up on a stand of white birch on your left," I told him. "Turn-in's about two-tenths past. Do it slow—the road after that's nothing but packed dirt."

"I got it."

I didn't have to tell him to check his rearview mirror, or to turn in sedately. Mack was a man who learned from anything he did, and he'd done enough things with me to understand that people can't talk about what they don't know. Oh, they *can,* and plenty do. But it wouldn't be the kind of information anyone else could use.

"In there," I told him, pointing to the right, where heavy brush made a natural garage. "We're going the rest of the way on foot."

I was proud to see him back into the spot I'd shown him. He was ready when I pulled a roll of camo netting from my carry-all. I handed him one end, and we snapped it out like a towel over sand at the beach.

The car became part of the scenery.

I started up the hill, Mack slightly behind my left shoulder. We walked less than fifty yards before stepping off the packed-earth road and into the forest.

The hill wasn't that high, but its top was just right for what I needed.

Once Mack saw me pull out what he probably thought was a pair of binoculars, his breathing changed.

Not enough for most people to pick up on, but I'd been listening for it—his nose had been broken a few times and you could hear a faint whistle when he didn't breathe through his mouth. For all Mack knew, I was setting up a sniper's roost. That wouldn't have come as a shock, or even have gotten him to ask questions—he'd seen me do things that had permanently changed the way he looked at the world.

We were up there for almost an hour. More than enough time for me to double-tap the laser range-finder with a built-in inclinometer that could compensate 60+/– a few times, and read off the numbers. The Bushnell Scout could be set for "bow" or "rifle," but I wasn't thinking about that kind of work.

Mack wrote down what I said, not pretending to understand things like "H-three-oh-five." Not asking me, either.

I scanned a left-to-right circle, then reversed direction. The distances weren't off by more than a couple of feet, but I wanted to be dead-sure, so I did the whole thing again. The numbers held.

The only surprise my scan turned up was a total absence of the "No Trespassing" signs you see tacked up on just about every plot of unfenced timber around here. Those weren't meant for hikers, just for hunters. Stray rounds were always a danger to people who lived anywhere within range of a deer rifle.

At least they used to be, before an ecoterrorist had killed a pair of hunters who'd been waiting in a deer blind. The FBI profile said that the shooter was probably a white male, ex-military, most likely suffering from PTSD, and "moon-phase delusional." Even with all that information, whoever was responsible was never brought to trial. Or even arrested.

We were back on the paved road in another twenty minutes. Mack dropped me off and went back to his work.

I walked up the long driveway to our cottage, ready to start mine.

As I walked in the back door, my eyes flicked over to the red circle Dolly had drawn around a spot on one of the terrain maps spread all over the butcher-block table.

The same area I'd just visited.

"What is it, Dell?" my wife asked, not even looking up from the papers she was marking in different colors. All her girls would use those same colors every time they were working on something together, but I didn't know what each one stood for.

No point in saying, "Nothing." It wouldn't be an acceptable answer. My wife was a human barometer, at least where I was concerned—she knew when the weather was about to change.

"Who threatened you?" I said. I can't sense the same things Dolly can, but when it came to death-math calculations, I could do quadratic equations in my head.

"Oh, that wasn't a *threat,* Dell." She made a brush-it-off gesture, not asking how I knew. "He just—"

"Who?"

Even Rascal growled.

"What is *wrong* with you?" she demanded. "Just sit down, baby. I'll get you some of my lemonade, and we can talk, yes?"

I didn't answer her, but I did sit down. I pulled a strip of rawhide out of my field jacket and tossed it to Rascal. He ignored it, keeping his eyes on Dolly—the mutt wasn't interested in a good chew any more than I was in a glass of lemonade.

"**B**enton," Dolly said, handing me a heavy tumbler of iced lemonade. "He's nothing. Not even a councilman," she went on, the contempt in her voice clearly communicating what she thought of the group of people who supposedly made all the political decisions for the town we lived in.

There's a mayor, too, but none of them really make decisions—they just follow orders. Around here, all of them usually run unopposed. When there's an actual race, the good-for-garbage-wrapping "newspaper" is careful to print an equal number of letters supporting each candidate.

That's probably the only reason anyone buys that paper anymore—to see their name in print. Or to clip coupons. Nobody reads that useless rag for news; for that, there's a blog called *Undercurrents*. Whether people liked it or not, I didn't know, but I did know it actually investigated whatever was going on. And that it had a reputation for no-bias digging.

I didn't know what funded it. *Undercurrents* didn't run advertising, gush over some moronic "wine festival," or even print "comments," the way most blogs did. Especially the ones that were replacing print newspapers all over America.

It's only been running for a few years, but it's built a reputation for sniffing out stories that prove true, even if nobody can figure who their sources are. Or where they get some of the photos they run.

I knew the answer to that last one. Mack had been working with a video ninja for quite some time. That was Mack's work, not mine . . . which is why I never asked him about it.

When I first encountered that young man, he was an expert voyeur—his back-channel footage of girls fighting each other went viral very quickly. I'd needed his skills on the last thing I'd been forced into doing.

Forced by Dolly, although she'd had no idea she was forcing

me into anything. Mack was her friend, not mine. I don't have any friends, not like she does. But anything that might protect my wife in the future was of immeasurable value to me. She already owned everything of ours, and she'd never want for money. But protection, that was a legacy beyond price. And Mack was a lot younger than I was.

"Benton?"

"Dell, in this town, voting is a sham. You know it as well as I do. Just look under the 'Vote for One' box—there's usually just one candidate listed. Even the DA's such a frightened little twit that he spent a lot of money putting up signs urging people to reelect him when he ran unopposed."

"I thought he quit."

"He did. There was this truly dangerous beast charged with all kinds of crimes—kidnapping, rape, torture. . . . But the girl, the victim, she was killed in a propane explosion just before the trial. And the DA wanted to drop the case! Without a live witness, he could actually lose, *ver lâche*!

"And that all might have gone unnoticed, but for two things: The girl was really liked by a lot of people—she worked on one of the fishing boats. Then *Undercurrents* got their hands on some in-house memos that showed him for what he—the DA, I mean—really was.

"He knew if the town drunk ran against him in the next election, he'd lose. Not just his job, but his government pension. You have to work—I'm not sure, maybe twenty-five years?—to lock that in at the max. So he took another government job, in another part of the state."

"I thought people never voted here."

"A lot of them don't," she said, disgusted with that lot.

"Remember that Web site I showed you? Oh, it would be *such* a hassle to mail a ballot."

"So?"

"So they don't pay *attention*. Mack says that the only difference in corruption between Chicago and this town is that Chicago's *proud* of theirs."

"Dolly . . ."

"Dell, what he said, *all* Benton said, was . . . Well, it wasn't even a warning, really."

"What did he say?"

"Dell, *stop* that."

I didn't say anything. I knew what she wanted me to stop, but all I could control was my conduct, not my temperature. I felt the coldness spread through me. And welcomed it.

"It was, you know, roundabout. Like, my 'people'—*as if*!" she interrupted herself to segue into that teenage-girl-speak without even realizing it—"shouldn't run around half cocked, whatever *that* was supposed to mean."

I didn't say anything. In my world, "half cocked" would be "full stupid." You either cock a weapon or you don't; that "half cocked" nonsense is what they show people at shooting ranges. Just like racking the slide on a semi-auto *after* you're inside a target's house, the way they always do in movies.

"He had to be talking about that logging road," Dolly said.

"Why would you and your girls care about that?"

"We *don't*. It's a lose-lose deal all around. Nobody wins . . . except maybe some lawyers who keep filing those 'Environmental Impact Statement' things. Or the insurance companies."

"Geological surveyors?"

"They get paid once. And both sides are going to pay for plenty of those, anyway."

"He found out who owns those parcels you've got marked off in red," I said, pointing at some of the plat maps.

"I'm only one of the owners," she shot back. "We've wanted to build a dog park out there for the longest time. One for real dogs. You know, like Rascal."

"Rascal?"

"Rascal," she said, in that dull-flat tone of voice she uses when anyone dares to so much as flirt with the idea that Rascal is one degree off perfection.

I retreated to silence. Dolly joined me in that, but she was still smoldering. Diversion was my best move, so . . .

"Then what's that thick line between the water and the road? The pink one?"

"A corporation has been buying up that land for years. The only houses out there—well, trailers, really—they don't get city water, and they can't drill wells that close to the bay, so their places aren't worth much. In fact, they don't get *any* city services: no electricity at the curb to connect to, which is why even the cable companies don't bother."

"They all run off generators?"

"Pretty much," she shrugged. "Propane can power just about anything. Heat, hot water, even barbecue grills. And they all have those satellite dishes for TV, so they're pretty self-sufficient."

"Some of them are still there?"

"That's the thing, Dell. Not really many, not now. And Tova—you remember her, she's in her second year of law school, but she comes home every summer—Tova says that if that strip of land was annexed by the town, they'd be entitled to city services, same as anyone else."

"So what?"

"So some areas don't *want* to be annexed. Some little town, about eighty miles north of here, it fought in the courts for years and years. It was a pretty exclusive area—I guess they wanted to keep it that way."

"But it lost?"

"Yes."

"So this corporation, you think it plans to build something?"

"That's the part that doesn't make any sense, Dell. What could it build? No condo would ever succeed along that strip. Who wants a place overlooking that sludge the bay vomits up, never mind *smelling* it? And with a logging road coming through, there's no way anyone could get approval to build there, anyway."

"But this Benton guy, he must have heard something, right?"

"Not from us. There was this piece in *Undercurrents,* though. That's how we found out one single corporation was buying up all that property."

"How *you* found out. So you weren't their source?"

"Well . . . I guess I was. I mean, we had a message sent to them. Just an e-mail. We wanted people to start thinking about . . . You know, just like you said: why would one owner want that land? But I told you, this wasn't like a formal meeting or anything. Benton just came up to me in the coffee shop."

"Doing you a favor, huh?"

"That's how he made it sound."

"Okay."

"Dell . . ."

"Don't fuss, Dolly. I just need to find out some things. And, me, I won't make *any* sound."

I'm no private detective.

In a village like the one Dolly and I live in, the phone book is where you look for names and addresses. The little book even has a separate section for businesses. Every kind of business you could imagine, from boatbuilding to aroma therapy.

Debt-collection agencies are listed, too—probably the closest thing to "investigators" around here.

I thought about that. Maybe there wasn't much need for private detectives anywhere—not anymore, not with the Internet offering all kinds of services, from skip tracing to "background." But local phone books will always exist, if only for advertising—a person looking for a lawyer will try the lawyer who took out the full-page ad first.

"It's like your own Web site?" I asked, trying to understand.

"No," Dolly said. "Your own Web site, it's called a 'domain' for a reason. You actually own it. Which means you have to pay for it. First you register the name, then you pay to *keep* the name. There's been a ton of lawsuits over people trying to use a celebrity's name for themselves. Tova says there's even a special court to decide who has the right to a domain name."

"So this Facebook, the whole thing is one domain?"

"Sure."

"Then nobody actually owns their own Facebook page?"

"What difference does that make?" one of her girls said. "It's not like they *charge* you for having a Facebook page. It's free."

How would these kids understand jungle law? I thought. *Nothing's "for free." And it's only yours for as long as you can hold it.* But I just shrugged, as if I had no answer to her question. Then I covered up by asking the girl, "Couldn't people just make up whatever they wanted?"

"Well, of *course*," she said, looking to the other girls for confirmation. "There's a whole TV show about that."

I just walked away before I asked any more stupid questions. I knew I'd never understand why all these people walked around glued to their cell phones, or texting madly about every tiny thing in their tiny lives, or carrying tablets so they'd be able to have a "conversation" with someone they didn't even know.

Some of their phones could actually do *all* of that. Like Dolly said, they had to be "connected" all the time. When I asked her how they could be connected to people who maybe didn't even exist, she gave me one of those Parisian shrugs that could mean anything, from "It doesn't matter" to "Who cares?"

"What if someone stuck a GPS chip in those phones? They'd know every place anybody was, anytime they wanted to know."

"They *all* have those chips, Dell."

"But . . ."

"Oh, they don't mind. And it's supposed to be a safety feature."

"Like if they're injured? Or even kidnapped?"

"No." My wife chuckled. "In case they lose their phone."

A jungle doesn't have to mean palm trees—it could be anything from a desert to a housing project.

A jungle is a place where your life is worth no more than your ability to protect it.

Even in this beautiful little village, jungle rules might apply—especially when privacy and self-protection were always at risk, thanks to the mania of some people to "stay connected."

This seemed insane to me. When I was still a child, I learned one thing that would never change: *all* secrets have value . . . to someone, somewhere.

I've never been arrested.

I don't ever expect to be. My fingerprints have never been taken, and the lump of scar tissue on my left wrist could look like anything from an industrial accident to a botched tattoo-removal.

In truth, that scar was from a branding iron. Yes, I've never been arrested. Not by the police. But I have been captured, and my captors knew mercenaries don't take prisoners.

They liked their work so much they prolonged it. My screams excited them as a woman might excite a man. All it took was tolerating the pain a little longer than they thought I could. Passing out came easily to me, but not as easily as the confidence of my captors came to them.

One of them, I knew, would return on his own. And that his death would be noiseless.

Torture isn't for information; it's for enjoyment. That had been part of my early training with La Légion, that knowledge. Within that knowledge was the certain truth—no torture victim is ever allowed to outlive his value. When death is the only possible outcome of any encounter, the most valuable knowledge of all is that it doesn't have to be *your* death.

I knew what Luc's work had been after the Nazis occupied France. I always heard his voice in French—*"Les Boches ont fait de certains d'entre nous des putains ou des assassins, à moins qu'ils n'aient fait que révéler ce que nous portions déjà en nous"*—but it always turned to English, as if I knew his native language should never leave my mouth: "The Nazis made some of us into whores, and some into murderers . . . or maybe they just brought out what had always been within some of us."

Dolly was quite a few years younger than me—a gap that seemed to widen every year. But she'd learned the truth of torture at a very young age, working in war zones where there were no sides, just enemies. Working with a rape bomb always attached to her belt, under her bloodstained white smock.

I don't know why my mind went to that place as soon as I walked in our back door that afternoon. The big TV screen was showing the sentencing of some creature who had captured women and kept them prisoner for years. Usually, the sound was muted, because Dolly wanted to follow world events in real time, and most of the "news" stations had scrolls running along the bottom of the picture. But this time, the sound was on—I could hear some woman reciting the details of the horrors perpetrated upon her, as if what she said would affect the sentence the creature was about to receive.

Rascal could protect Dolly from a lot of people, but not once they had been allowed inside the house. That had happened, years before. Dolly never knew why that foul young man had been so "disturbed" that he'd blown himself up with a rudimentary pipe bomb he had been building in his bedroom. Some of her girls even cried when the news got out.

Dolly wouldn't have expected tears from me. My wife had no respect for my knowledge in some areas of life—every not-for-work piece of clothing I owned was something she'd bought for me. But she knew I'd seen that young man in our house, more than once. She knew I'd lied, cheated, stolen, burned, killed. All in my past, but not erased from my skill set.

Dolly knew I didn't do any of that work for fun. And she knew that if a roomful of people contained one person who *might* harm her, and I was short on time, blowing the whole place up would have been my solution.

I knew she was already kicking herself for just saying the name "Benton" to me.

There's always more to any town than its image on a tourist's postcard.

Who would advertise that the underbelly of their little village is no different from that of any big city? Clean air, pure water, no traffic congestion, friendly people, sights to see—*that* was the picture they wanted to paint.

But if you were tuned to the right frequencies, you'd know that picture wasn't so much altered as it was selective—what it would never show was what every spot on this planet has in common: predators and prey.

I don't mean "crime." If you read the local newspaper, you'd be so confident of your own safety that you'd never close your windows or lock your doors. But nobody with functioning brain cells would confuse promotional swill with what Parisians would call *reportage.*

The collective who put *Undercurrents* on the Internet had built a reputation for telling the truth, and anyone who cared about "news" went there for it. That's probably one of the reasons for its reputation: not just that it was free, but that it wouldn't run ads or endorse candidates. "It doesn't even demand you feed it cookies," I once heard one of Dolly's girls say, amazement in her voice.

Later, when I asked Dolly what that meant, she told me that all these "free" Web sites always got something in return, some little packet of information that was worth money to someone. "Data mining," she called it. "Most kids are so used to it that they set their browsers to accept cookies and run Java scripts, so they don't have to wait to log on to some site."

I just nodded.

"Why are you asking me, Dell? I know you have . . . I mean, you know all about this stuff, don't you?"

"Only secondhand," I told her. And that was the truth: Once I'd answered his coded questions, the cyber-ghost who prowled through "secure" networks undetected had helped me many times. First, he told me I would be getting something in the mail.

Not mail at the house: I had to drive almost three hours

to pick up a key hidden exactly where the instructions said it would be waiting. I used that key to open a box in a little post office that stayed open around the clock. Not to sell stamps or anything: the only part that stayed open was the area where the boxes were.

Inside that box was an envelope with four more keys. Each one opened a different box—the largest size they had—in that same place. When I was finished, I had four sealed packets, each bubble-wrapped inside one of those Priority Mail cardboard boxes.

Back in my basement, I put all five keys in my little hydraulic press, and waited until they were fused into a single lump. Careful work with a scalpel opened each of the boxes. The four pieces inside snapped together like one of those Lego sets, then became two halves. There was no way to make a mistake; every connector was color-coded. Still, I worked slowly and carefully.

When I was done, I had some kind of little computer. Besides a keyboard, it only had two buttons: an orange disk at top left, and a yellow one at bottom right. Like some kind of fax machine that could only dial one number.

The first time I pushed the orange disk, the screen lit up.

```
|<Ack>|
```

I typed in one letter.

```
|>Y<|
```

And hit the yellow button. The response was instant; the instruction explicit.

```
|<To use, snap pieces together. When finished, dis-
connect. Ack>|
```

As before, I just typed:

`|>Y<|`

Then I saw:

```
|<IP changes, both ends. Your local cable will always
be final connect-send point, but untraceable—dead-
ends in Estonia. Use only to ask questions and
receive responses. Ack>|
```

I had to read that a couple of times before I understood that the ghost could send messages to me through our local cable network, but any attempt to trace the source of what I'd receive would be futile.

As soon as I typed in `|>Y<|` the little screen went dead.

I disassembled the machine. The fused-together post-office keys went into an acid bath. When it cooled, I pulled the container out of its housing by the handle. After dark, I put it into a channel I'd cut into a big rock in the woods behind our house, then poured metal-eating liquid over the whole thing.

I would never waste the ghost's time on anything I could do for myself.

Apparently, this guy who'd said something to Dolly was considered a great catch for the village, a big fish they'd lured in. There'd been plenty of newspaper coverage a few years back. George B. (Byron) Benton was born in 1969, to John and Barbara Benton of Bethesda, Maryland. Graduated from Princeton 1988, then an M.B.A. at the Wharton School in 1990. Worked at Thackery & Associates in New York City until 1999, when he moved to Portland and founded PNW Upstream, a hedge fund.

According to the newspaper's back files, he had a waterfront house on Lake Oswego—about as upscale as it gets—but he'd visited this place a few times and "fallen in love with life on the Coast." Permanently relocated here in 2006.

The photograph they ran with the story wouldn't be what he looked like today. A studio shot, white male, late thirties, stylish haircut, carefully trimmed mustache, very nice suit. Whatever he looked like now, he wouldn't have that mustache—nobody around here wears one unless he also has a beard in a matching color.

All I could find out about Thackery & Associates was that it was an investment bank with a long, unsullied history. Never had to be "bailed out," like some with bigger names.

Typing "PNW Upstream" and "Hedge Fund" into the search engine got me the simplest Web site imaginable—the equivalent of a listing in the phone book. But it confirmed the date it was opened, its managing director—Benton—and a street address in downtown Portland. There seemed to be no way to invest, or even to ask about investing.

That was as far as I could go on my own. I activated the machine in the basement, typed in everything I already knew, then:

```
|>Connect 2?<|
```

I didn't know who the cyber-ghost was, much less what time zone he'd be sending from, so I never expected a message at any particular time, unless I asked for a reply ASAP. This time, I did.

The response was waiting an hour later, the info all loaded onto the little screen.

I copied it off as quickly as I could, knowing that I couldn't leave the line "live" for long. And that as soon as I touched a single key, *any* key, the message would disappear.

```
|<Connect (verif, anon. sftwr contact ↔)>|
```

Then came a long list of names. A couple I recognized, most not. I tapped three keys:

```
|>Thx<|
```

. . . and watched the screen go blank before I took it apart.

Then I sat down and looked over the notes I'd taken. I knew that "verified" connections meant Benton had contacted all the names on that long list using some "anonymizer" program. That didn't mean they were connected to each other, just to him. Not encrypted, just not easily traceable to any specific ISP.

I took my list upstairs and showed it to Dolly.

"This is a 'Who's Who' of political power in the whole county," she told me. "I can tell you that much without even going online. Some of the names I don't know, but I'm guessing they're heavyweights—not the kind of people who run for office, the kind who finance those runs."

"Could you . . . ?"

But Dolly was already banging keys on her laptop before I could finish asking her.

"Everything from dentists to architects," Dolly said, pointing at the screen of her tablet.

"Some small fleet owners, a café—the big one, where they do those readings by local writers—even a bed-and-breakfast."

"But they all have money?"

"I . . . guess so. I mean, to get on *this* list, it's like joining a club. And the membership requirement would be either money or power."

"Not the same?"

"I don't think so, Dell. Not necessarily, anyway. Like, say, somebody could run for Town Council, that's some power, sure. But if he was just a tool of people who put up the money to get him elected, and he had to do what they told him to . . ."

"How much?"

"How much?" she repeated my question, making it her own, to me.

"Money."

"Oh. I guess that depends. This place, it's like, I don't know, in a permanent state of détente. There's hard-core right-wingers, and there's some just as committed to peace-and-love, even if they have to wage war to bring understanding to the unenlightened."

"Fringes, then?"

"Fringes with overlap, Dell. If the liberals who write those 'ban all guns' letters to the paper don't actually try and make that a *law,* the right-wingers content themselves with writing letters calling the liberals a bunch of wimps. Ignorant wimps. See?"

"No. I really don't, Dolly. You're saying . . . what? It's like some argument in a bar where people call each other names but never throw a punch?"

"Sort of. The *really* rich people have more than one home— they only live here for part of the year. And the *really* poor people don't vote. There's some businesses that make money, but there's just as many, maybe more, that are really just . . . hobbies, like. You know, those stores that sell used books, or the artist studios that don't sell enough to pay the rent."

"But even those, they depend on tourists?"

"Sure. That's why they brought Mack out here. In fact, he's a perfect example: The liberals say 'homeless' like it's some sacred status, and the conservatives say it like they're all a bunch of bums too lazy to work. Mack keeps track of them. The homeless. So he's helping them *and* keeping them from making a scene outside any of the businesses at the same time. That pretty much sums up this place."

"So you don't need money to get into politics?"

"You need *some* money. Not much. Not unless you have an opponent, and most of the time, you don't. That's where the money comes in—making sure everyone knows who *their* candidate is. No point putting your own money against much bigger money."

"So why would he say you shouldn't be running around half cocked?"

"Who?"

"Benton, Dolly," I said, very patiently. I was calm and soft-voiced, but my wife knows me better than anyone.

"Oh! I don't know, actually. I mean, it was no secret that some corporation was buying up that whole strip of worthless land. Like I said, it was in—"

"Right. And you wanted to know—?"

"Those are *public* records, Dell. It isn't like this corporation was trying to cover its tracks, anyway. The only thing people are wondering about it is *why*. And that's just gossip, not some . . . investigation."

"Not like whatever you and those girls have tacked up all over the place, then?"

"Dell, it's nothing."

"Uh-huh."

"You don't believe me!" she said, putting that little pout on her face that she knew always worked with me.

I pulled her onto my lap, put my arm around her, said words I know she loves to hear.

But I *didn't* believe her, not for a second.

Rascal made a little growling sound.

Dolly hopped off my lap, just in time to open the back door for three girls. I knew there would be more of them on their way, so I went downstairs.

Buying up a tract of worthless land didn't make sense. It couldn't be what was underneath it, like that patch of dirt calling itself the Central African Republic where Hutu *génocidaires* might find more hospitality than in the Congo—provided they picked the winning side.

But I knew the Darkville Rules: When it comes to land, there's no such thing as "worthless," it's only a question of what it's worth to take it. Or keep it.

And whoever was buying up all the land knew that not hiding himself was a good way to hide his objective. A Judas goat never gets to make up his *own* mind, so you couldn't call him a traitor. But the trick worked just the same.

I spent a lot of time thinking about that.

I knew there were ways for any Web site to collect information about anyone who clicked on it. Not a lot of information, probably. But maybe enough to finger Dolly as the instigator, working backward to the source. Maybe this was how Benton had known Dolly and her crew were poking around. Only I couldn't see why *Undercurrents* would be cooperating with anyone seeking *their* sources.

Was he just guessing? Or carpet bombing, covering all the possibilities? Dolly said he hadn't really warned her off. He was just being friendly, asking her to get all the facts before she made up her mind.

I didn't believe that, either.

"There's a way to tell if a hedge fund is open to the public?"

"Sure," the lawyer answered. "Take me a minute."

Ever since he'd won an acquittal for MaryLou in a trial that had all the elements for national news coverage—"Star Softball Pitcher in School Shooting!"—Bradley L. Swift occupied the top spot on the statewide criminal defense pyramid.

It had been an unwinnable case: MaryLou walked up to the high school's heartthrob, shot him in the head, put down the pistol, and sat there waiting for the cops. But Swift had proved the "victim" had been the leader of a rape-initiation gang, targeting the school's low-hanging fruit by sniffing out absence of self-esteem like predatory bloodhounds. And Mary-Lou had believed her little sister was next in line.

Dolly had used her local network to dig up some ugly truth; I'd used my past to put some heads up on stakes. The town had changed, and so had Swift.

"I'd appreciate that," I said.

It didn't even take that minute.

"No. In fact, it even says that the fund is currently oversubscribed—they won't be open to new shareholders for at least another year *after* it declares earnings. And, so far, they show nothing but some minor expenses. Not exactly an encouragement.

"You could put yourself on an e-mail list, and they'll notify you when they're ready to sell more shares. *If* they ever are. I figured you wouldn't want me doing that."

"You were right. Thanks."

"You . . . heard something?"

"No," I told the lawyer. "Neither did you."

J ust one more set of questions for the ghost.

You can put all kinds of security on a Web site, but if anyone with higher skills than yours was looking, your security would be about as effective as trying to dam a river with barbed wire. So I opened up my little machine.

```
|>HF capital? Share ownership?<|
```

I didn't expect an instant answer, so I disassembled the machine and went back to work on something I was building. I could feel Luc nodding his approval of my design . . . and that old man's approval never came easy.

It looked just like a golf bag. But I could unsnap the top and pull another bag out from inside it. The outside bag was gaudy, red and white, with some big logo on it. The inside one was black and gray, in a blotchy pattern. In darkness it had the trick-the-eye quality of the best *trompe l'oeil.*

One pattern for transporting to and from the job, the other for actually doing it.

The bottom of the workbag was a spongy foam that would safely cushion even a piece of fragile glassware dropped into it. The inside walls were a series of Velcro flaps, set so I could cover the first thing I dropped in with another flap, and close it as firmly as I needed each time. The top of that first flap would be ready to silence the next thing dropped into the bag, and so on, all the way to the top.

I could carry a thirty-kilo load of loot with the shoulder strap, and the contents wouldn't make a sound.

That would leave one arm free. And both hands.

"He followed her here. He says he'll follow her no matter where she goes."

"And she doesn't want that?"

"Dell! Sometimes I don't know what's going on in your mind. Laura's my friend. I was just telling you what she told me."

"Why tell you in the first place?"

Dolly spun and walked away from me. I expected her usual three steps before she whirled and started in again, but I was wrong—it took four this time.

"I said she's my *friend.* Friends tell each other things."

"If she's your friend, she knows you."

"I just *said*—"

"I don't mean know you like to say hello to, Dolly. I mean, if she's a real friend, she knows *you.* Knows how you are inside."

"You think Laura wants me to do something—is that what you're saying?"

"I don't know," I said, throwing up my hands, palms out, to ward off whatever she was going to say next. "All I'm saying is, I don't know how *well* she knows you."

"And . . ."

"And that's why I asked."

"Asked *what*?"

"Dolly . . . Dolly, just sit down and listen for a minute. I know you really like Cordelia. I'm not saying anything against her. *Or* Laura. I'm just asking, how does this guy always manage to find Cordelia, every time?"

"You think she . . . No! She's a beautician. Or a hair stylist. Or whatever it's called. But, to do what she does, she has to have a *license,* okay? She has to register with the state. That's public information. He doesn't exactly need CIA connections to look it up."

"How quick does he find her?"

"How quick?"

"Yeah. She's been here, what, three, four years?"

"So?"

"So he's been looking all this time, and now he's found her?"

"Oh. Yes. That's what happened. That's why she only just told Laura about it."

"There's a law against that, right? Stalking, or something."

"That's only if he *does* something. He can *watch* her all he wants."

"She has a Facebook page?"

"So—you *do* listen once in a while, huh?"

"Dolly . . ."

"No, she *doesn't* have a Facebook page" was my wife's tart response. "She isn't in the phone book. She doesn't even have a landline, just her cell. And she's changed her e-mail address, too. More than once. But now that he's found the place where she works, all he has to do is follow her home one night."

"Sure. But what makes you think . . . ?"

"He walked right into the place—they do men and women both, so it didn't seem strange. The girl at the front pointed him to her station. Probably figured she was doing Cordy a favor—her chair was empty. He sat down and told her he wanted a haircut. She said she wasn't cutting his hair. Ever. And you know what he did? He complained to the manager!"

"She shouldn't have to—"

"Oh, she didn't. I mean, the manager, Liz, she told the guy he wasn't welcome in her place. She's tough, Liz. We all went down to Legal Aid, but they said there was nothing we could do unless he had a record. A record of assaulting her, I mean. Or if she had some kind of Order of Protection."

"Couldn't she get one?"

"She tried. But the court they sent her to, they said she needed proof that she was in immediate danger."

"Wasn't she?"

"Not as far as *they* were concerned. When he beat her up the last time, that's when she took off. All the times before that, she never reported him to the police. *Now* she would, but he's not going to do that again."

"Why are you so sure?"

"When he . . . when he beat her up, it was when they were living together. So that would be 'domestic violence.' The way I understand it is that the cops *have* to arrest someone when they're called out on a case like that. Around here, the way they get around the law is, they arrest them *both*. That means the woman has to have her kids get picked up by CPS. If she has a dog, the dog has to go to a shelter. And even if they cut them both loose, it all depends on whose name is on the lease. Or who owns the house."

"I didn't know any of that."

"Why would you, Dell? It's not like you're . . . I don't know . . . 'interested' in that kind of thing. But the cops, they're *supposed* to be interested. Once they passed a law about 'mandatory arrest,' the cops use the threat of taking the woman in, too. As soon as they hear that, most women will forget about pressing charges."

"They don't live together anymore."

"No. No, they don't. But she—Cordy—she still gets the shakes even *talking* about it. He told her—before, I mean—he told her that if she ever tried to get away from him, he'd find her. And he did. He even sent her a letter last week."

"Isn't that enough to . . . ?"

"No! It was just one of those stupid 'Can't we try again?' cards you can buy in any store. It's not against the law to ask someone who broke up with you to give you another chance."

"How did she meet him?"

"Why does that matter?"

I just looked at her. She was close enough to touch by then, but I didn't reach out my hand—I just waited.

"She used to live not far from Eugene. There was a pool-room close by. Not some dive, a very nice place. They even had leagues and everything. This man—Donny, everybody calls him—he's very good. At pool, I mean. Won all kinds of trophies and stuff. That's how he got to meet her. They ended up on the same team—looking back, she knows that wasn't some accident—and they even won some league championship. The team, I'm talking about."

"Huh!"

"What does *that* mean?"

"Nothing, honey. It's just that he's the kind of creep who follows women around. Not because he loves them, because nobody leaves *him,* right?"

"Yes."

"So I was just curious how he got together with your friend."

"Dell. Dell, I am *serious* now. I was *not* trying to get you involved with this. We'll handle it."

"Who's 'we'?"

"Just me. And Laura. And Bridgette. He's not going to threaten any of *us.*"

"Okay."

She gave me one of her "I can see right through you" looks. Only she couldn't. So it was like when one of those teenagers always around the house says, "Oh, my mother will *kill* me if she finds out." That girl's just amping it up—she doesn't think for a minute that her mother's going to take her life.

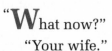hat now?"

"Your wife."

"Bridgette? Who . . . ?"

"Nobody. Not yet, anyway. But my wife just *had* to go and tell her about her friend, Dolly's friend, I mean, and Bridgette wants to trap this guy with—"

"Wait! Slow down. Just start from the beginning."

So I told Mack everything Dolly had told me. Maybe amping it up just a little.

The house was dark, but that didn't mean he wasn't there.

"There's a nice spot just down the road," I told Mack. "Drop me off there. Then go over to the poolroom. The fancy one, with all those colored tables. Here's his photo. If you spot him, ring the number I gave you. Ring it *once.* Then move off and put the end of a lighted cigarette to the photo. One *poof!* and it'll disappear.

"But keep watch. As soon as you see him move, push the number-seven button on this," I told him, handing him a burner cell.

"Then what?"

"Then snap this piece of plastic crap in two, pull out its chip, and scatter the pieces on your way over to pick me up again."

They take trophies.

This guy earned his, I guess. Sure had enough of them, scattered all over the front room of the house he lived in. A couple of them were heavy—glass crystal, etched with his name and whatever he got them for. I'd brought the bag because I didn't want to make any noise as I dropped them all in, one after another.

Still no vibration from my phone, so I had time enough to find half a dozen different cue sticks, racked point-up on his bedroom wall like they were standing guard. They were really nice ones, the kind that you screw together. The one with the gold-inlaid butt-piece was by far the fanciest.

I took all but that one. And I still had enough of the padded cushions inside the golf bag so all I needed was a flat rock behind his house and a few cracks of my tomahawk to turn his fancy cue into fragments.

As I worked, my mind flashed to when I'd vowed to always carry that tomahawk with me in the field. Back to when I'd used it to fashion the crude crutch that got me to the field hospital where Dolly's team had set up. I didn't know it was there—all I knew was that I had to get as far away from the blast scene as I could. When I came around, there I was. And there was Dolly.

Maybe I was more superstitious than I'd ever admit.

As soon as I finished, I went back inside and scattered the cue shards all over his top sheet. Then I pulled the bedspread back over it.

It was almost three hours before my phone throbbed.

Mack was at the pickup spot way ahead of time, like I expected.

"What happened?" he asked, as I slid into the front seat.

"Tomorrow" is all I said.

I was back inside the house before Dolly. So I didn't even have to bribe that mutt of hers into silence.

"This is a rule of life," Olaf had once told me. "Any terrorist can be terrorized."

"How do you know that?" I'd asked him.

"Physics" is all he said, as if that one word answered all the questions in the universe.

Maybe he was right. I'd never seen anything that contradicted him. So I was ready when Dolly dropped the question on me, just before I fell asleep. When you . . . Well, I guess I only know about me and Dolly, and she always called sex just another kind of communication between people who loved each other. "You can't *make* love," I'd heard her explain to a group of those girls once. "You can have sex if you get talked into it. To 'prove' your love, something like that, you know what I mean. But if you really love someone, and they love you, too, sex will show up all on its own. It's like a play: if a character makes an entrance at the wrong time, it ruins the whole thing."

"Put a ring on it, Tontay!" one of them cracked.

"Anyone can *buy* a ring," Dolly shot back.

"You're saying we should all be virgins—"

"I'm not saying anything like that." Dolly turned to face the girl who'd been expecting a different answer. "All I'm saying is that sex isn't love. People can have sex, but they're not 'making love,' see? Virginity isn't some medical thing. You can be first-time pure in your heart no matter what you did with your body before . . ."

She let the sentence trail off, settling over her girls like a comfort blanket over a baby.

None of them noticed me as I slipped past.

Later, I thought about what Dolly said.

And I realized she'd known I was there all the time. She was talking to me, too, not just to her girls.

So we waited until we . . . finished, and she was curled up inside my arm, before she said, "Donny left town."

"Who?"

"Donny. The man who had been stalking Cordelia."

"Oh. Maybe he was just passing through."

"Stop it, baby. I don't know what you did, but you made him go."

"Me?"

"Oh, go to sleep," my wife whispered.

I didn't go far.

Those cursed woodpeckers. Not the red-topped kind in the cartoons. These were flickers—big birds, with a black patch on their throats and salmon-colored underwings.

They had a whole forest to bang away in. And I'd been good to them, too—I made a bunch of nesting boxes and stuck them up on square stakes of pressure-treated lumber, about eight feet off the ground. You'd think they'd be satisfied with all that. Not a chance. Some of them pounded on the bat houses, too.

Now, *those* I really cared about. Where Dolly and I live is a long way from where I'd been hit with malaria, but mosquitoes really spook me. Even standing water gives me the creeps. So I put together the bat houses very carefully. I followed all the instructions to the letter—even if the small opening wouldn't keep some birds from nesting, the depth would. Then I applied coat after coat of flat-black, and fastened them to much higher stakes, with a three-piece sheet of green plastic riveted under the box to help keep the insides cool no matter what the day-time weather was.

And it worked. Sometimes you could hear the bats at night. Most of the time they were noiseless, but they gobbled every mosquito around. In the summer, the girls would always be asking Dolly how come her yard was never buggy. She'd tell them about the bats. Some did that "ee-you" thing. Bats were just so disgusting.

"You don't have to play with them," my wife would say.

"They only come out at night, anyway. And if you like mosquitoes, there's plenty of places where you can go and find all
you want."

But those damn flickers were relentless. I stood there and
watched one of them hammer away at the sides of a bat house
for ten minutes straight. Like he was drilling just for the hell
of it—he'd never find a single bug inside that pressure-treated
wood, but he just kept at it, anyway.

At first, I figured if it was okay with the bats it was okay
with me. But one day I saw some of the green plastic dangling
from its rivets. That's when I realized that, if I wanted to keep
things the way they were supposed to be, I had to be as relentless about maintenance as the flickers were about drilling.

There wasn't any other option: I couldn't exterminate the
flickers without putting the whole place out of balance. I didn't
know what role they played, but I knew they were there first.
The bats were the intruders, and I was the one responsible for
bringing them in.

So, every couple of weeks or so, I made the rounds, checking on the bat houses. Most of the time, they were fine. When
they weren't, I used an aluminum ladder to get up high enough
to put them right.

Every time I did that, I wondered if those damn flickers
were watching, waiting their turn.

When I got back inside, I went down to my basement and
assembled the machine.

|<1,000 shares @ US$5,000. Full as of 2011. Only
investment activity, purchase 100% share of TrustUs,
LLC. Cost $225K. Remainder still in Fund.>|

I hit |>Thx<| and unsnapped the two halves.

Five million dollars. Two hundred and twenty-five thousand to buy total ownership of that LLC. The other $4.7 million and change just sitting there, waiting for . . . what?

People with money always want more money. Some just gamble blindly; some think they're getting inside info.

But this was tying up a *lot* of money, like putting greenbacks in Mason jars and burying them in the ground.

I could make guesses, but that's all they'd be.

"Benton" kept running through my head.

I tried writing down some questions, but I had to make them precise. The cyber-ghost had no use for adjectives.

So I'd have to wait until Dolly was alone upstairs.

"How much land have they bought up, that LLC?"

Dolly didn't bat an eye. "So far?"

"Yes."

"Reach up and take down the plat map, Dell. The one with the strip running along the bay. It's marked in orange. . . ."

I brought the map over to where Dolly was sitting, laid it down in front of her, put a hand on her shoulder, and watched her uncapped gel pen as she traced it out for me.

"Starts here," she said. "Looks like someone just made a random choice to buy that lot to give his single-wide a home, but it's actually the borderline between our village and Bayside Bountiful."

"What's the—?"

"That unincorporated slice that runs all the way up through here," Dolly said, anticipating my question, her fingernail tapping the point around a foot away from where the thin orange line started.

"It's all these trailers? The ones that don't get city services?"

"Except for this spot, right at the end. There's nothing there, and it doesn't look like there's ever going to be."

"I don't get it. What's all this got to do with your dog park?"

"I don't know. Not yet," she said, in that promise-threat voice that comes out of her mouth every time she smells a rat. "But we're going to find out before this is over. There's got to be a reason why one corporation would want all that land. And if a town votes that it *wants* to be annexed, and the town next to it wants that, too . . . well, it's going to happen."

"How can a corporation vote? I mean, you can't own a town, can you?"

"I don't know. But Tova says a corporation is just like a person when it comes to some things. So maybe there *is* a way."

"You think it's something like a trade? This 'Bayside Bountiful' place, if it becomes part of the town, it gets those services—electricity and all—but it'd also have to pay taxes."

"Sure. But if it had all those services, then the land would be worth more, too. And that's just it, Dell. Worth more to who? What good is electricity and water and garbage services and all that if you're not going to *build* something?"

"That's why we went to *Undercurrents* in the first place, honey. They're famous for finding out stuff that nobody else does."

"You mean that nobody else prints."

"I guess that's fair enough. But they've got all kinds of sources, in all kinds of places, and once it goes up on their blog, it's a sure thing that everybody will know it. Maybe it's not even fair to call it a blog—it's more like a real newspaper than anything we have around here."

"And they'll keep digging?"

"Sure. They're famous for that. It may be public record that this corporation is buying up that whole strip of land, but until they started asking questions about *why* anyone would do that—

just like we're doing here, you and me—lots of people wrote to them. Public letters that they've printed, not private messages like the one we sent them."

"How do they know the difference?"

"The difference between . . . ? Oh, okay, I see what you mean. Wait a second."

Dolly's tablet snapped into life. A color photo of the ocean, with the word *"Undercurrents"* throbbing below the surface. Dolly clicked on it, and a page opened up. It was the same image, but now it had buttons running from the lowest left up to the top, then all the way across and down the right side.

Across the top were buttons for topics, like "SPORTS" or "POLI-TICS." The side buttons were smaller: "LETTERS TO THE EDITOR," "OP-ED," stuff like that.

Dolly tapped one of the buttons on her screen, and a whole bunch of conditions popped up. Like, if you wanted to write an op-ed piece, it had to be no more than twelve hundred words, and the author's name and qualifications had to be displayed. For stuff like personals, they had some really clear warnings about not taking anything at face value, not being responsible for misrepresentations, even some legalese about "assumption of risk."

At a spot somewhere below the ocean image was a blinking red light marked "CONFIDENTIAL" that opened into three different options:

Information—with a warning that anything you sent there was going to be checked out before it would be allowed.

Photos and Videos—with or without sound, but with the same warning.

Investigation and Issues—for people who wanted the blog itself to look into something. That last one was *very* clear: you had to send something that was in the public interest, not some private beef you had with a neighbor or anything like that.

"See the e-mail address for that section?" Dolly said. "It

starts with 'https://,' not 'http://,' like most Web sites. So it goes to a secure server, and you don't have to keep whatever address you send it from. Just send it, and nuke the address—it's not like you'd be expecting an answer, anyway. Either they'll start their own investigation or they won't."

"That's the one you used?"

"Uh-huh. And even if they could finger the IP, it wouldn't compromise us—Tova sent it from the public library in Fargo. I mean, she had her younger brother send it, actually—he's a senior in high school."

"I get it," I told Dolly.

And I did. Benton *was* warning her off, but he'd been too oblique about it. Otherwise, she never would have mentioned it to me. And why pick Dolly? Even if he had someone in City Hall who told him she'd been in there checking records, that info would have been worthless on its own. No way any one clerk could keep an eye on everyone who came in to check for a building variance, or when some LLC went into business, or any of the thousand other reasons people would be using its public-access records.

And, like Dolly said, all those public records are online. She'd hit that CONFIDENTIAL button anyway, so how could Benton know who'd been asking questions about the land buys?

Benton was PNW Upstream's boss. So he'd know that fund already owned TrustUs, LLC, which had been buying all that land . . . but there was no way he'd think Dolly knew it, too.

So I was left with this. *Undercurrents* had a lot going for it. A reputation for "pure" journalism—factual reporting, without bias—and total protection of all its sources. But any leak can reverse its flow, and the most trusted news source could get an infection, one that could turn fatal if it wasn't treated.

There's only one medicine that can stop the virus all traitors carry.

Undercurrents had always been about investigation, not self-promotion.

There was no masthead. No "staff roster," no titles, no . . . nothing. I went back to my own poking around—asking the cyber-ghost to find out who owned the domain or anything like that would have been insulting the value of his time.

But the domain wasn't even a dot-com; it was a dot-org, registered to TPE8YU, Inc. The contact person was Xiaun Constell, with an address somewhere on Nauru, and the phone/fax info was as blatantly phony as everything else. The area code for each was very different . . . and nonexistent.

They'd set it up so any attempt at incoming messaging was blocked, but they were very clear about the message their outgoing sent.

Still, there had to be at least one valid e-mail address to receive incoming. More than one, actually—how else could their editors get any given reporter's story?

Maybe they'd never actually gotten together in the same place at the same time. But, "collective" or not, there had to be someone at the helm. Or the hub. No way they'd release anything without double-checking, and there had to be a way for X to send in a story, and Y to open it and decide which Z would be assigned to check it out, without notice to X.

Sure, X would know the story would be fact-checked, but wouldn't know who Z was for any given submission. There wasn't any other way they could protect themselves.

At some point—maybe *past* some point—everything you do is an act of faith.

Olaf had absolute faith in physics—a life spent testing it

against all situations and substances had never revealed a single flaw.

I couldn't trace my faith in the cyber-ghost back that far. I never knew for sure he'd even be at the other end when I contacted him. But, so far, that connection had held, unbroken, for years and years.

And he was all I had.

|>TPE&YU? Info, A&A?<|

"A&A" was "Any and All." If the ghost couldn't get past that first barrier, no point in asking any zoom-in questions.

Even for the ghost, it wouldn't be an instant hit-back. So I had time to activate one of our "agency's" local assets.

"What?"

"I need to talk with you. Say where and when."

"Hour and fifteen minutes. Last place."

When Mack's car pulled in, his all-white pit bull jumped out of the passenger window and began slowly walking toward me. She would have kept walking, but Mack called out "Minnie! Friend!" and the dog instantly dropped into what most would see as a "sit" position. I saw it for what it was: launch mode.

When Mack got to his dog, he bent down and whispered something to her, then waved me over.

I didn't waste time. Careful to make no sudden movements, I reached inside my jacket and handed over a copy of that newspaper photo of Benton.

"You might know someone who's skilled at surveillance photography," I said. "This is an old picture, probably a posed shot. It was copied from a newspaper, so it's all grainy. Black-and-white, too. What we—the agency that gives us assignments, I'm saying—what *it* needs is a few fresh shots. As recent as possible. Color. Reference-scaled."

"Why do we need this?" Mack said. He wasn't asking an actual question; he wanted to know what story to tell the video ninja.

"We don't. That's why the shot has to include other people. No sneaking around this guy's house, no night work, nothing like that."

"He's not comfortable enough to work daylight. Not yet."

"You're saying, it's got to be dark?"

"Yeah," Mack said, a little on the defensive. "But it *doesn't* have to be the . . . the stuff he used to take pictures of."

"Relax," I told him. "There's no way I want his assignment to be taking pictures of just one person, anyway. If anything happened to that person, it'd add up pretty quick."

"Something's going to happen?"

"I don't know," I lied.

"Benton," he said, staring down at the photo. "I never heard of—"

"He threatened Dolly."

Mack's face went stony. His dog made some low-in-the-throat noise, picking up on something, just not sure what.

When Mack said, "How many shots do we need?" he was dealing himself in. But before I could answer, he made it clear what he *wasn't* dealing himself in for: "How many shots of *different* people, I mean. You know, photo or video?"

The first time I got Mack into some bad stuff, it was because Dolly wanted me to protect what was so important to him. So now he's walking right in, to protect something that's important to me.

Later:

```
|<Server in Finland. Top-level secure. Worldwide
but  separate-slotted.  Reporters/anarchists/oth-
ers. No cross-traffic. Incoming redirected. Single-
access pickup.>|
```

I wasn't going to insult the ghost by asking "Could you?" questions, so I hit keys quickly:

```
|>Local blog |||| Undercurrents |||| When started?
Who pickup? How many senders? Arrival/departure
date for all?<|
```

I knew the ghost would already have some of that info, so I waited.

```
|<Senders = 18. Pickup = 1. Opened 6/6/2002. Full
list 48 hrs.>|
```

Undercurrents had been around even before Dolly and I moved to this village. So whoever was in charge now might not be the person who started it. That didn't matter.

I'd been trained to do many things.

But that training was all depth, no width. So I knew a great deal of different ways to do the same thing. But outside that narrow band, I was ignorant.

When I was still a boy in years, but old enough for the recruiter to pass me along, he did almost all the talking. And the first officer to address us as a group echoed the truth of my life.

As all the instructors did at the beginning, they would use several languages. I only could understand part of the French, but I knew every word of the English.

"All of you who stand before me at this moment are ignorant. You know nothing of what you must learn if you are to survive what awaits you. To be ignorant is nothing to be ashamed of. Every man lacks knowledge of some things. No man has knowledge of all things.

"Here, we will teach all you need to know. But this teaching is all we can do. That is our job. Yours is to learn. And here is your first lesson: The line between ignorance and stupidity has nothing to do with intelligence. Not here. Not where you will be going. The line between ignorance and stupidity is the line between life and death. We cannot teach a stupid man. Why? Because a stupid man is a man who refuses to learn. A stupid man will soon be a dead man.

"That choice is yours. A choice you will have to make many, many times. So decide now. Pick the one path you will walk. Once you have made your choice, you have no option to change it. You need not tell us what choice you have made. That, you will show us."

So I didn't even know where to start. Or how to do it. Pictures of Benton would be good for one thing, but that one thing only.

Something connected to that forest land. That had to be what Dolly had sent in to *Undercurrents*. She was no investigator, either. So why not have those in the business of digging up facts do the work for her?

That's when I knew who I had to talk to, and why I needed Mack to come along.

"It's Spyros, the old man; he's the one I have to talk to."

"Okay."

"So your job is to get Franklin away from wherever I get to do that. I know where they're going to be working today, but I don't know how close—how *physically* close—to each other they're going to be."

It's not like Spyros is brain and Franklin is muscle. It's true the old man knows all there is to know about trees and stuff. And it's true that Franklin can throw boulders around like they're hollow movie props. But the old man is as strong as hell. And Franklin, he never *was* stupid. Nobody bothered to try and teach him anything. Except for football stuff.

"I got it."

Mack parked where the road ended, at the bottom of a long slope of trees. Near the top, that's where they'd be working, I thought.

We could hear voices while we were still climbing. More than one. The closer we got, the clearer they became. I couldn't make out the words, but I didn't like the tone. I motioned Mack to move behind me. I couldn't see if he signed anything to Minnie, but the white pit bull put herself between us.

"What d'you say, big man? You're a cinch to win!"

A young man's voice. Not one I recognized.

Another one: "Come on, stud. I mean, you like eating pie, right?"

One more: "Hey, maybe he's never had any. You like the way good pie tastes, Franklin?"

"I don't—"

Just as I stepped out to where they could all see me, Mack

cut off whatever Franklin had been about to say with: "How would *you* know? The only way you'd ever get close to pussy would be at the animal shelter."

Mack's voice was flat and hard, the kind of hostile calm that scares people like them.

All three whirled. None of them liked the view.

"Who're you guys supposed to be?" the first one said.

"I'm a friend of Franklin's," I told him. "A good friend. And this is a friend of mine"—quickly nodding my head toward where Mack was standing. "He wanted to meet Franklin, so I brought him with me. That's a problem for you, maybe?"

"We never saw you before."

"You don't want to see us again," Mack told him, very calm.

I watched their hands. Twitchy, but not ready to reach for anything.

Franklin opened his stance, but stayed as rooted as one of the trees he was working on. He wasn't sure what to do, not yet. But I knew what he'd do if any of the three punks moved toward me, and I didn't want that.

"Tough guy, huh?" their spokesman said. "I'm not fighting no pit bull."

"Off!" Mack snapped out. Minnie hit the deck. Mack looked at the guy who'd been doing all the talking for the three of them, holding out two empty hands. "Feel better now?" he said, his voice as empty as a hollow-point slug.

"Look, we were just having some fun," the spokesman said, turning to me, as if my age would make me more reasonable.

"Have it somewhere else," I told him. "We don't like people having your kind of fun."

"We can do whatever—"

"Whatever isn't the same as *wherever,*" I said.

"You own this property?" another of them whined. Not tough, looking for an excuse to go away.

"We're *standing* on it," I said.

"Mr. Dell, they weren't doing anything," Franklin finally said. "Really. They were just—"

"I know," I assured the giant. Then I dropped my hands to my sides, stepped off to my right, and told the three punks, "We're all done talking."

Minnie was still flat on the ground, but she never took her eyes off them. Mack rotated his head on his neck. The audible *crack!* was as loud as a gunshot in the still air.

They all walked off, their leader muttering under his breath. Bullies need to save face, but this lot wasn't stupid enough to make threats loud enough for us to hear.

"Gee, Mr. Dell, I didn't expect to see you."

"Actually, I'm looking for Spyros," I said. "It was Mack who wanted to meet you, so I brought him along."

"That's a pretty little dog," Franklin said. I didn't see what gesture Mack made, but the white pit shot toward Franklin, leaping up at his chest. The giant caught her in the air, spun her around, and scratched her behind her right ear. "See, Mack! She likes me."

"Of course she does, Franklin. She knows who likes *her,* too. You and me, you and me and Minnie, we're going to be pals."

"If you're Mr. Dell's friend, then you're *my* friend, right?"

"Right," I said over my shoulder as I was walking off. I didn't look back, already punching Spyros's number into my phone as I walked. He couldn't be far away—I'd seen his truck parked next to Franklin's before we started to climb.

He wasn't.

"What?" came snarling through the earpiece of my cell.

"It's Dell, sir. I wanted to consult you on something, and Dolly said you were working in this area, so . . ."

I'd said the magic word. The old man was waiting for me, sitting on a downed tree. His greeting didn't change, though.

"What?"

"You know Sector 27? That chunk of land Dolly and her crew bought to build a dog park? Inside a much bigger one . . . 303."

"Do I know it? I was the one who told her it'd be perfect."

"Something's going on there. I don't know what."

"With the land?"

"Not that land. With the land along the strip, just across the road from it."

"What could be going on there? All the trailers are gone, except for that one at the west edge. And that one—it's a meth lab. Either the cops'll find it, or it'll blow up," the old man said, making it clear that either result would suit him equally well.

"Some company's been buying all that land. The strip, I mean."

"So?"

"So Dolly and her girls traced it down. Then they let the paper know—"

"I didn't see nothing in the—"

"Ah, I should have said this Internet thing. *Undercurrents.*"

"I don't bother with that stuff."

"It doesn't matter," I told the old man. "Here's what does: When Dolly sent the info to them, they ran it. And now they're doing their own investigation. The deal with them is that you can send something in—info, photographs, whatever—and they may run with it or not. But, either way, they'll never tell anyone where it came from."

The old man didn't say anything; by then, he knew there had to be more.

"The guy who runs the group who bought all that land, he told Dolly to keep her nose out of it."

"He *told* her?"

"Not those exact words. He made it sound like a friendly warning. 'I hope you aren't running around half cocked,' something like that."

"And you want to show him some land he might be interested in?" the old man asked, as subtle as a crowbar to the head.

"Me? I wouldn't do anything like that. But I sure would like to figure out what's so damn important about that strip."

"Look, just because I like your wife doesn't mean I lost my eyesight. So don't play me for some brain-dead nursing-home case, okay?"

"Yes, sir."

He gave me a long look. Then he just nodded his head, as if we'd agreed on something. "I'm telling you, that strip ain't good for—"

"I'm not arguing. But the land Dolly's crew owns, it's on the hillside that looks down toward the bay. The only thing it could be looking down at is that strip."

The old man dry-washed his hands. Big hands, as dark and gnarled as the ancient trees he loved. "I told Dolly I'd be poking around over that way," he said. "The only access is pretty rough now, and there's no place to park. She knows her club would need to buy some more property to make it work."

"I'd appreciate that, sir."

"You were a soldier, am I right?"

I just looked at him.

"That 'sir' thing," he said, "you didn't learn good manners in no prep school, 'respect for your elders' crap. You don't make noise when you walk. So I figure, you must've . . ."

I nodded. Let him take it any way he wanted.

"It's better if you hold it like this."

Franklin's voice. He was showing Mack the best way to handle the lumberman's ax he was using to reduce fallen dead-wood to chunks that could be moved away from the live roots they'd been impeding.

"This way?" Mack asked, swinging with his shoulders, not just his arms.

"That's *good,*" Franklin encouraged him. "Mr. Spyros said we have to give those long roots more room."

"Hey," I said, so they'd know I was coming. I'd had to learn to do that—I'd once made Dolly nearly jump out of her jeans years ago. "You never made a sound," she'd said, hands on hips like I'd done something wrong.

There wasn't any point explaining that moving through brush like cigarette smoke through a mesh screen was ingrained in me. Too many years of training, too many years prowling hostile jungle—if they knew I was coming, they'd be waiting. Those times when fear was my most cherished friend. Now I always warn people I'm coming.

If I want them to know, I mean.

Franklin and Mack turned in my direction. Minnie was already looking, not making a sound herself, the tensed mus-cles twitching all along her hindquarters.

"Franklin's going to come over and show me and Bridgette how we can make a better yard."

"Franklin knows his stuff," I said to Mack.

"You know who's coming for a visit, Mr. Dell?" the big man burst out, unable to contain himself any longer.

"MaryLou?" I said. A safe guess—there wasn't another per-son on this earth who could get Franklin so excited at the pros-pect of a visit.

"Yes! She's got four weeks off. And now that I've got my own place, she wouldn't have to—"

"Why don't you bring her over for dinner?" Mack asked him.

"You and . . . you and your wife?"

"Sure."

"I bet she'd love that," the giant said. What he didn't say was that MaryLou would love the idea of Franklin's having a friend like Mack. The only other friend of his she knew about was me, and I wasn't her favorite person. MaryLou knew what I could do, and she didn't want Franklin learning any of it. Unlike most, she knew Franklin could learn all kinds of things.

"Then it's done," Mack said.

The giant bent down and patted Minnie's shovel-shaped head. "MaryLou is going to love *you,* too," he promised the pit.

"Just make sure she understands this isn't some kind of . . . social-worker thing, okay?" I told Mack.

"MaryLou's not *that* suspicious, Dell," Dolly said.

"Not of you, honey."

"*You're* the one that's suspicious of everyone," my wife said. And I had no comeback—it was the truth.

"MaryLou knows I keep my promises" was the best I could do.

"Well, there you go. Isn't that enough?"

"You're probably right," I lied. "Still, I'd really appreciate it if you'd just . . ."

"All *right,*" my woman said, as if giving in to a stubborn child. The truth is, she's the stubborn one in our family. Once Dolly plants her feet, a steamroller would bounce off her. She didn't know exactly why MaryLou was so confident that I'd keep my word, and it wasn't something she needed to know.

I'd kept my promise to MaryLou when I tracked that pile of toxic waste to his new home in Denver.

He wasn't calling himself Ryan Teller then. I don't know what they put on his tombstone—or even if he got one.

So MaryLou believed that, when I said I'd do something, I would.

If she had so much as suggested that the boy she'd killed was "bothering" her, Franklin would have pulled his head off his body. But MaryLou was nothing like her foul little sister—she wouldn't use people, especially a man she knew truly loved her. And she knew I was a different species—I wouldn't care what I had to use to get something done.

MaryLou had come so close to throwing her life away on a psychopathic prodigy. Maybe that's why she was so fiercely protective of the only person in her world that she knew would never betray her.

When're we gonna see some damn action?"

I didn't know why that fool who spoke only the few words of French that La Légion required us to learn worked so hard at letting the rest of us know how eager he was to see combat. But even though I was still a very young man, I'd already learned enough to know he wasn't broadcasting to any of us—he was convincing himself. Trying to, anyway.

"That's not ours to decide," Patrice told him, moving his head in the direction of the officers. His voice was low, but it carried.

Carried a message. More than one.

Idrissa shifted his body. Only a few inches, but it was a clear signal to those of us who knew him—not as a person, as a warrior.

The man so eager to see action wasn't going to return from

any mission we were sent on. Not because he would act foolishly in combat, endangering the rest of us. He'd never see combat—he wasn't going to survive the journey to reach the Blood Zone. How we explained his loss, that would be for later. But we could all see he was radioactive, glowing in the dark. Better if he was under the ground than walking it beside us.

In our work, there were no guarantees, only empty promises. We knew the truth—we wouldn't last any longer than the weakest of us did. We all knew that the best we could hope for was to increase our chances of survival. La Légion had its inflexible rules. We could all recite them by rote, but not a one of us would hold them higher than our own, single rule: do *anything* that might tip the odds in our favor.

So we always paid strict attention to scouting reports, but not necessarily so we could follow them. That would depend on what was known about the scout.

Some snakes are harmless, some are venomous. What we called a "carpet viper" is the same dirty-brown color as the trails we walked, and less than two feet long. But if one bites you, death is certain—its venom causes internal hemorrhaging. All the medics could do was to inject painkillers. A silenced bullet was kinder, and it preserved the meager supply of painkillers for the rest of us.

A python could be ten times the viper's size, but not really dangerous—it wouldn't attack anything the size of a man, and it couldn't kill with a bite, anyway. So the rule was: *any* small snake, you kill it.

But it would be Idrissa's blade doing that work, not my pistol. No silencer was ever as noiseless.

Too much patience can keep you silent forever.

I had to wait for the scouting reports to come back. But, in *this* zone, I trusted the scouts.

So it wasn't impatience that made me put together the

machine. But it was my training that made me disassemble it when I saw no message from the ghost.

I was trained to move from one world to another, and return as if I had never left. But when I wanted to *stay* in that new world, I'd had to learn new rules.

When you cross such a barrier, you must become what is expected each time—reentry is the most difficult phase. Sometimes, the barrier is so wide that you might have weeks, even months, to study, listen, learn . . . and blend. But when two worlds run parallel through your life, there's no time at all— you are *always* a resident of both.

In one world, people will speak glowingly of a man who never breaks his word. A man with such a reputation can be trusted, whether to repair your car or to tell you what medications will prolong your life. You can even look up a reputation on the Internet. That such reputations can be purchased never occurs to the trusting.

"Trust" is situational. A reputation for always keeping your word is your only protection—it fills what otherwise might be taken as hollow threats with actual menace, and menace changes behavior. Whether that filling comes from honor, ego, or treachery doesn't matter. Nor whether the threat is screamed, whispered, or unspoken.

Dead is dead. No difference whether the body rests in a mausoleum or is never found.

No difference to the dead man, sure. Not necessarily so to his killer. A "No Trespassing" sign could be a hollow threat. But a village surrounded by heads impaled on stakes sends the clearest of messages: only the skulls would eventually become hollow—never the threat.

I've known a lot of men whose students called them "sensei" or "sifu." I've seen knife fighters up close, and snipers at a distance.

Combat covers all that, and more. But it always narrows down to this: pattern recognition and balance disruption.

In the field, you are both aggressor and defender—a balancing act with only a hand-held pole to keep you centered. When that same pole must be used to strike or to repel, its *next* move must counteract precisely or your median is lost. And you fall.

The mother bird who fakes an injured wing to draw predators away from her nestlings is acting on instinct. The soldier who deliberately changes the pattern the enemy expects—visual or audio—has been trained to draw predators closer.

You might lure an enemy squad into an ambush, but you wouldn't call in an air strike on your own position.

Without information, patience is useless. You could be waiting for the enemy to walk across your trip wires, but if you don't know what's coming, you might be patiently waiting for your own death.

I'd never use my Dolly as bait. But if I asked her to call off whatever she was up to this time, I'd have to explain why . . . and I couldn't.

I could ask her to just trust me, and I knew she would. But the next time? And the time after that?

I could spend the rest of my life behind layer after layer of protection, but Dolly couldn't. Or wouldn't. With her, those were the same thing. The life she'd dreamed of in this little village on the coast was a life of peace, not confinement.

Telling her to "be careful" would be like telling a screaming maniac to "calm down."

I couldn't pretend I was interested in attending those endless meetings she was always going to. And I couldn't hang around the kitchen when her crew was working—that would spook them bad enough to leave, and then I'd be alone with Dolly. Alone with Dolly and her questions that I couldn't answer.

So I got Mack to invite us over.

"Mr. Dell!" Franklin blurted out his surprise.

"He didn't come alone," Bridgette said, flashing her bright, confident smile.

"Dolly!"

"MaryLou," Dolly said, ignoring Franklin as she pulled MaryLou's head down to kiss her once on each cheek. She'd taught all her girls that French nonsense, but at least it wasn't some phony air kiss—MaryLou wasn't a girl you had to be delicate with.

My wife introduced the two other women to each other, leaving me and Mack and Franklin to do whatever we were supposed to do. I guessed that would be to sit down, so I did.

Bridgette didn't make any big deal out of the cold cuts and greens she pulled out of the fridge. Dolly had brought along a big tote overflowing with fresh baguettes. MaryLou pulled one apart, scooped out the inside, slathered on something that looked like mustard, and stuffed it full before she handed it to Franklin. The giant blushed. Nobody noticed.

Bridgette and Dolly did pretty much the same . . . only they were already into their third bite before it dawned on me and Mack that we were on our own.

There was a pitcher on the table that looked like one of those cans you carry to the gas station, except it was glass. Franklin picked it up by the handle and filled everyone's glass— MaryLou's first, then all the way around until he got to himself. MaryLou gave him a wink . . . the only thing that made that weight tremble his wrist even slightly.

"Do you know a French toast, Dolly?" Franklin asked. But

instead of answering the way she did her girls when one of them had asked the same question years ago—"Yeah. Maple syrup"—she said, "Sure I do: *Mon ami*"—she tipped her glass slightly toward each of us in turn—*"ami des nôtres."*

No translation required.

"You know what you'll be doing after graduation?" Dolly asked MaryLou.

The tall, rawboned young woman shook her head. "I don't know. I mean, I could try out for the Olympics—they're supposed to be reinstating softball—but it might be a long time to wait. Maybe go after a master's, then find someplace to coach."

"You'd be great at it," Dolly assured her. "When we used to watch games together on TV, everyone got an education just listening to you."

"Probably have to take a course at finishing school first." MaryLou smiled. "I don't have the right style to handle pampered little princesses who worry more about their makeup than their stride."

"If they didn't listen to *you,* they'd be just . . . stupid," Franklin said, stumbling a bit over the word that had been his unspoken middle name most of his life. Not always *unspoken* inside that house he was raised in. The only reason his drunken excuse for a father stopped beating on Franklin was that he didn't need tea leaves to read his future if he didn't.

MaryLou was supposed to be gay. I say "supposed to be" because that's what she played herself as. All through school, the same way. Maybe it was a "You don't like it, just make your move" thing, maybe it was just her way of keeping distance. But Franklin had saved a damn fortune to take her to the senior prom. And Dolly told me MaryLou never had a girlfriend.

Mack doesn't give away much, but Bridgette was like a tough charm-school graduate who could send off messages with the smallest gesture. And all hers read the same: "Gay, straight, whatever, why would I give a damn?"

Even Minnie and Rascal seemed to get along. They weren't pals—not yet, anyway—but as much as they loved to snatch chunks of roast beef out of the air, they didn't fight over them.

"I know you don't have smoking in your house," I said, standing up and pulling a pack of cigarettes from my jacket. "I'll be back in a few minutes."

Mack knew I didn't smoke, but he'd seen me smoke when I needed to be someone else. And when MaryLou got up to follow me outside, Franklin's face told me he wasn't surprised. So, either he was a lot smarter than anyone thought, or Mary-Lou had gotten the message to him.

Maybe even both.

I walked a short ways off, far enough so that our voices wouldn't carry. Then I fired up a smoke without offering one to MaryLou—she'd been an athlete since she was a child, and I wasn't going to insult her intelligence.

"Franklin's not going to get hurt," I told her.

Her harsh face told me that I'd guessed right. And every word she spoke next underlined that. "Because you're going to protect him?"

"I'm not going to *use* him," I said, echoing what I knew was always in MaryLou's mind when it came to the man who loved her.

"You could pass any lie-detector test, couldn't you?" she said. It wasn't a question—she was making sure I understood she wouldn't believe anything I'd say.

"I'm not taking one. I haven't lied to *you,* have I? About anything?"

"No, I'm not saying you have. But something's . . . off about you. I don't know what it is, but I know nothing's going to get between you and what you want to do."

"Need to do," I said, underlining the difference.

"Yeah, I get that. But Franklin would do anything you asked him to do, 'Mr. Dell,'" she half sneered. She wasn't disrespecting Franklin's trust, just warning me off.

"There's no part for him."

"Then what were you talking to Spyros about?"

"Nothing that you have to worry about."

The tall girl with the pale-blue eyes turned to face me. I matched her stare, minus the warning.

"Tell me something," she said, very softly. "If you thought Dolly was in danger, and you could protect her by killing Franklin, you'd just do that, wouldn't you?"

"Him, you, anyone else."

"Easy as that for you, huh?"

"Yes."

"And if you were planning to do that, you'd lie to my face, right?"

"Yes."

By then, I'd lit another cigarette. Just in case.

"You know I'm gay, don't you?"

"No."

"No?! You think, just because Franklin—"

"No, I think you played it like that because it was the only way you could be yourself in that school. You didn't need a girlfriend, but you needed a way to make boys keep their distance. And a way to tell everyone to go fuck themselves if they didn't like it."

"I . . . I'm not sure what I was. Am, I mean. It's not like boys would be beating down the walls to get at me, anyway."

"Franklin would be a lot harder than any wall. And Franklin, he sees you beautiful."

" 'Sees me beautiful'—what is that supposed to mean?"

"It means that's the way his eyes work: they connect to his heart. He loves you."

"And I love him. But . . ."

"I'm not going to get him involved in any—"

"You want to know the truth?" she said, clasping her hands behind her, as if she was afraid she might do something stupid with them. "I'm a . . . I'm a virgin. I never much liked boys. Or girls, either."

I didn't say anything. I wished she was having this conversation with someone else.

"Franklin wants to marry me," MaryLou said.

"He's wanted to do that for a long time. But he wasn't ready. In his mind, I mean. He's only got his father for a model when it comes to being a husband. And he'd rather die than have you live like that piece of garbage made *his* wife live. But now he's found something he's good at. *Real* good at. He makes a nice living, too. And he's got his own—"

"Damn!"

"What?"

"I can't do it."

"Do what?"

"Not what you think. I can't come back here. Not after what . . ."

Her voice trailed away.

"It's not the same place, MaryLou. There's no trace of any of them left. Your so-called father moved out probably ten minutes after she took off. He can pick up his Disability check anywhere."

I didn't have to spell out "she" for her—MaryLou was never going to hear her baby sister's name out of my mouth.

"It's a paradise, now, this place?" she said, not sparing the sarcasm.

"No. And it'll never be one. You believe in Paradise, go to church. You only have to remember one rule."

"Rule?"

"Rule," I repeated. "You can handle just about anything. But I know, if you hear some punk make a crack about Franklin, you're going to throw down."

"Be better than asking *him* to."

"That can't be your job," I told her. "Franklin may be slow to pick things up. *Some* things. But once he does, he doesn't drop them."

"All through school—"

"I know. Punks said things. Boys and girls, both. But behind his back, not to his face. So he ends up with the same job you do."

"You mean the 'rule' thing? Not to . . . ?"

"Right. He's got a little apartment, and he's saving every dime, MaryLou. Just like he did for the prom. Only, this time, it's for a house he's going to build."

"Oh!" She brought her big hands around to the front, clenching and unclenching.

"I would never *use* Franklin," I said. Thinking, *Not unless I had to.*

She was silent.

"Dolly would kill me," I said.

MaryLou's smile was her own. I hadn't seen it before. But now I could see a piece of that beauty Franklin had always seen.

It was well after midnight by the time we left.

"Hold my hand!" Dolly demanded, as we walked ahead of Franklin and MaryLou.

I didn't ask why, just did it.

When we got back to our place, she explained it to me.
But it wasn't the first thing she did.

Nothing from the cyber-ghost in the morning.

I didn't know what time it was wherever he was, or even if it mattered . . . just so long as he knew it mattered to me.

That thought brought me up short. I was getting so lost in what I had to do when I encountered the target that I was in danger of not paying enough attention to how to get there.

More of La Légion's training: *Always approach with caution, but never with fear. Caution will protect you; recklessness will kill you. Fear will only paralyze you, but the result will be the same.*

Dolly knew everyone in town, but asking for her help would tell her too much. I didn't know anyone I could talk to that I hadn't already asked, one way or another.

I don't trust the Internet. Not because I was worried about some "hacker"—the ghost had a real-time monitor on all the lines going in or out of our property—but because I couldn't rely on it. One person says . . . anything at all, I guess. Another person sees that, and writes an article that quotes the first person like he was some legitimate source. Then someone else refers to the article in what *he* writes. It keeps picking up speed, spinning around and around like a centrifuge, splattering what's inside all over its walls.

Everything merges together. Digging core truth out of the mess that's left, who could do that?

There may not be totally trustworthy truth in anything. It feels more and more like that all the time. But there are universal truths, and I'd learned many of them before I was even old enough to want a woman.

I realized I wasn't seeking the whole truth, just looking for a path to a piece of it.

So I went to the library.

The reason people around here look at *Undercurrents* is that the newspaper prints only what it is told, not what it discovers. But I saw enough to see that Benton was an important man. A wealthy one, too.

What the newspaper also told me was that he was a homosexual. Not from this "reading between the lines" things people claim to be able to do, but from his own public statements. When he was interviewed for a "profile," he'd been quite clear about that. Not only did he live with his "life partner," he was a big supporter of same-sex marriage, and had donated considerable amounts to the effort to make it a federal law.

That hadn't happened yet; it was still a state-by-state decision when that interview had been done. So he also contributed to the campaign to get the same benefits for a "life partner" as for a spouse: health insurance, Social Security, the right to inherit if one party died without a will.

"The way the law is written now is insane," the paper quoted him. "A *single* gay man or a *single* lesbian can adopt a child. That is, a single *half* of a family unit. The other half of that family unit is going to do his or her share of parenting, from changing diapers to helping with homework. But if the parties ever decide to separate, for any reason, only the one whose name is on the certificate has *any* rights.

"He or she could even bar *visitation* with the child, and the courts would not intervene. Don't we have enough children rotting away their lives in foster care, moved from place to place like furniture? Don't they deserve parents?"

"Is that why you and your partner have never adopted?" the interviewer read her question from the sheet her editor would have told her not to deviate from—the one Benton would have memorized.

"No," he had responded. "We intend to do so as soon as we can be legally married. And, yes, I know: we could simply drive up to Seattle. But we both believe this would be morally wrong. We live *here,* we expect to spend the rest of our lives here. And we would rather stand our ground and fight than run away."

All the right words, in the right places. Most of those benefits he wanted made sense to me, but I had to read the parts about "the right to sue for wrongful death" and "loss of consortium" a couple of times before I felt I understood everything he was talking about.

When I did, I was even more grateful that Dolly had married me. She owns everything on paper, but until I read what Benton was fighting for, I never realized all the advantages. Not taxes—that wasn't something that mattered. But I *really* liked thinking about how a plane crash or a drunken driver could put some money in my wife's hands. It would be like I was leaving her something in a will I'd never write.

Benton was also a major backer of what the paper called "the arts." Everything from bringing in authors from out of town to speak at the library, to the huge art center where they put on plays and had exhibits of paintings. Only residents could display their art: sculptures, blown-glass creations, all kinds of stuff. Each one with a price tag, in case anyone wanted to buy it.

Benton's checkbook was always open, and always to the right page.

Everyone took it for granted that he didn't have to work. Nobody seemed to resent that. In fact, just as the paper said, the town was proud a man like him had chosen our village as his home.

I'm usually someplace else when Dolly and her girls are working on their projects, even if "someplace else" is my basement.

But when I got back from the library, I had to navigate the whole gang of them. Dolly gave me a "keep walking" look. Rascal did a quick inspection to see if I had any rawhide to bribe him; when I didn't, he walked over to where Dolly was sitting and stretched out at her feet.

I would have kept going all the way to the basement, but the voice of one of the girls cut through the separating wall like it was looking for me.

"Look! That evil little crowd, you see what they're doing?"

"I don't get it," a young woman said. I recognized MaryLou's harsh voice. I hadn't seen her when I came through the kitchen, but I hadn't been looking around. Anytime I had to come in while they were all doing something, I did it that way. Nothing dramatic, but enough to deliver the message: I wasn't interested in checking them out so I wasn't worth their attention.

"Are you for real?" another girl snapped. "Look at her Facebook page. Look! It wasn't enough for them to post messages that she was a pig. And a slut who'd do anyone for free. Now they're saying if she had any school spirit she'd hang herself—that'd make a great yearbook photo."

"I saw it," MaryLou answered. "What I don't get is why she lets them do it."

"How *could* she?" Dolly echoed MaryLou. "Can't you, I don't know, 'un-friend' someone? Or block them off your page?"

"That wouldn't make a difference," another girl said. "They'd just make up new names for themselves. They can tag her, too—every time her name gets typed in, it shows up on her page."

"So why *have* a damn page?" MaryLou said. "What does she get out of it? Why would she even look at it?"

"Not have a Facebook page?" another girl said, as if such a thing were beyond imagination. "That's like telling the world that you don't have a single friend."

"That's pathetic," MaryLou said, disdain coating her words. "But even if you're *that* pitiful, why not just let it sit there? Why *look* at it all the damn time?"

The big room went silent.

Maybe none of them had an answer. Or all of them remembered that MaryLou was a killer. She might not have been convicted, but the boy she shot wasn't coming back to complain about that.

There was a tentative little tap on the door, like whoever was there wasn't sure they'd be welcome.

"What?" MaryLou's voice—it sounded like she'd been taking elocution lessons from Spyros. I looked at the mirror I keep mounted in the corner before the hall to the basement steps. MaryLou was at the door. I couldn't see who she was talking to.

"I wanted to talk to Dolly. I heard you could—"

"You 'heard'?"

"It's okay, MaryLou," Dolly said.

As Mary Lou moved closer to me, a girl stepped gingerly past us. All I could see was that she was stringy-haired and fat—in youth culture, chum to always-circling sharks.

"They know me," the girl said. "I don't mean we're friends or anything, but . . . I guess I think *everyone* knows me now."

"I recognized your picture," one of the girls said. "From Facebook. You're—"

"Petunia," the girl said, her voice already breaking around the edges. "You know, the one they all call 'Tuna.'"

"That's enough!" Dolly growled. Rascal growled, too. He

couldn't tell what was making Dolly angry, but, whatever it was, he was ready to nail it.

It was quiet for a couple of seconds.

"Come over here," MaryLou said, her voice still hard, but a comforting kind of hard. "Sit down next to me."

I heard some noises, people moving around.

"I don't know what to do . . . ," the girl was saying as I turned away from the mirror and headed for my basement.

This time, the ghost was waiting. Not the ghost himself, just the trail signs he'd left before he vaporized.

When I assembled the machine, there it was:

```
|<Originator shielded, still active. Funnel system,
wide at top, filters down, narrows to Originator.
Any member: contribute, initiate fact-checking,
internally contradict or oppose inclusion, but not
a democracy—Originator sole controller of released
content. Opened w/ 29 cleared for encryption. 2002
+3; 2003 <>; 2004 +9; 2004 +4/-5; 2006 +4; 2007
<>; 2008 +1; 2009 +1/-4; 2010 -20. 2011–2014 <>As
of 1/2015, 22 currently cleared.>|
```

I moved quickly, eye-scrolling. *Undercurrents* had grown, but it wasn't a linear process; some years, more members were removed than added. High was forty-five members in 2008, housecleaning started the next year; it had been pared down since then, and was now seven less than when started. No indication as to why members were removed or added.

It kind of *felt* like it was all young people to me, but if this "Originator" was an old-school investigative reporter, then maybe more like a classroom than a collective. A course you could take for life, and flunk out of at any time.

|>ID on 1 added 2009?<|

By the time I went back upstairs, everyone was gone, with only the glow of Dolly's tablet breaking the darkness.

I sat down next to her, waiting for her face to stop scrunching from concentration. When it did, I asked her, "How do you get something to the people at *Undercurrents*?"

"Me, personally?"

"Isn't it the same for everyone?"

"You mean, like, do I have a private contact there?"

"Yeah."

"No, Dell. Remember what I showed you? You just tap Confidential, then Info or Investigations. Anyone can do it."

"Do you have to give your own identity?"

"They don't *want* you to do that."

"But those . . . 'cookie' things? Wouldn't they . . . ?"

"You don't have to allow cookies. I told you—you can even run script blockers, or go through one of those anonymizer services. They don't care."

"Huh!" is all I said. I wasn't any computer genius, but the ghost was way above anything most people could even imagine. And if he could get into their main server, he must be able to . . .

It only took me a few minutes to snap the machine back into place. Even less to ask the ghost what I thought I already knew the answer to.

|>Does using 'confidential' button to send info ID
sender?<|

I climbed into the charcoal jumpsuit, grabbed my helmet
and gloves, and went back upstairs.

"Won't take long" is all I said to Dolly. She'd known from
what I was wearing that I'd be wheeling my motorcycle out of
the enclosed space behind the garage.

"**D**ell, is everything okay?"

"Why wouldn't it be?"

"It's almost three in the morning, baby. You come up here,
see me working, sit there, patient like you always are, ask me
a couple of questions I've already answered, go back down to
your basement, and *now* you're going out?"

"There's something I want to look at."

Dolly gave me a look, but she didn't say anything—she
knows I don't need daylight to see things.

I rolled the motorcycle to the road, made sure it was in neutral, and let it go. I had to brake it pretty hard as I neared the
bottom of the hill. Then I unclenched my left hand to pop the
clutch in second gear, sparking the bike to life.

It didn't make much noise. It wasn't fast, either. But it was
good for what I wanted—no cop would give a rider wearing a
helmet, faceplate, and gloves a second look.

I guess Benton could afford any house he wanted, especially
around here. And no gated community would fit a man building the public profile he'd been working on. So it was easy
enough to glide by and pick up some intel.

Good-sized house, but not a mansion. Three stories, down-sloping yard. Professionally landscaped by people who knew what they were doing. Not Spyros's work. I couldn't say how I knew that, but there was something missing—it was just too geometrically strict to have come under the old man's touch.

There was a heavy-gauge wrought-iron fence all around the front of the house—black, with a touch of gilt around the more elaborate pieces. A wide driveway leading to a big garage, with what looked like a separate apartment above it.

No floodlights. No dogs, either—my headlight would have reflected in their eyes, and there was no barking noise. But that driveway was at least a hundred meters long, so maybe he had a more sophisticated system in place, closer in.

Circling behind, I could still see the top of the house, but that was all. On the back side, the slope was a lot steeper, and fully wooded.

That was enough for now. The ride had cleared my head. Focused it, too. I couldn't go where I had to in daylight, so I'd have to wait a full twenty-four.

I couldn't use Dolly's ragged old Subaru without leaving her stranded. And worried.

But for my next trip I wouldn't need a car; I'd need an alibi. So I pulled out my disposal cell, and went to work.

"What?" MaryLou's raspy voice—I guess that was how she responded to any visitor, even one on the phone.

"I'd like to talk to you."

"About what?" she said, telling me she knew who was calling. And that I hadn't woken her up.

"Not on the phone."

"Come to—"

"Can't," I cut her off. "Tomorrow, anytime past noon you say, anyplace you want. I only need about five minutes."

"You know where I am. Ten in the morning."

"Thanks," I said. It was just a reflex—the dial tone was already sounding in my ear.

One more call.

"You're up with the sun, right?"

"Sometimes *still* up," Mack answered, telling me he was ready to move right away if that's what was needed.

"Nine a.m. Earlier, if you have to be somewhere. But you need me to go along on one of your visits, which is why you're picking me up at nine."

I waited for the signal to tell me that Mack had disconnected. Then I wheeled the bike back home.

Whenever I had to return the bike to its nest, I always had the same poor choices.

I could gun it until I had enough momentum, then cut the engine and coast, but that would make more noise than I wanted. Or I could walk the bike up the hill. It wasn't that heavy, and I'd done it before. But the risk was that some good citizen would see a man pushing a motorcycle, and stop to see if I needed help.

The street almost never got pedestrian traffic, unless you counted all the "Look at me! I'm working out!" joggers and speed walkers who come out with first light. They never came out at night—what was the good of dressing up if there was nobody to watch your performance? I was dressed for the shadows, and the bike was that dull gray that blended itself down to near-invisibility, day or night.

So I pushed it all the way. Took a while: I didn't want to vary my pace, so I had to walk slow, letting my stride adapt to the steepness.

Dolly arched her eyebrows when I came in the back door, but she was too absorbed in some papers spread out on the table to ask questions.

Rascal was satisfied with the rawhide I tossed at him.

I went to our bedroom, put everything I'd been wearing into a blue drawstring bag, took a hot shower, and closed my eyes.

Kept them closed all the way to the bed. Dolly would do the lights-out check of the security when she was done.

I thought I'd be awake awhile, anyway. Lots to think about. Always is when I have to do something I'm not good at.

But my night-luminous wristwatch said it was almost six in the morning when the weight of Dolly on top of me woke me up.

After that, I didn't have much to do but hold on. I remembered my hands on Dolly's bottom, I remembered . . .

"Lazy bastard," from Dolly, just as I drifted off to the cushion of her whispered chuckling.

When I came around, it was a couple of minutes past seven.

I found Dolly in the kitchen, but she wasn't working on her project. She was working on breakfast.

"Perfect," I said, after a bite of the omelet she'd slipped onto my stoneware plate right from the pan.

"Best you ever had, huh?" she said, winking to make sure I knew she wasn't talking about food.

"Best anyone ever *could* have."

That got me a kiss . . . and a little basket of croissants.

I sipped my white-grape juice as my wife bustled around doing whatever she does when she cooks. It was a moment of such sweetness that a familiar blanket dropped over my thoughts. *If this Benton is a threat to my Dolly, he's a threat to . . . everything. But until I know who the players are, I can't cut into the game.*

"Where're we going?"

"Franklin's house."

"At this hour? He'll be at work."

"He's not the one I need to speak to."

"Got it."

A few minutes later, Mack said, "I don't know her. But I've met her. Maybe I could help . . ."

"Not with this," I told him. "You're going to drop me off a couple of blocks from where they're staying. I don't think it will take long, but you don't want to wait around."

"Why not? Where Franklin lives, that's one spot where nobody would even look twice at *my* car—once they're sure it's a white man behind the wheel, that is."

"You're not wrong. But it'd be better if you drifted off. I'll call you when I'm leaving, and you can pick me up two blocks north of here," I said, pointing to make sure he knew the direction I meant.

MaryLou must have been watching for me—the door to the house popped open a crack as I was coming up the packed-dirt path.

I stepped inside, closed the door behind me. I'd been in Franklin's place before, but it looked different, somehow.

"Find a seat," MaryLou said.

I took a corner of the couch. She folded her long body into a lounge chair, but didn't recline it.

"I need to borrow Franklin's truck tonight."

"Why didn't you ask him?"

"I would. And he'd say 'Sure.' But he'd say something to you about it, and I wanted to get any worries out of your mind."

"Meaning, you're not going to be doing anything where Franklin's plate number could cause trouble for him down the line?"

"Nothing," I assured her. "But I don't want Dolly to know where I'm going, so I can't use our car."

"I'm supposed to help you do something that—"

"—will protect Dolly," I finished whatever she was going to say. "But I don't know if the people I need to speak to will help me do that. And I wouldn't want Dolly to—"

"—worry about it? The same way you wouldn't want me to worry about what you might be up to in Franklin's truck, right?"

I gently placed my right fist into my left palm and bowed slightly.

"I've got a better idea," the suddenly falcon-faced young woman said.

Franklin's pickup was a work vehicle.

No back seat, so MaryLou was kind of squeezed between us. But it never occurred to me to ask her if she wanted the window seat. I'd already given her the directions, right down to what the odometer should clock, so I closed my eyes and leaned my head back.

I could hear them talking, but I tuned out everything except the sound of it. When I felt the truck come to a gentle stop, I opened my eyes. We were at the beginning of what I knew was about a quarter-mile of driveway.

"I'll call as soon as I'm done," I said. To the both of them, I guess.

It was only a couple of minutes before I saw the lights in the house I was approaching.

Johnny opened the door.

"Where's your car?" he asked, telling me they'd picked up on my approach way before I'd tapped the telegraph key mounted on a block of dark wood they'd put together to make a doorbell.

"I got a ride," I told him. "When I'm leaving, I'll call to be picked up. No reason to bring strangers any closer to your home."

"Why not give us a call first?" That was Martin, Johnny's partner.

"Because you'd ask me why I wanted to talk to you, and I didn't want to explain that over the phone."

Johnny stepped to the side, ushering me in.

"You want something? Coffee? Tea? Cognac?"

"No, thanks. I just want to sit down with the two of you and ask a couple of questions."

"No harm in asking," Martin said, just in case I was thick enough to miss that they weren't necessarily going to answer.

Their living room was probably bigger than our whole house. It didn't matter what I thought of it—what I *knew* was that it was all put together the way *they* wanted.

I had only one card worth playing, and I wouldn't get a second chance once I put it on the table, faceup. Before I could get fully centered, Johnny jumped the gun. "Dolly's not with you? Is there anything . . . ?"

"She's fine," I said. "For now, anyway."

"What does that mean?" Martin asked, his tone somewhere between frightened and dangerous.

"It means that someone said something to her. Friendly-like, but—"

"But what?" Johnny cut me off.

"What he said was something like 'I hope you're not going to go running around half cocked.'"

"Dolly *will* do that," Johnny said, smiling.

"Sure," I said, holding his eyes. "But you know me. I'm not like Dolly, am I?"

"No, you're not," Johnny said, dropping the smile. He *didn't* know me, not really. I'd been at their nursery quite a number of times, to pick up flowers for Dolly. Even a couple of trees, and other gardening stuff.

I knew I had better standing with Martin ever since I recognized the battered hulk in his garage as a Facel Vega. I think he was used to his partner's making fun of his "project," and there wasn't a trace of meanness in the way Johnny said *anything* to him.

Besides, they both adored Dolly. Always greeted her with a kiss on each cheek. That might have looked affected to some people, but they wouldn't be people that mattered.

And it didn't matter to them what I was, or whatever I might have done. They knew she was safer with me in her life. How they knew that, I don't know. I don't even know how they decided I wasn't interested in how they lived, but they acted just as sure of that, too.

I think I probably was prejudiced against homosexuals when I was younger. The only ones I ever ran across when I was a street kid in Paris were always asking the same question. Different words, but the same question: What would I do for a hot meal? Or a bottle of wine? Maybe a nice, warm place to live? Or they skipped right to money.

They scared me.

After Luc took me out of the gutter, I guess I never thought about men like that again. Not until I was a *légionnaire.* There was this big guy. Rhodesian. Called himself Hondo. Patrice had warned me about what this guy was. What he'd done to a couple of the weakest ones. If you were . . . raped—what else could it be called?—you couldn't go to the officers. That could result in a number of outcomes, none of them good for you.

We set him up. It was easy. Patrice explained it to me. "Those kind, they're all alike. And that makes them think the whole world is the same."

"Homo guys, they think everyone's a . . . ?"

"No, lad. Men like him, what they think is, everyone lives under the same tent. If you're strong enough, you can take what you want. If you're not, people will take from you. There's no middle; you're one or the other. No," he added, before I could even get the question out, "different people want different things. Sex, money, land—it doesn't matter. You've seen that plenty of times yourself.

"Hell, you're part of it. We all are, here. They pay us money for what? To take things they want. If they want land, we take that land for them. That means killing. Not a one of them would care if any of us wanted to rape a woman—even a little girl—those who're left over after their men are either gone or dead."

"I wouldn't—"

"Ah, no *man* would do such things. But there's plenty with the same equipment as us," Patrice said, cupping his crotch to make sure I didn't miss his point, "and they'd do . . . well, they'd do anything they thought they could get away with. And call themselves 'men' for doing it.

"And it's not only us, I don't want you to be thinking that. The savages, they do that all the time. It's part of the way they fight their wars between themselves. A woman from one tribe, she gets pregnant by rape from a soldier of a different tribe, she's got the enemy's seed in her.

"We took a village once. When we went through it, we found a dead woman. Not dead from our bullets. She had a sharp stick . . . stuck inside her. You could see she was pregnant, from her belly, but she was all bloody down . . . down there. Probably tried to stab that baby inside her, so she'd never have to look at her own poison-blood child."

"Mon dieu!"

"There's no God in here, son. Or, if there is, he's one blood-thirsty bastard. But who am I to talk? More than one priest held our weapons for us. When we came calling, they knew what we'd be out there doing. I never understood it, not really, not the way it's told. Catholics being driven out by Ulstermen. Maybe so, but not for any . . . religious reason. We want the bloody Brits out; the Orangemen, they know what their fate would be without the Queen's soldiers. Remember what I told you? About the curse of the Irish?"

"It's not drink; it's revenge."

"Aye, that it is. A blood feud. Blood that will never stop flowing. You know why I joined this pack of misfits. Mickey was my mate, all the way back to when we were little ones. When they killed him, I had no path but to take vengeance. I won't be able to go home for a good while."

Hondo came up on us one night. Patrice told the big man he was finished. With me. For the time. He walked off. Hondo turned to watch him go, and I had my dagger deep into his right kidney before he realized I'd been holding it all along. Patrice had showed me how to darken the dagger. It was second nature to him—anything that might catch a glint of light had to be darkened. That's why he'd told me to never wipe blood off the blade—dried, it was almost black.

The big man was already dying when Patrice ran over and hastened him along.

Any feelings I'd ever had about homosexuals being degenerates, or bent on rape, or cowards, they wouldn't have survived my first work as a hired gun.

When I left the Legion after the five years you had to serve, I'd learned a lot about people, but I had only one skill. A cluster of skills, really. But only one market for them.

I signed on with a unit that was working jungle. The pay was much better, and the bosses didn't think we were scum. Or, if they did, they kept it to themselves. We all need sleep just as much as we need food. We can only go so long without either. Bosses, that's what we called them. We didn't wear uniforms, and we didn't salute. But we were all a vicious lot, and a boss who closed his eyes at night wanted to be able to open them the next day.

One of the men in my squad told us his name was Pinky. He went into great detail about how a certain place in his body had turned pink from being used so much. You could tell immediately that *he* hadn't been used at all—anything anyone ever did to Pinky was by invitation.

He was a hefty man, but he moved like a poisonous snake. Smooth and silent. Pinky thought rifles were for cowards. He carried three pistols, one on each hip, the third in a shoulder holster. Another strap held the tube silencers. All of his pistols were the same. H&K, chambered for NATO rounds.

Pinky would get *close.* He'd drop two or three of the enemy before they realized they were under attack.

And I'd seen him standing, his back against a tree, dispensing death from each hand. No silencers then. Not much use in a firefight. The man was either fearless or seeking death—the way he fought, it was impossible to tell.

In the jungle, there's a deep, powerful belief in magic. I don't know what went through the mind of a hired rifleman at the sight of native boys wearing pink chiffon scarves, reeking of perfume, charging headlong into bullets. Despite dropping one of them after another, they would keep coming, as if the rifleman were playing some lunatic's video game.

Their belief in magic would hit the rifleman as surely as his bullets hit those crazy boys.

When we all went our own ways after that job was done, Pinky was still alive. But not before he shot a guy named Abel. The man he shot had called him some kind of name. I didn't hear anything but the cough of the shot. One shot.

Nobody did anything. Nobody said anything. This wasn't La Légion. We had none of their lies controlling us, no orders to never abandon our wounded or our dead.

We just walked off, in different directions.

I learned a lot from Pinky.

From watching him, I mean. How he handled whatever came his way. Maybe he'd once wanted to prove something to himself, but, whatever that test might have been, he knew he'd passed it.

If Pinky asked you if you wanted to "put it where it's nice and pink" and you shook your head, he would just shrug. And leave you alone. That was Pinky: he'd either leave you alone or leave you dead . . . and that was *your* choice.

Maybe what I had learned branded me in some invisible way. All I know is that Johnny and Martin accepted that I had no feelings about what they did, how they lived, or even how they came to be that way.

That last part was something I figured out for myself. It wasn't a choice; it was in you or it wasn't. Like being born with blond hair. You could dye your hair, but you'd still be blond underneath the covering.

I never had their feelings, but I realized that didn't make me anything special. I loved Dolly, and it seemed I'd never had a choice about that, either.

"**A**re you sure you wouldn't like something to drink?" Johnny asked. "I'm going to brew some tea for Martin and me anyway. . . ."

"No, thank you."

"All right," he said. "Let's just get to it, whatever it is."

"Do you know anything about a man named Benton? That's George B-as-in-Byron Benton. Hedge-fund guy. He started something called PNW Upstream in Portland. Mid-forties, looks a little younger, maybe. Moved to the village we—me and Dolly—the one we live in, about a dozen years ago."

"Why do you ask?" Johnny said. Like he was just curious, not probing.

"He's a danger to Dolly."

"And you . . . ?"

"Shut up, Johnny." Martin sliced into whatever his partner was going to say. "You're sure?" he asked me.

"Yes."

"Whatever you want, just say it."

"I just did."

"That's all you want? Whatever we know about . . . him?"

"Yes."

Johnny walked over and sat down next to Martin and put his hand on his partner's arm, telling me he stood with Martin. All the way.

"We don't know him," Johnny said. "But we *know* him."

"I'm sorry. . . ."

"He's a fraud," Martin said, no emotion in his voice.

"He doesn't really manage a hedge—?"

"He's not gay," Johnny said, making it clear he was telling me a fact, not expressing an opinion.

"Then why would . . . ?"

"He's an infiltrator," Martin answered me, trying to speak a language he thought I'd understand. "Where you live—actually, all along the coast—it's political suicide to be 'homophobic.' Or even not a liberal. You have to support the 'arts,'" he went on, hitting that last word with a light acid bath. "You have to be eco-conscious; you have to recycle, you have to be a 'Dem.' You have to write letters to the editor, even if nobody reads that rag. And it goes without saying that you have to support 'gay marriage.'" He didn't spare the vitriol on that last phrase.

"Aren't there plenty of . . . I don't know, people who call everything *they* want 'small government'? Like lowering property taxes, or being against abortion, or . . . ?"

"Yes," Johnny said. "No shortage. But Martin said 'political.' Which means you can leave out all the trailer trash—not my term—because, whether you're white or Mexican, if you don't have money, you don't vote. Nobody runs for office as a Republican or Democrat at the local level—everybody's 'nonpartisan.' Makes it a lot easier to control all the decision making. How many *local* Republicans do you think you'd find in Chicago?"

"Okay, but why the masquerade, then?"

"That's a good question. But I can tell you this for sure: Martin and I had dinner with George and Roger—that's the man he lives with—a couple of years ago, and they are *not* a couple. They may be partners, but not romantically. I don't mean they gave it away by *not* camping it up—that's not a test, that's a personality.

"But when you've lived your whole life as we"—he pushed his shoulder against Martin's—"have, you just can . . . feel some things. Especially between another couple. I'm not talking about some 'gaydar' nonsense. That's a signal you deliberately send out, and theirs was the opposite: a cover-up. But I can tell you this. I can tell you this, for sure: those two are the first closeted fag-bashers I've ever met."

"They *hate* . . . you? I mean, not you personally, but—"

"That's right," Martin said. Like he shouldn't have to say any more than that.

"That's a lot to go through, keeping your face on all the time," I said. "They can't be doing it just to fit in—it wouldn't be worth it. You have any idea what this Benton could be planning?"

"Not now we don't," Johnny said, softly. "But you already said the magic words, Dell. And you can take this to the bank: we *will*."

"That's a bank that doesn't draw interest," Martin added, just in case I missed the point.

"I don't want Dolly to know," I said, just in case *they* had.

"Can you say why?" Martin asked.

"Yeah. Dolly's no good at keeping emotions off her face. She's already sorry she even told me what Benton said to her."

"And if something were to—"

"That's enough," I told them both.

"We're entitled to protect Dolly, too. We're *obligated* to. You don't say you love someone—and we *do* love her!—and not stand ready to prove it."

"You already are," I assured them. "There's things you're good at that I couldn't ever learn to do. And there's some things I'm good at. We're each working our part of the job."

"And what we don't know won't hurt us?" Johnny said, half sulking.

"It won't hurt *Dolly,*" I answered, handing him a blank business card with a burner-cell number on the back. "Okay?"

We shook hands. All of us.

I believed them. And I knew they believed me.

Now I knew.

On the drive back, I kept thinking how most folks would think being gay was something you'd hide, not fake.

But, the more I thought about it, the better I understood—or, at least, thought I *could* understand—why MaryLou had played that role all through high school. And how Franklin could sense things even if he couldn't spell them.

Dolly wasn't home. I went right to the basement, snapped together the machine, and . . . Yes. While I'd been away, the ghost had visited.

```
|<(1) Confidential senders all ID'ed at their end.
(2) Member added 2009 = R/N Rhonda Jayne Johnson.
S/N changes, floating IP. DOB = 2/2/1987. Contacts
back-channel for PNW, ongoing. Approved for ><
question-phase, check-out ><*only*. Grad 0 State U
this year. Concentration: economics. Also: coach-
ing athletics, empha soccer. Accept'd MA program.>|
```

Then a lengthy list of vitals, from birth certificate to transcript to address. And a photograph.

There was something off about the photograph, but I couldn't put a name to it. I knew better than to try and print anything off the machine—it didn't have a connector port, and any message would disappear within a minute or so after the ghost's system would tell him I'd viewed it. I needed that time to copy off the information.

I did that. Then I stared at the photograph until the machine blinked off. I wouldn't need a printout to keep the image in my head. The career Olaf had started me on had forced me to learn that skill. Being caught with weapons could always be explained. But a photo of the target, that would do its own talking. Whoever was in such a photograph was soon to be dead, and clients of professional assassins expected anonymity to be part of every contract.

Dolly wouldn't be surprised if I didn't come to bed. Sometimes, I can't sleep—not with film strips being pulled across the underside of my eyelids, forcing me to watch a slow-motion movie. Most of the time, I could follow the script. Could be something I'd done that I wasn't proud of. Or something that had been done to me. I *had* to watch.

But a replay of whatever my life had been before the "retrograde amnesia" the doctors in that clinic had told me I already had when I was brought in—*that* had never come up on the screen. Still it *could,* I told myself. Maybe that veil would lift. Maybe I could learn . . . I don't know what. Or even why I cared.

After a while—I don't know how long I'd been there, and they wouldn't tell me—I left. I always thought of it as "escaped," but there really was no security, not even a fence. The drop from my window was cushioned by the soft, carefully tended grass. It was dark, but you could hear the shadows. Some of the other kids said those shadows were grown-ups who had been there for years and years, wandering the grounds after night came. I wasn't afraid of shadows. Not afraid enough to remain caged, anyway.

From some place in Belgium to the gutters of Paris. A different kind of cold. A ravenous wind always blowing. Then Luc found me.

I used to think about what I'd do if ever I found that "clinic." I knew things now that no child could ever know. I had skills no child could ever be taught. Tools no child could ever use. I could make whoever was in charge tell me whatever I wanted to know . . . if they knew it themselves.

I was good at that. One time, I was alone in a hotel's penthouse suite with a man who owned the hotel, and a dozen more like it. He was rich enough to travel the world on his yacht; he kept private jets in different places, and employed a security force powerful enough to overthrow some small countries. I needed to know where and when a massive arms shipment was to be delivered. If he wouldn't tell me, I'd put a venom-tipped round into his brain.

"You can't be serious," he said, not a hint of anxiety on his face or in his hands. "You kill me and you'll never get out of here alive. And even if you managed that . . . You're a professional—you *have* to know you're already on video. You'd be hunted down sooner or later. Then you'd be boiled to death like a lobster."

"I get the coordinates, or you get dead," I said, just as calmly. I had good reason to be: A man who buys too much security never thinks that what he paid for, another could pay for as well. Pay *much* more—traitors don't come cheap. That's why my job was to get the information and pass it on over the satphone I had with me. Then put the rich man to sleep.

But the threat to kill him was a bluff. Dead, the traitor inside his organization would be of no more value to the people who had hired me.

"You can kill me, I suppose," he said. "But you'd just be killing yourself, don't you see that?"

"I won't ask you again."

"Didn't you hear a word I said? Are you *insane*?"

"Not as long as the shot they gave me is still working," I answered his question. "I kind of know what it is, some mixture of lithium and Thorazine, some other stuff, too, I think. But I don't know the formula. Only they do. That's why I have to do this. They're the only ones who can keep the voices away, so I have to do what they say."

My voice had already started to wobble, so I made a concentrated effort to separate my words. The rich man didn't miss what he thought I was trying to hide.

"Please . . ." is all I could get out by then.

I could see inside his head just as he thought he could see inside mine. *This man is a lunatic. A robot. What's one arms shipment, anyway? Not worth my life.*

He told me. I let him hear me speak it into the phone, my voice barely getting the words out.

And then *I* got out. But not before I put a flat metal box on his desk.

Even if that clinic still existed, even if I could find it, it was all so long ago. I could think of a hundred reasons why no records about me would still exist. And not a single one why they would.

I learned this very early in my life: all knowledge isn't power.

I might know how to break into a fortress, but if I didn't know where the fortress was . . .

So I knew a lot of things I'd probably never have a use for, but that didn't mean I'd ever throw them out. A man I served with told us that New York cab drivers who were Sikhs would always be left-handed. Nobody had to ask him why that was so; he wasn't drunk enough to fall over, but he'd had enough liquor to believe that we were all spellbound by his stories.

"See, all Sikhs have to carry this little curved knife in their turbans. It's a religious thing with them. Now, all the cabs have these bulletproof shields behind the front seat. So you can't do nothing from back there. What a robber does, he jumps out as soon as the cab stops, then he walks around to the driver's window, holding out money, like he never saw the slot in the shield, see? The driver rolls down his window, and the robber pulls his piece. Or a razor, or whatever. Now, a Sikh, he'll have his own blade out and a big rip in your arm before you can blink. But, see, that only works if his blade is on his left, 'cause that's the side he'll have closest to the window."

I knew I'd probably never have a use for that, even if what the loose-mouth told us had been the truth.

"How come he didn't have an accent?" I asked Olaf later. "He said he was from New York, but—"

"If he was from Brooklyn, or Queens, you would hear an accent. But if he was raised in Manhattan, his voice would sound the same as if he was raised in Chicago, or Cleveland. It's not like being from Boston—that carries an accent that does not depend on what part of the city you grew up in."

"Oh" is all I said. That was enough—it was usually what I said after Olaf told me something.

But that photograph . . .

"He says, if we give him an image that's already online, he can find out a lot more."

Mack, repeating what the video ninja told him.

The only image I had was in my head, not online. And, somehow, I knew even if that photo was online there wouldn't be a match.

Something off, but I couldn't feel my way through to it.

I knew her name, where she went to school. I've hunted down men with far less information.

But jungle law always came first. "It is not tracks that will give you away." Part of Olaf's legacy—he'd known he couldn't tell me everything in the time he had left, so he'd focused on correcting mistakes before I made them.

"Even a fool knows not to leave trail signs after he has finished his work," he said. "It is the *entrance* you must control. You already know about things like trip wires, land mines, deadfalls. That is not enough to protect you when you work outside this environment.

"When you hunt in a densely populated area, even your *vibrations* must be masked. Every question you ask sends out tremors—you cannot know how far they reach, but every pattern you disturb is a potential alert to your target.

"An alerted target may flee, or may lie in wait. It is never enough to move silently. You must be beyond quiet, beyond stealth. That means any job with a time limitation, you refuse."

Around here, a Subaru is so common it wouldn't be noticed. But if I told Dolly I needed to use her car too many times, *she'd* notice. Mack's car was a generic, once—now it was so torn up that it might as well be flying a flag. Franklin would lend me his truck in a second, but the license plate would be a problem. Martin would lend me one of his rides, only none of them would work for what I had to do.

If I traveled without a car, it would take me longer. That wasn't a problem. Longer to get there—so what? But not being able to *leave* quickly—that could keep me in a place I didn't want to be.

"Let me make sure I understand this," MaryLou said.

Her tone was more suspicious than friendly. Still, I'd already told her this was all part of protecting Dolly, so she'd hear me out.

"You want to . . . have a look at . . . this girl, only you can't let her see you, and you can't go around asking questions, either. Am I right so far?"

"Yes."

"And you came to see me because . . . ?"

"Because I don't know anything about colleges. Campuses, things like that. I could never look like I belong, like a student or a teacher. I don't know how to talk like they do. I might as well paint myself green."

"That could work," she said.

"If you don't want to—"

"Jeez, you really *are* an alien! What I meant was, that's one of the school's colors. They're so sports-crazed that if someone was walking around wearing a duck's-head mask, the campus security people wouldn't even get a call."

"But how . . . ?"

"It was a *joke,* okay? I should have known you wouldn't get it. You probably don't even have a sense of humor."

"I probably don't," I admitted. "But I don't need one, not for this."

"What *do* you need?"

"Your help."

"What do you want me to do?"

"I don't want you to do anything. I want you to help me with your mind. You know what I want. Can you tell me anything that would help me get it?"

MaryLou was quiet for a minute. I could see her thoughts: *This is a dangerous man. But not a sarcastic one. He wouldn't*

*waste time coming around to play games. He scares me, but . . .
his word is good. He keeps his promises. And this is for Dolly.*

"Let me think for a couple of minutes."

I didn't move. She hadn't been asking permission, and I
couldn't go wrong being quiet.

"You're dressed okay," she finally said. "You mind being
my father for today?"

I shook my head "no."

"I drove Franklin to work, so we can use his truck. It's not
that long a drive."

"Just tell me what to do," I said.

She stood up and looked me over, carefully. "Are you carrying a gun? I can't see it if you are."

"Yes."

"Then you'll have to—"

"I'm carrying a permit, too."

"Let's go" is all she said, plucking the keys to Franklin's
truck from a hook screwed into the wall by the door.

"If they see *me* looking around, they won't think twice about
it. And this woman, she wants to be a soccer coach, you said?"

"Yes."

"Okay. Well, if anyone in the athletics department recog-
nizes me, I'll just tell them my father drove me down to give
the place the once-over."

"Like you'd be transferring, maybe?"

"Sure!" she sneered in sarcasm. "They've got a super football program, and they support the holy hell out of track-and-
field, too. But if you want the best deal for girls' softball, you
want the Southwest. Texas, Arizona . . . like that. Still, I could
be getting married. . . ."

"That makes sense."

"The story?"

"I didn't think it was a story."

The sun turned her blue eyes even paler as she half-turned from her position behind the wheel. "It wasn't *that* long ago."

"The whole town stood up for you, MaryLou. You think they wouldn't want you back?"

"I don't want to *be* back. This place . . ."

I kept quiet. MaryLou didn't have a reason in the world to ever return to where every memory was a lie or a terror. If it wasn't for Franklin, she'd probably never even cross the border. Franklin, he'd follow MaryLou into Hell wearing a gasoline overcoat if she asked him. But she never would. And the only place where Franklin would ever feel like his world was in balance was working for Spyros.

Another puzzle. For another time.

MaryLou rolled Franklin's truck into the parking lot, zipped down the window, and handled the security guy as easy as she handled anyone who stepped into the batter's box against her.

"Which way to the softball team?"

"You mean, like, the locker room?"

"No, I mean the field," she snapped off, just short of bratty. "I'm here to see Coach Marrone."

"Oh. Well, she'll be in her office, this time of day."

"And that would be . . . where?"

The guard pulled a laminated map from a side pocket, mused over it for a second, then said, "You want Building Nine. Just walk to the other side of the lot; there's one of these 'You Are Here' things, and you can—"

"Thanks," MaryLou said, as if she'd just been mollified. And just in time, too.

"This isn't the way to Building Nine," I said.

"I'm not going there. And neither are you," she told me, taking my arm the way a daughter might, giving me one of those "I can't take you *anywhere,* can I?" looks to complete the picture.

We ended up outside a stand-alone brick structure. It was so covered with different signs, I couldn't even figure out what it was for.

"Fan stuff," MaryLou said, reading my mind.

"They'll have . . . ?"

"Yes. Or tell me where to find one. School's over. The girl you want, she's a grad, right? This year?"

"Yes."

"Wait for me outside. Don't lurk—stroll around, but don't go far."

"Got it," she told me.

I wasn't sure what she'd gotten, but that leather bag of hers was big enough to carry a twenty-kilo package of heroin, and she was strong enough to swing it like it was empty. Her body language told me we should get going.

"Here," MaryLou said, reaching inside her bag, and handing me a book with heavily padded covers and "2015" in huge gold letters on the front.

"What am I . . . ?"

"It's a yearbook. Her picture will be in it. Probably alphabetical order. I couldn't open it up to check while they were looking at me."

I knew the girl would look older than her classmates—the ghost's info put her in her late twenties—but I wasn't prepared for such a severe separation from "student."

The inside photos were in color, with stuff like "Debate Club" under each one. Rhonda Jayne Johnson was dressed like a businesswoman in her mid-thirties, dark hair pulled back into what I guessed was some kind of bun, dark lipstick making her lips thinner than I expected, sharp cheekbones. And not smiling.

The photograph the ghost had sent was a girl maybe half the age of the one in the yearbook. In that one, her hair had been fixed into two long pigtails, and she was wearing some kind of school uniform—a blazer with a crest over her left breast. Her lips were much fuller, face a little softer, more rounded.

But it was the same Rhonda Jayne Johnson, beyond doubt.

Then it hit me. The photo the ghost had sent didn't make sense. He would have known I'd need to recognize her by sight. And the dates didn't match, either: how did some schoolgirl get herself cleared to drop info into the *Undercurrents* funnel?

"What you needed?" MaryLou asked.

"I think so."

"You want to . . . ?"

"No, no," I assured the tall girl. "I may have to look some other places, but I can go there myself, no problem."

"Give Dolly my—"

"Why don't you drop me off and come in? That way you can tell her yourself."

While MaryLou was upstairs having some of that tea Dolly brews different ways for different people, I was in my basement, putting together the machine.

|>Photo last sent: how recent? Seen by CIF?<|

I had just started to disassemble the machine when the screen flickered, as if the ghost had been waiting for me to ask those questions.

```
|<Photo current. DK seen. Possible. URL rotating,
but always off (.cr). CIF = IP local, but could be
masked. No address confirmed.>|
```

The screen went blank. I unsnapped the slides, reboxed the machine, and started my mind working on why the Commander-in-the-Field—the ghost would know I'd meant the boss at *Undercurrents*—hadn't seen the photo he had sent me. And where the ghost had found it.

But before I threw another |> his way, I wanted to consult an expert. And as soon as MaryLou was gone, I would.

"Could you take ten, fifteen years off the way you look?"

"Dell, I know you're not asking a fashion question. And even if you were, I know you're not asking about me," she said.

The "you better *not* be" ending to her words was unspoken, but as clear as a red skull-and-crossbones sign on a little black bottle.

"No, no. Don't be absurd," I said, using a word that would tell her that I was working, not playing. "I was asking if there's . . . I don't know, makeup tricks, stuff like that. Not a disguise, exactly. But some way a woman almost thirty, say, could have a picture taken of herself so she looked maybe half that?"

"A *photo*? You know there's computer programs that could retouch anything. So . . . Wait! Are you talking about those software programs that they're always showing on TV, like how a kid who went missing ten years ago would look today?"

"No, precious. I mean something that would work like that, only in reverse. Ten, fifteen years *before* today."

"Well, that's even easier. Anyone with Photoshop could do that much. Some of the girls who come over here do it when they're being silly—see how they'd look with different-color hair, or purple eyeshadow. . . . What do they call it? A 'cyber-makeover,' that's it."

"Not a photo, Dolly."

"How much time would they have?"

"I don't understand," I said, now even more lost than I'd been when I started.

"Well, if you lost a lot of weight, that would—"

"No," I cut her off. "Something where you could look like one age, then go into another room and come out looking like you were much younger. Not *you,* I mean—"

"Yes. Sure, you could. Depending on certain things. Like, if you were really skinny, you probably couldn't add weight that quick. But if you wore your hair differently, or had it cut, or—"

"Your clothing, too?"

"Well . . . up to a point. And that would depend on how well other people knew you, how close you were standing. . . ."

"Say you never met. In person, I mean."

"You're back to that cyber-thing again?"

"I guess. . . . On a computer, you could look like a grown-up to one person and a kid to another, right? I don't mean a baby, just like a teenager to one and an adult to a different one."

"Sure," she said. Unsaid: Who *wouldn't* know that?

"Then why . . . ?"

"This isn't like you, Dell. Just ask me whatever it is you want to know. Why be so . . . delicate about it?"

"I wasn't trying to be. I just don't know the questions I'm supposed to be asking."

"Really?"

"Yes. I have a photograph—an actual picture, I'm saying.

Then I have another picture, but that one's in my head. And in that one, the same woman looks like a kid just starting high school."

"Someone you remember from . . . ?"

She cut herself off before she reopened a wound. A wound I always told her I didn't have.

"Okay, like this," I said. "The picture where the woman looks like a . . . girl, *that* one's the most recent. But when she"—a lightning-flash thought warned me against even mentioning *Undercurrents*—"applied for a job, she used a photo that made her look much older."

"What good would that do her? Sooner or later, if she got the job, she'd have to show up for work."

"What if the job . . . what if the job was one she could do from home?"

"It doesn't matter. I can't think of any job where you wouldn't need a résumé of some kind. Credentials, references, stuff like that."

"There must be—"

"Cyber-sex!" Dolly burst into what I was saying. "It's like phone sex, where the man just *imagines* what the woman he's talking to looks like. It's like that TV show the girls go on about. Some slob who never goes out of the house pretends he's this sixpacked hunk with a Ferrari in the garage. Even has his picture on his Facebook page, too. Only it's all a fraud. And some of it can get real ugly, like if some vicious girls get together and make up a dream lover for another girl. Then, after they get her hooked, they humiliate her by putting up the whole story for everyone to see."

"That's . . . Well, that's cruel, sure, but—"

"You don't understand." Dolly was so angry that her words ripsawed out of her mouth. "Do you know what some of those poor girls end up doing? One girl, she got 'played' into believing that this guy from a town that was a couple of hundred miles away was going to take her to the prom, so their first date would be 'special.' When these disgusting little . . . when those miserable swine who thought it would be such fun to just *torment* that girl, they had this nonexistent guy post on *her* Facebook page that she must be insane to be telling anyone he'd ever take her anywhere except maybe to a 4-H Club if he wanted to win a blue ribbon in the pig contest. . . . Do you know what she did *then*?"

I didn't even want to guess.

"Well, *do* you, Dell? She killed herself! She put on her pretty prom dress and went out to the garage. She ran a hose from the exhaust into the car, closed the windows, and started the engine. Then she cried herself to death."

"What happened to . . . ?"

"Those other girls? *Nothing.* They were just playing a 'prank' on her. They never meant for any such thing to happen. One of them was so upset, they put *her* under a doctor's care! Some of the others, they even wanted to go to the funeral!"

If I'd been one of those girls standing in the same room as Dolly right then, I would have been frightened. My sweet, loving wife's face had tightened into the mask of a fanatic about to push a detonator switch.

"Some people just can't take it," she snarled, imitating those she despised through clenched teeth. "You remember, that professional football player, he was a *huge* man, but he was so . . . so pressured by this other one—his 'teammate'—that he had an emotional breakdown. Guess how much sympathy *he* got!

"Everyone circled the wagons around the man who'd bullied him. 'Bullied'—there should be another word for what he did. He *threatened* that other player, even said he was going to do things to his *mother.* And this was no new thing for him, either. The bully, I mean. But all these 'commentators' said,

Well, that poor boy, he should've just punched the bully in the mouth. This is a *man's* game, you know?

"I looked up some of those tough guys. One was a cokehead, another one a wife beater. And the toughest of them all was the one who ordered an underage prostitute from room service!"

"It goes both ways?" I said, making sure Dolly would hear it as a question, not a statement.

"What are you . . . ?"

"I mean, do boys kill themselves, too? Teenage boys, if somebody plays that kind of evil little joke on them?"

"I guess they . . . could. But, now that I think about it, I don't remember ever hearing about one."

"Because boys are, what, stronger-minded?"

"Hah! No, baby, it's because girls can be so much more vicious. Everyone knows some old biddies who could draw blood with their gossip. But this is different. The young ones today, there's *nothing* they won't do."

"Oh," I said, as if I'd just learned something. Maybe I had. I'd seen girls go after each other, clawing like wild animals. But the girls who hounded that teenager into suicide, there was nothing wild about them. They may have been as cold-blooded as cobras, but reptiles don't torture for fun—they just go after what they can kill, and avoid those who could kill them, moving as quick as a triggered reflex in either direction.

"So, if a grown woman got herself all dressed up and made up her face to look like she was just a kid, that could be her idea of a . . . ?"

"A bully wouldn't do that, honey. It sounds more like one of those 'escorts' that are always posting pictures of themselves."

"You mean . . . ?"

"Yes," my wife said, a little calmer now. "*Une putain, non?* That is part of what the customer buys. That . . . fantasy, I guess you'd call it. A man could be treated like a cash register by his own wife, but if he dares to spend some of his own money for the right whore, he can be King of the Castle. The boss. Master. Snap his fingers, and she'll do anything he commands."

"That's only a—"

"It's as real as the customer *believes* it is, Dell."

I knew she was right. A "window girl" in Amsterdam once paid me a lot of money to make her "man" dead. She told me she was used to doing anything the buyer wanted. "I'm just an actress," she said. "It's a movie. I play a role. And I have to *sell* it—I have to make the buyer *believe* it."

"So he'll come back?"

"He'll come back to *me*. And when he's with me, he's . . . I don't know, a big movie director, a race-car driver, an athlete. . . . Whatever he wants to be, that's what he is."

"That's expensive?"

"It depends. If all he wants is for me to make all those excited little moans, that's not such a big deal. But if he wants to be a slave master . . ."

"So you *make* money? And you give most of it to . . . ?"

"*Most?* I give it *all* to him. I'm not a slut, I'm a *slot*. Customers don't see that part. I say 'slot' because that is all I am to him—one of those cash machines. Different people make deposits, but he's the only one who can make withdrawals. If he *wants,* he might even give some of it back, like when I beg him for new shoes or something."

"Why kill him, then? I'm sure there's plenty of others—"

"Not anymore," she said, flicking on a light in the dark hotel room I'd been paid to meet her in. The left side of her face was scabbed and twisted; her upper lip on that side couldn't cover her teeth.

"Candle wax," she said. "He heated it first, so I could see what was going to happen. Then he gave me a shot of heroin before he poured it over my face. When I came out of it, the pain was so horrible I just screamed and screamed. This," she said solemnly, pointing at her face, "this is me now."

"But if you were earning so much money for him . . ."

"Oh, he could always get other girls. He always *had* other girls. This was a lesson. So other girls would know what would happen to them if they ever crossed him. They'd go from movie stars to skags that had to work in dark alleys just to make enough money to pay their rent and eat."

"What had you . . . ?"

"I hadn't done *anything*! And he *knew* I hadn't. He really didn't want to do this to me, he said. But it was like an . . . investment. That's what he said, just before he . . ."

"You must have been holding out, right? I mean, for what you paid the broker to get this done . . ."

"I *earned* that money," she said. You could drop a fresh slab of raw meat on her voice; it would still be good a month later. "You don't even want to hear what I had to do. In fact, you'd have to *pay* me to tell you about it." She kept talking, but a weird note throbbed inside her voice: "That's what they want, some of them, just to have you tell them. They all want the same thing, only some of them like it packaged differently."

I slitted my eyes. As if she could read my thoughts, she flicked off the light.

"You'll do it, then?"

"Yes."

"I know what you're thinking."

I didn't say anything.

"You're thinking: Doesn't she want him tortured? Or acid poured on his face? Or even cutting off his . . . ?"

I stayed quiet.

"All I want is for him to hear my name. Not my name, even—just the one he gave me. I want him to hear that 'Heidi' paid for it. Before you kill him. You can do that?"

"Yes."

"And you will?"

"Yes."

She'd never know. I mean, she'd know he was dead—that news might never make the newspapers, but it would be all over *her* world in a couple of nights. The streets with their bright windows if the customer could pay enough, and dark, twisted little alleys if he couldn't. She'd never know if I said her name first, that part.

I hadn't. I might have, only I wasn't going to spend weeks scouting for a chance to get him alone. I knew the gambling clubs had doormen, and security people working inside. But once you left the club, none of that protection left with you.

Still, maybe she got her money's worth—the first shot from the little subsonic hardball probably did it, but the suppressor might have choked it down far enough that he could have still been alive for the few seconds it took me to empty the magazine into his eyes.

I don't know when the brain shuts down. There wasn't any blood; after I used my Saran Wrapped boot tip to roll him face-down, he just looked like a drunk using the gutter as a hotel room. He was already dead, but it might have taken him a few seconds to close off completely.

Later, I thought that if I'd just walked away after the first shot, he might have been found and taken to the hospital. They might even have saved him, but he'd be a drooling lump of flesh forever after that.

I tried not to think about how Heidi might have liked that even better.

Hours later, alone in my basement, I kept working—probing the darkness of my mind.

"Cui bono?" Always the assassin's first question.

You might think this a contradiction. But I had always heeded Olaf's words. If there was only one person who profited, it wouldn't take the police long to start looking at that person. And anyone who paid others to kill for him leaves a human chain of potential informers. If one of those links broke . . .

I worked on my breathing until I slowed my heartbeat down to what the best snipers need for their work. Then I started on my list:

- ✓ Benton wouldn't have threatened Dolly if he hadn't somehow known that she was the source that had started *Undercurrents* looking into all those land purchases.
- ✓ The only thing each land parcel had in common with the others was that they were all connected.
- ✓ But even if all connected under one ownership, they were just as worthless as they were before.

LEAVE IT!

I came out of wherever I'd gone with a start, that inner-screamed warning still echoing. I knew what that meant— I'd come to a fork in the road, and not recognized it until I'd already gone too far down the wrong one.

Trust it. I could feel those words. Luc's? Olaf's? It didn't matter, not then. If you try analyzing the motives of a man shooting at you before you dive for cover, you might as well shoot yourself. I went back to where the road had forked:

- ✓ The *Undercurrents* boss was the narrow end of the funnel. That same narrow end became the nozzle that sprayed out assignments.
- ✓ You'd have to be cleared to be able to pour anything *into* that funnel.

√ And whatever you poured in, *that* would have to be cleared, too. "Fact checking," the old newspaper guys called it. I knew what they called it because the Internet was full of their complaints that it isn't done anymore.

√ The only way the CIF could check out Rhonda Jayne Johnson would be to check out the info she submitted. He must have done that many, many times before he let her drop anything into the funnel's mouth.

√ That would have been a long-term investment. . . .

THERE! my deep-wave subconscious screamed. Loud enough to wake me up.

I knew there was no point reaching out to the ghost so soon.

Oh, he'd pick up whatever I sent, but he wouldn't stay around after he answered—that's why I had less than a minute to write it down before the screen would flicker a warning, then go blank. I didn't understand how he did what he did, but I knew he wouldn't tolerate "conversation" again so soon. An open connection was against all his rules, and his rules were the only ones that mattered.

But I wouldn't need a cyber-genius for some of what I needed to know.

When I went back upstairs, Dolly was alone in the kitchen, tapping on her tablet, Rascal at her feet. The sun was just coming awake in the east. Soon the birds would start their screeching for their breakfast.

I never look over Dolly's shoulder when she's working, unless she asks me to. It wouldn't be right. I have my basement; what privacy did Dolly have?

"Hungry?" she asked, not looking up from whatever she was doing.

"Just want some juice," I told her as I opened the refrigerator and poured myself a glass of that red-orange-colored stuff that Dolly made herself. I didn't know what was in it; she called it "jungle juice." I knew some of her girls liked it, but she didn't force it on them. Me, she kind of did. I knew I was supposed to have no less than three full shots a day when I was home.

"That's not breakfast."

"It's all I—"

"Then open the breadbox and tear off the end of the baguette in there. It's yesterday-fresh."

I did that.

Then I sat right across from Dolly, chewing slowly, washing every bite down with a sip of her concoction.

"What?" she finally said.

"I didn't say anything."

"Dell, how long is it going to take you to learn? You think I can't hear you talk just because you don't speak out loud? I know you could sit there for hours, waiting for me to finish whatever I'm doing. I'm not going to be able to finish *this* for a few days," she said, hitting a key that made her tablet beep. "So?"

Arguing with Dolly was always a waste of time, especially when she was right. "Remember when you told me about how people could pretend to be other people on . . . Facebook, and stuff like that?"

"Yes," she said. She said it patiently, tapping her nails against the butcher block so I'd know she really wasn't.

"You can do it with pictures, too? Of yourself . . . Well, not really of yourself, pictures of someone else."

She made a "Get on with it" noise.

"Isn't there a way to tell if someone stole a picture?"

"Sure," she said, leaning a little forward. "It's so easy that I don't know why these kids don't do it. Or maybe it's that they *won't* do it. I think . . . I think it's like those crazy karate movies—you know they can't really be flying around and kicking each other ten feet off the ground, but you never say that."

"Why not?"

"Because *everybody* knows it. So if you say it like you're telling them something you know, they go, 'Like, who *doesn't?*,'" my wife said, switching to that teenage-girl voice that comes out of her mouth as naturally as French does—Dolly's bilingual in English. "There's a term for it: 'suspension of disbelief.' You volunteer to do that when you go to one of those movies. Or read a *Batman* comic, stuff like that."

"So they don't check pictures people say are theirs because they're afraid to spoil . . . whatever it is they're doing, yes?"

"I guess that *must* be it. I mean . . . Come around behind me, Dell. I'll show you."

I watched as she tapped some keys. A whole bunch of photos appeared.

"Who're they?"

"It doesn't matter. Some girl who put her picture on Facebook."

"So why . . . ?"

"Wait," Dolly said. She used her finger on the touch pad, grabbed one of the images, and moved it up to the top of the screen. "See?"

"It went into . . . Huh! That picture, it's not really her. The girl on Facebook just now, I mean. Right?"

"Yes. It's no more complicated than that. You find an image you like, then you move that image onto your own page, and, just like that, that image is *your* image."

"And you could have different images for different names, then?"

"I'm not sure I—"

"That's my fault," I said, squeezing my wife's shoulder gently. "What I meant was, if you can use any image you want to be 'you,' then you could be a whole lot of 'you's."

"Sure."

I moved Dolly's hair off the back of her neck so I could kiss her. Then I went down to my basement.

I sent this:

```
|>Rhonda Jayne Johnson + Benton?<|
```

And this time, I waited.

```
|<Communication conf. Irreg. G4S, each time.>|
```

Not exactly pen pals, then. But what "goods for services" did they exchange? Cash would work, but if the *Undercurrents* reporter was feeding info to Benton, it wouldn't be through e-mail. So that schoolgirl photo was, what, a disguise? Not a chance. If a damn *picture* wasn't good enough to fool anyone, how could she hope to pull that trick off in person?

I knew there was a time limit for keeping the line to the ghost open. Had to be. I didn't know where the border was, so I just jumped:

```
|>Shares of PNW Northwest + Rhonda Jayne Johnson?<|
```

The response came back so quickly that the ghost must have been waiting.

```
|<10K U$, invested 2011. No value change.>|
```

The machine's screen blinked, which I took to mean "Shut down!" I disassembled it, thinking this Rhonda Jayne Johnson had a lot to gain if that hedge fund skyrocketed. That would explain her tipping Benton to whatever was going on with the *Undercurrents* investigation. But what could she tell him that he couldn't just go online and read for himself?

It was easy enough to find her—campus security is all about protecting schools from lawsuits, not protecting students.

At three in the morning, the parking lot was empty. The closed gate would keep cars out, but I wasn't looking for a parking spot.

The grounds were pretty deserted, too. Most of the windows in what I knew was a dorm building were dark, nobody on the well-lit paths. One of those electric-powered golf carts the campus police patrolled in could show up around any corner, so I passed up the temptation to move in the shadows and just strolled along. My only disguise was a hooded poncho, the kind you wear if you want to be ready for a sudden shower. It was in the school's colors, one for the body, the other for the sleeves. The entire back was covered with an image of the school's mascot.

A cop would need to get very close to see the clear latex covering my hands, but I wouldn't let that happen: if I let them pull in close enough to ask me some questions, they'd know I was no student.

I never considered one of the administration buildings. They'd have all their records computerized, and double-locked down. Besides, I didn't need any medical or financial info, just an address.

The dorm I picked didn't have a single lighted window on the second floor. I couldn't take that to mean they were empty—

anyone inside any of the rooms could be asleep. Or stoned. Or doing something that worked better in the dark.

So I held the rubber-ringed cup against the door, alert for any sound. But the burglar's stethoscope sent only silence to my ears.

I inserted a blank plastic card with a magnetic strip correctly positioned, then tapped the little random-number generator until a green light showed.

The push-button LED flash showed that what I thought would be a room was actually some kind of suite. Four rooms, each with its own bath, and a big common area with a pair of sofas and stain-free carpeting in some bluish shade.

I turned on the tablet I'd been carrying inside the poncho, and let it search for a signal. The WiFi only took a second to connect. I plugged in the thumb drive, waited for a window to open, and typed her name into the Student Directory box.

Rhonda Jayne Johnson had an apartment just a few miles off-campus.

That was a lot of work for a little bit of information, but with a last name like hers, I wanted to narrow the search for when I got back home.

Oregon's DMV sells the data it collects, so all I had to be was an insurance company registered with them. I already was that—there was only one agent in the office Dolly and I visited to ask about a "personal" letter Dolly had received, promising to beat any price offered by a company with a "national reputation." While Dolly got the guy to come outside with her to show him her Subaru, I told them I'd wait.

Like I'd guessed, his computer was already on, so I didn't even need the password-recovery program I always carry when I visit strangers.

Rhonda Jayne Johnson's school address checked against a blue 2014 Audi TT. Insured full-boat, down to zero-deductible.

Driver's license showed no tickets, no accidents.

The license photo was the same one the school's yearbook had. No point trying to match it for other names—even if she had some kind of personal page, that same photo under another name wouldn't help me.

Feeling as if I should have done better on my own, I reluctantly snapped the machine together.

```
|>Where photo obtained? Does not match target's
driver's license.<|
```

I left the machine on. If the ghost was watching his screen, I wouldn't have long to wait.

I guess he wasn't.

"I apologize for just showing up," I said to the man whose size overlapped the width of the door he'd opened at my knock.

"Mr. Dell! You never have to—"

"It's good manners to let folks know you're coming." Mary-Lou's sandpaper voice cut him off.

As Franklin stepped back to let me in, I said, "She's right," to the behemoth. What I didn't say was that I hadn't called because MaryLou was perfectly capable of answering his cell phone herself if he was in the backyard or someplace else. And equally capable of telling me that this wasn't such a good time for me to drop by.

"Sit down," Franklin said, pointing to the one armchair in

the front room. It was big enough to hold even his bulk, but not him and MaryLou both—and she jumped onto the sofa a split second before the man she loved turned around and joined her.

"The reason I didn't call first," I started, holding MaryLou's eyes long enough for her to understand that I wasn't there to ask Franklin to do anything dangerous—or even to leave the house—"is because there's things about this town I don't understand, and I need to understand them. It's the only way I can protect my wife."

"Dolly?" they said, in a single two-timbre voice, ready to anaconda-wrap around the unspoken threat of whatever might make me worried about the woman they both loved.

"Yes. I can do whatever has to be done, but I have to cross some ground to do it, and I don't want to step in a sinkhole."

It was language they both understood, in their own ways. Before Franklin could respond, MaryLou put her power pitcher's left hand on his forearm in some signal they'd worked out between them. "What do you need to know?" she asked.

"What's most important here? In this village? Not some umbrella thing, like finding happiness or making money. Specifically. What counts the most?"

"There's more than one answer," she said. "Depends on who you ask. But if you take making money off tourists out of the mix, it's a safe bet you're talking about either sports or the 'arts.'"

I didn't miss the sarcasm on her last word, so I knew more was coming.

"Not pro sports," MaryLou said, just to make sure I was paying attention. "Here, it's college. We've got big-time teams in Oregon at that level. Nationally ranked, all that. But the only pro team in the whole state is basketball, and that's way up in Portland."

"Okay" is all I said—to MaryLou, soccer wouldn't count.

"But when it comes to *any* kind of art, that's going to get supported," she went on.

"You mean, like, painting, or . . . ?"

"Photography, or sculpture, or music, or acting, or . . . you name it."

"And there's money for all that?"

"They will always *find* the money," the young woman said.

"Because art stuff doesn't bring in money, and sports pay for themselves?"

"They pretty much do," she said, just a light frosting of defensiveness over her voice. "This town may be just one of a hundred little feeder streams, but college ball, that brings in *serious* money."

"Especially football, right?"

"Right," she said, stroking her man's forearm. "If they paid college athletes—which they *should*—Franklin could have made a fortune."

"I don't want—"

"*If* he wanted to," MaryLou said hastily to squelch Franklin. "But we all know what Franklin wants to do. What he's so good at already."

"I just started," the big man said. "I won't be good at it for a long time. But I don't care. Someday, I'm going to be good enough at it to have my own business."

"Spyros says you're a natural," I told him. "He says you've got a special touch that you can't learn—it's got to be in you from the beginning."

"He told me something like that, too," MaryLou added.

Franklin's face flushed. It would take him another lifetime to get used to any kind of praise that wasn't coming from a football coach.

"I'd never go against Mr. Spyros."

"Who said, 'against'?" I asked him. "The man's not going to

want to work forever. And what do you think he's training *you* to do?"

"You mean . . . ?"

"Of *course* that's what he's saying," MaryLou jumped in. "A man has a business all his life, he doesn't just walk away. Either he sells it off, or he gets someone to run it for him, stays on as a partner or whatever."

I nodded my head gravely, to make sure Franklin would understand I was dead-serious.

He immediately turned to MaryLou. "Then we could get—"

"This is fine for now," she said. I could tell it was a conversation they'd had before.

"So what's the biggest draw?" I asked her. "Of the arts thing, I mean."

She didn't hesitate a second. "Probably writing. Poetry, short stories, books—anything like that. It's kind of a hold-together." Seeing the slight raise of my eyebrows, she went on: "One guy draws comics, another one writes the stuff that goes in the balloons. Or some kid wants to make a little movie, and he needs a script. Even the ones who paint, they need . . . titles, like."

"They teach this in school?"

"Some of it, sure. But most of it's in those workshop things. Like, the library will have a night class. Learn to write your own story—that's always hot stuff," said the young woman who wouldn't ever want to write her own.

"Who pays—?"

"I guess that depends on what you're talking about," she cut in. "They have those open-mike nights in a few of the bars. Excuse me, *cafés*—the places that serve hard stuff, they get their crowds from guys who want to watch the game on the big-screen, convince themselves the girls who wait on tables are shaking it just for them."

"So the big money—say, to build that Performance Art Center—that's all from taxes?"

"Taxes? Oh, you mean, like, property taxes? Some of it, I guess. But they're always applying for grants. And the Town Council has money it can set aside for stuff like that, too."

"People don't vote on that?"

"I don't . . . I don't *think* so, but I couldn't swear to it."

"Thanks," I said. To both of them, even though Franklin hadn't said much of anything.

As if he realized that, the big man said, "Would you like something to drink, Mr. Dell? We don't have liquor, but we've got all kinds of—"

"I'd take some apple juice in a second, Franklin. But you've got to stop making me feel like I'm a hundred years old first, okay?"

"What did I do, Mr. Dell?"

"That's what he means," MaryLou said, affectionately. "Why not just call him what I do—'Dell'? That's your name, right?"

"Actually, it's Adelbert," I said. "But that's a tongue twister. Anyway, my friends call me Dell, you're right about that. So . . . how about it, Franklin?"

"Sure," he said, coming off the couch like a floating feather. Any fool who assumed his size made him clumsy wouldn't stay fooled long. "Apple juice, right . . . Dell?"

"On the nose," I said.

It's not always about money, I thought to myself on the drive back.

Olaf didn't have to tell me that part. Even if I didn't know it when I started working as an assassin, I knew about it long before I walked away from that life. Jealousy, revenge—motives like that I'd probably expected. But that last job, the one where I first learned Dolly was a real person, that had been an act of mercy.

Not on my part. I did it for the money, as always. But the people who hired me, they knew it had to be done, knew it was their duty to a man they loved—they just couldn't bear to do it themselves, or even to watch it happen.

So I told myself that even the slightest chance Dolly could be prosecuted was something I had to avoid. But lying to yourself never works. So—here's the truth—just like those people who had hired me in San Francisco: I couldn't take it.

I had never expected to die a hero's death. Before Dolly, my greatest hope was that it would be quick one.

I didn't need one more chance to tell her I loved her. If I hadn't proved it by now, words would change nothing.

"Why didn't you just ask me about all that?" Dolly said, after I finished telling her about my visit to Franklin and MaryLou.

"MaryLou doesn't have all your connections here. You know what's going on more than she ever could. But she knows some things about this town that I couldn't get from you, sweetheart; she's got one source you don't—she grew up here."

Dolly nodded her understanding, but she didn't say a word. That was up to me, she was making it clear.

"I've gone as far as I can, I think," I said. "I can maybe get more stuff"—I didn't bother telling Dolly where, or how—"but there's no way to . . . I don't know, connect the dots, maybe?"

"Why don't we just make a list of what we *do* know, first? Then at least we'll know what we *don't* know, okay?"

It was my turn to nod. Dolly snatched one of those pads she's always writing on, the kind where the paper is crosshatched, so it's really a bunch of little boxes. That's the same stuff I use to work out anything I'm trying to design. Luc always made his own designer's paper. It wasn't something he liked doing, but it was a necessity to be precise. A tool, so no different from keeping a knife honed.

But that paper—now I could just buy the same thing. And once Dolly saw me sketching on that pad, she had to have a whole mess of them for herself.

No sitting on my lap, playing secretary, like she does sometimes. I didn't have to tell her this job could turn nasty, and turn me into something a lot worse.

"Okay," she said, "this is for sure. We know there's something wrong with this Benton guy."

"Yes."

"Not just because he said . . . ?"

"Nothing like that," I interrupted. Not just to keep Dolly focused on what had been her own idea, but to keep her away from the truth: it was *everything* like that. "Keep going."

"You said that one of the reporters for *Undercurrents* must be feeding stuff to Benton?"

"How else would he know who was responsible for the tip in the first place?"

"So it *is*—"

"No, honey. It's a lead, not a connection. We know which reporter because we know she's been in contact with Benton. *And* she bought shares in his hedge fund years ago. But all that fund has done is spend money, not make any. So there has to be some huge financial score in this—something worth investing not just money but a lot of time, too."

"In that strip of land? How could there be? It would take . . . I don't know *what* . . . to make it worth a dime."

"I don't know what, either. But I know the guy's a fraud."

"How? Ever since he's been here, he's done nothing but—"

"Martin and Johnny told me."

"When?" she demanded.

"A little while ago."

"They never said—"

"Neither did I, right? I thought I could get some help from them without bringing you into it, but now there's no choice."

"Dell . . ."

"They're not gay."

"Martin and Johnny? Have you lost your mind!?"

"No. Not them. Benton and his supposed 'partner,' *they're* not."

"That's silly. I mean, they're always in—"

"So you couldn't tell, either. Any more than I could. But Martin and Johnny, you think *they* couldn't?"

"I'm not . . . I mean, I wouldn't . . ."

"This is about money, Dolly. Somewhere inside, that's what it's about. And it's got to be a *ton* of money. Benton's playing a long game. He's already rich, so it might even be for more than just paper money."

"I *still* don't see—"

"Me, either. It was your idea to write down what we knew."

"But you just said Martin and Johnny told you—"

"Yes. But now that I told you, *we* know."

"What else, Dell?"

"Rhonda Jayne Johnson, that's the name of the informer. She just finished her senior year at State, but she's probably ten years older than her classmates."

"You know where she lives, then?"

"And the car she drives. But none of that really helps. If we can't put together the big score Benton's been playing for, we can't do anything."

"Why do we have to do anything if all he's after is money? He wouldn't be the first one who wanted more just for the sake of having it."

"We have to do something because you're in his way."

"Me?"

"You or something you're connected to. It has to be. Why else give you that friendly advice in the coffee shop?"

"I don't see it, baby. Maybe he was just—"

"Men like him, they never 'just' do anything, Dolly. I don't know much about a lot of things, but men like him, I do. I've known a lot of them. They're all alike. Not in how they look, or even what they want. But there's one thing that's in all of them: they don't see people; they see *things.* Like chess pieces, or rocks, or buildings. Doesn't matter unless what they see is some kind of obstacle to where they want to go. To them, that would be a beaver dam blocking a river. You don't negotiate with beavers; you don't buy them off. Not when a few sticks of dynamite . . ."

"Dell, I'm scared."

"Me, too."

"Damn it! I'm not scared of this Benton, and you know it! I'm scared of what you get like when you think I'm in . . ."

"Why?" I said, trying to keep bitterness out of my voice. "That's the only time you never *have* to be scared, isn't it? When I go back to . . . what I know how to do. The one thing I'm good at."

Dolly put her head in her hands. When I touched her shoulder, she whirled and slapped me hard enough to make me . . . *NO!* screamed in my head before I could spin with the slap and . . . I wouldn't allow myself to even *think* about what I'd come so close to doing.

"You are not allowed to ever do that," my wife said, as calmly as she had once removed bullet fragments with only a flashlight to guide her hands. "Do you understand me, Dell?"

"Dolly, I would cut off my—"

"Ah, you stupid man! You think I meant you are not allowed to hit me? I hit *you,* didn't I? And you deserved it." She gently pushed me until I was sitting in one of the chairs. Climbed in my lap. Dropped her voice to a whisper. "Don't you *dare* ever think you're only yourself—your true self—when you're at war. That's not you. That was never you. You're a good man. In your heart, in the way you act. You're the man I love. If you're nothing more than a man who earned a living by . . . by doing what you did, what does that make *me,* then? Some whore who loves a man only for what he can do for her?"

"I—"

"Sssshhh, my husband. I know what you're going to say. I always know what you're going to say before you say it. Not the exact words, but what's behind them."

She stood up. Held out her hand. Said, "Come with me, Dell. We'll finish that list later."

"**A**re you all right now?" she whispered in the dark.

"As soon as my face heals, I'll be."

"Liar! You couldn't *be* any better, could you?"

"Don't be so sensitive," I said, much more softly than I pinched her.

"Ow!!"

"Who's the fraud now?"

She kind of laughed deep in her throat, and slid her head onto my shoulder. "First we sleep," she said.

"**I**t has to be the land," she said a couple of hours later.

"I think it must be that, too. But you and your friends, you bought it for next to nothing."

"That project started before Benton ever came here. And we've still got plenty to do before we can make that dog park we want."

"Nobody's ever offered to buy it from you?"

"Not from me. And not from any of the others, either. We made our own 501(c)(3), so there's no secret about who—"

"That number, what is it?"

"Number? Oh. A 501(c)(3) just means we're a nonprofit. The idea was to buy that parcel first, and then start raising money for the other things we need."

"Like an access road?"

"Yes. Physical things. But also stuff like insurance. Everyone swears to Heaven their dog is peaceable, but . . ."

"So it's still years away?"

"Well, not *that* much. Maybe, I don't know, four or five. Our lawyer—"

"Lawyer? You mean like Swift?"

"It *is* him. I mean, we know we can trust him. And he said it was simple to incorporate, but we might have to go through the County Attorney's Office to get permits and things like that."

"The County Attorney . . ."

"Oh, he's *nothing* like the DA. It won't be a problem. He *wants* there to be a dog park. He's on our side. But he's the kind of guy who wants all the 'i's dotted and the 't's crossed."

"The reason you know nobody's tried to buy the land from you, that's because you'd all have to vote on something like that?"

"That's right—no single member could sign a transfer deed; it would have to be the corporation itself. Or an 'authorized agent,' I think Swift called it, and we haven't even picked one yet."

First I made sure that MaryLou was going to be around for a few more weeks.

Then I started fabricating a face shield for a motorcycle helmet that would accommodate night-vision goggles.

It was three days before I was sure it would work. My motorcycle is an old 600cc Honda. It doesn't look like much of anything, and its battleship-gray paint makes it hard to get a good visual. It never made much noise to start with, less now that I've rewrapped the exhaust pipes.

Even if a cop did see me on the road, there wouldn't be anything to make him suspicious. A helmet and gloves, that's standard gear. And compared with the way some people ride around here, I'd scan as Good Citizen on all counts.

The bike would cover maybe a hundred and twenty miles before I'd need fuel. Not much range, so I'd need some luck along with the gasoline. The ghost had said the boss of *Undercurrents* was somewhere within the same range as the school.

First, I had to make sure that Rhonda Jayne Johnson's school address was still good.

"**D**amn!"

"What's wrong?" MaryLou asked.

"The address, it's in that apartment complex."

"So?"

"So I can't have you drop me off now and just wait for a phone call to come back and pick me up. There's no cover close enough. And I can't go into an apartment as quiet as I could a house."

"*Break* into, that's what you're saying?"

"Not what you think. If she's there, I could see that without going inside. And if she's not, she'd never know I'd *been* inside."

"There's only . . . maybe eighty apartments in that whole complex," MaryLou said as she circled the block. "You see what I'm saying? It's kind of an X-pattern, ten, twelve units a floor, two floors."

"That only makes it worse."

"Worse? Why? You could just walk up and look at the building directory. Every apartment will have a name next to a buzzer or something."

"She could keep her name on an apartment even if she lived somewhere else. As long as she paid the rent, the landlord wouldn't care."

"The landlord is the school," MaryLou said confidently. "We have the same kind of setup where I go. I don't use it myself. Those're off-campus housing, and I'm not much for partying. Anyway, there's an athletes' dorm. Much nicer. And it's part of my scholarship."

"So you're saying, since she just graduated, she'd have to leave?"

"Didn't *you* say she was going for her master's? That'd be enough to let her keep the place."

"Okay. But her name on the door wouldn't tell me anything. Even if it's there, it doesn't mean *she* is. And this whole area, the one we just drove through, it's no good for what I need. Some places, I could find cover in a bad neighborhood or even in some brush. Or I could just be a homeless guy, sleep on a bench or something. But if they're not scared, campus cops are worse than regular ones."

"Yeah," she said, half to herself, "same as my school. They know they're not real cops, so they snoop into everything. One of them even made me show ID when I was coming back after the library closed."

"Just let me out, then. Circle the block a couple of times. If I can find her name in the directory, we won't know anything. But if I don't, at least we'll know where *not* to look."

MaryLou nodded, then spun the wheel of her truck with one hand and coasted to the curb.

"Her name's in the directory, all right. Building B, Number 17."

"Doesn't help at all, then?" MaryLou asked me.

"Not really. The only good thing is that the complex isn't new. There's actual buttons, not some electronic scroll."

"What does that mean?"

"In some of the new places, there's a touch screen. You tap the apartment you want, and it goes right to the cell phone of whoever lives there."

"What's the difference?"

"Those kind, the person you're looking for would know someone had been there, even if she wasn't there herself at the time."

"Oh. Okay, but what good does that do them? I mean, you touch the screen, it rings someone's cell phone. They're not around, but their Caller ID tells them nothing except they had a visitor—someone who tried to visit, anyway."

"Yeah. Anyway, it doesn't matter. We're no better off than—"

"Get behind the wheel," MaryLou said over her shoulder, as she slid gently to the curb and went out the driver's door in one smooth motion.

"She's there," MaryLou said as I was pulling away from the curb.

"How do you know?"

"The apartment's full of stuff. Nice stuff, too."

"How could you . . . ?"

"I rang her bell. She buzzed me in. When I got to her door, I could see it had one of those big one-way mirrors, not some little peephole. She looked me over for a little bit, then she just let me in, like she didn't want to have a conversation through the door."

"She didn't act surprised?"

"Not . . . not really. I mean, she didn't know me, but I guess the idea of someone who she hadn't seen before ringing her bell wasn't anything new."

"What did you tell her?"

"I apologized for coming over so late, but I was thinking of transferring to her school. To play soccer. And someone in the Student Union told me she was going into the program for coaching, so . . ."

"She didn't think that was kind of weird?"

"I don't know what she thought," MaryLou said. "She wasn't nervous or anything. I could see she bought the story—I never have to tell people I'm an athlete. I could play volleyball, tennis . . . anything I wanted. I never played volleyball in high school, but I still got calls from recruiters. I'm a 'natural,'" she half sneered in contempt for what she must have been told a thousand times.

"Anyway, she was very nice, but she didn't waste much time before telling me I'd gotten a bum steer. She was interested in coaching, sure. She'd never played herself. She just thought it would be—what did she say?—ah, 'a different path to upper management.' Her undergrad work was all in economics, and she'd researched opportunities, so . . ."

"That's perfect, MaryLou. Here I was cursing myself for being such a damn dope. When I was on my second pass around the area, I saw the parking area. It's not a garage, just slots with a roof over the top. And her car was right there, Slot B-17. And the license plate was a match—no chance it belonged to anyone else. But it was too late to call you on your cell, and . . ."

"What's next?" is all the big girl said.

"I got her!"

Dolly was so excited I thought she'd burst out of her jump-suit. She gave off that sweaty-sweet natural perfume that only shows up after she's been working for hours. Working hard. At something that really matters to her. Rascal was even a little charged up, but he stayed on his sheepskin rug, next to where Dolly had been.

I could see that her tablet had something on its screen, but before I could tell her to calm down, she grabbed my hand and hauled me over to the butcher block.

"Look!"

It was a Web page, with a swirling ribbon running across the top. I don't know what kind of coding it took to make the ribbon change colors as it moved, grow narrower or wider, and have little starbursts of light mixed into it, but I guessed it wouldn't come cheap.

I watched it for a couple of seconds before I saw the embed-ded *My Magic Can Be Yours.*

"Use the wand," Dolly said, impatiently pointing with a lipstick-red fingernail at a three-dimensional pentagram that took up most of the screen. "See it under the ribbon? Just drag it to any of the points. Don't click it on, just do a mouse-over."

"This isn't really my—"

"Oh, for . . . ," she muttered, hip-checking me aside and sit-ting down. "Watch," she said.

The wand hovered over one of the pentagram's points. "Har-ness the Power!" came up.

"If I click *that* one . . ."

The screen filled with tiny little thumbnails.

"And I pick any one I want . . ."

A woman on all fours, facing straight ahead. She was wear-ing a black blindfold, each wrist separately bound to what looked like an ebony stake. Her lips were parted, the lower one in an invitational pout.

Dolly tapped quickly. The same woman, posed differently in a dozen photos, but always restrained.

"Okay?" Dolly asked. Meaning, was there any point in making me look at the whole menu?

"Okay," I told her. Meaning, I'd seen enough.

Dolly tapped twice, and the screen went back to the pentagrams.

She touched another point. The mouse-over came up "Spoiled Brat." The first thumbnail was the same woman, in some kind of expensive-looking lingerie, with an anklet of diamonds impossible to miss.

"More?"

I touched the back of her shoulders.

Dolly kept going:

"Private School."

"Mistress in Charge."

"Best Date Ever."

"Country Club Gala."

"Voodoo Priestess."

"All Business."

"See Thru the Window."

"How many are there?" I asked Dolly.

"I don't even know yet," Dolly answered. "That pentagram is really a bunch of them. They rotate, take turns coming to the front. But there's at least . . . four times five, so twenty, minimum."

"And they're all her?"

"Every single one. I used the Bertillon method. I know there's all kinds of science for facial recognition, but, no matter what you do with your face, the distance between the pupils of your eyes, that never changes."

"Unless you had so much work done—"

"Yes. Some women went so far that their eyes look sideways, like a lizard's. But not *this* one. She's too young, for one thing. Remember when you asked me about a woman who could look fourteen or thirty-four? That was a question about pictures, not people. This one, she uses a different name for each . . . persona, I guess you'd call it. That's the 'magic,' see? The client makes her into whatever he wants. But when I scanned in that yearbook photo, all I had to do was size it to the right dimensions for each Web site."

"Huh! How many pages did you look at before you found this?"

"Probably thousands. But I'd be at it for another five years if I hadn't stuck with the one-woman ones. No 'escort' stuff— they usually have dozens on every page, so the customer could get his choice. Or it's some stupid whore who thinks she can screen clients on Craigslist or Facebook. I used terms like 'I can be . . .' Or 'One is all . . .' Like that. No 'specialists.' I knew it had to be a public site or we weren't going to find it, no matter what we did."

"That's her, Dolly. She's the same . . ." My voice trailed off as I felt my wife slump her shoulders, like a fighter who couldn't go another round. Not just exhausted, emptied out.

"I need Dolly out of the house from, say, nine to as long as you can keep her."

Mack didn't ask why. Probably didn't want to know. But he hit his cell as he put some distance between us, talked for a couple of minutes, then came back to where I was standing.

"She says it'll be easy."

"You called Dolly?"

He gave me a look I couldn't read. "No," he finally said. "Bridgette."

"I'll be back later," Dolly said, smacking the side of her hip to tell Rascal to heel at her side.

"I'll send that new info to *Undercurrents* inside an hour," she assured me.

"Perfect," I told her. "I'll probably be later than you. There's something I have to look at."

She was as curious as Mack had been.

It was 21:25 by my watch when the monitor showed Franklin's truck pull in.

By the time I wheeled the motorcycle outside, they were both standing behind the tailgate.

"We'll have to grab some planks to make a ramp," I told them, pointing at the bed of the truck. "There's lumber in the—"

"How much does that thing weigh?" MaryLou cut me off.

"Probably around four fifty," I said.

She made a kind of snorting noise, then unlatched the back of the big pickup and said, "Bring it as close as you can."

I pushed the bike until the front wheel was almost touching the bed. "You jump up there," she ordered. Then she turned to Franklin. "Ready?"

If he said anything, I couldn't hear it.

They each took one side of the handlebars and lifted the bike until the front wheel was sitting on the bed.

"Hold it steady," she told me.

I grabbed the handlebars. I couldn't see where they grabbed

the rear of the bike, but as soon as I saw it come up I began walking backward. It fit with plenty of room to spare.

"Can you lay it on its side?" she asked me. "It doesn't have to be all the way, just enough so it won't show."

Before I could answer, Franklin leaped into the bed and took the bike from me. He pulled it over toward himself until it was below the rail of the bed and asked me, "Is this far okay?"

"Sure."

By then, MaryLou was next to me. "We've got a bunch of tarps back here, and if we take that . . ."

Franklin shoved a roll of thick tree limbs into the empty space between the side of the bike and the floor of the bed. MaryLou had covered the entire bed with a heavy tarp. "No point scratching it up," she said.

It didn't take much more wood to wedge the back wheel. Then the bike went under a blanket of more of the tarps.

We all jumped down. Franklin opened the driver's door. MaryLou climbed in, and he followed her. When I got into the passenger-side seat, he was behind the wheel.

"Let's go," MaryLou said.

W e off-loaded the bike, reversing the way we'd put it in the bed.

"It's a little before midnight," I told them. "We already know her car's still in its slot. By now, Dolly's e-mail to *Undercurrents* about the rumor that the same group that bought up that strip of land by the bay is connected to one of those 'green' organizations is already in their server. We know the person feeding info to Benton is this Rhonda woman. She couldn't count on always being the one picked to investigate, but she's always notified, so the boss is playing some game with her. Which means she has to know how to find him."

"That quick?" MaryLou asked.

"I don't know. But the only way to find out is to follow her . . . if she leaves, and we can't know that she will. So you and Franklin go wherever you want, it doesn't matter. I'll meet you up the road, that spot we picked out. I won't be any later than five in the morning, win or lose."

"What if that girl doesn't go out tonight?" Franklin said.

"Then I'll try again."

"How many times?" from MaryLou.

"As many times as you're willing," I said to them both.

The rumor that Dolly had sent to *Undercurrents* wasn't just a fraud to draw Rhonda Jayne Johnson out; it was a safety play.

Benton had warned Dolly about not running around half cocked after the hard info about someone buying up a whole strip of worthless land had been sent. This latest e-mail wasn't just soft info, the kind still worth checking out—it was dead wrong.

If Benton moved Dolly from "threat" to "gossip" in his mind, he wouldn't be warning her again. Why would he? The more nonsense she sent to that ultra-blog, the less *anything* she sent would be respected. Probably not even get past whatever BS screens they had set up.

But Benton would still be notified. Enough gossipy garbage and he'd figure out that Dolly really didn't know anything. She wasn't investigating; she was just passing along anything she heard other people speculate about. That would move her all the way down the threat scale and up the other side. All the way to "Diversion."

Hell, if she kept on gossiping, he'd get what he wanted, and it wouldn't cost him a dime. Next time he ran into Dolly in that coffee place, he'd tell the barista the drinks were on him.

I didn't have long to wait.

Or far to go. The target wasn't on the highway more than five miles before she turned off.

When she turned off the road, I turned off the bike's headlight. A two-lane blacktop could make following a car a lot trickier, but only if the driver's rearview mirrors showed anything.

Traffic was so light at that hour that the only danger to me would be some drunk who crossed the dividing line. I kept the rear light of the bike on, to warn off any idiot who believed intense tailgating made him a Le Mans candidate.

The taillights on her little blue Audi were a beacon I could have followed even without the night-vision goggles, but when she turned off again, I was glad I had them; the road she was following was still two-lane, but it curved through what looked like a forest on both sides.

When she turned again, she slowed way down to follow a narrow path. I gambled on that being a driveway, the kind Martin and Johnny had. So I pulled off the road, stashed the bike quick, and cut through the woods in the same direction she'd been headed, following the sound of her car. I left the helmet with the bike, but kept the goggles on.

Good thing I did—she parked her little Audi right in front of what looked like a giant log cabin, but I could see it wasn't any slapped-together build. The whole place looked like money—subtle money. It took me a few minutes just to circle it, and the stained-glass windows on the left side completely covered a tower of some kind. It was high enough to be a second story, but when I got around the back, I could tell it was an atrium. There was a greenhouse back there, too. No grow lights, so not a marijuana farm. I guessed the angle had been picked to grab the sun's rays for a few hours every day.

On the far side, a stand-alone garage, built of the same kind of logs. Cedar-shingled roof on it, too, just like the house.

I made my way back to the bike, pulled it upright, and walked it against what could be oncoming traffic for what I guessed was about a quarter-mile before I crossed the road and started it up.

After that, I was a man out for a ride. Headlight on, goggles in the saddlebag.

Franklin's truck was easy to spot, parked overlooking the ocean. No cop would even be curious about it—the hour was late, but the surf was foaming, and a man and a woman were inside, very close together.

"Did you get what you wanted?" MaryLou asked, on the drive back.

"Yes" is all I said. And I wasn't lying—all I wanted was to be able to find my way back, and that was so easy I wouldn't need the data recorder I wore like a wristwatch.

"When are we coming back?" Franklin asked.

"Soon," I said, wondering how he could know that I'd need a ride again. Maybe MaryLou had told him what she'd figured out on her own, and he just spouted it out. Or he was on the scent, same as I was.

It didn't matter. Because what he said told me what I needed to know: They were going to go the distance with me. They didn't need to know what the job was to be in on it. Together.

Dolly usually slept right through when I got in very late, knowing if everything else failed Rascal would always be between her and any intruder.

Not that night. She wasn't in bed. Or even at her workstation. She was lying back in the oxblood leather recliner in what she insisted on calling my "den." I don't know if she'd been sleeping, but she was wide awake when I walked in. Rascal's sharp bark hadn't been a warning—he could detect me coming easy enough. He just wanted to register his unhappiness at being away from his usual post.

"Dell! You know where I was tonight?"

"No" is all I said. She was charged up about something, and I didn't want to get in the way of whatever it was.

"There was a meeting of the Town Council. An open meeting, I mean. I always go to those when something hasn't yet been decided—we have to bring a show of force to get them to *really* pay attention. Otherwise, it's the usual bunch of cranks who just want their three minutes at the microphone. It's so much worse now that the local cable channel actually carries whatever goes on. Now they think they're celebrities.

"But that's not what I need to tell you," she went on, as if I'd interrupted her. "A man waited his turn. No one knew him. He was nicely dressed, suit and tie, not the way people do around here—not even the council members or the Mayor. He said he had an announcement to make concerning the whole town. Everyone went quiet.

"He said his name—I don't remember it, but it'll be on the record of the meeting—and he was the authorized spokesman for TrustUs, LLC. You know, the one that's buying up all the—"

"Yes." I had to interrupt her then. Otherwise, she was going to talk around whatever she had to tell me, like an airplane circling in to find the best spot to land.

"Well, guess what? He said his corporation was willing to *donate* that land to the city."

"Provided what?"

"That's what everyone wanted to know. I mean, if they were giving us the land, we'd have to make it part of the city to accept it. So there'd have to be power lines run, maybe even water pipes. That could cost a lot of money, and the taxpayers would have to cover it. And how much taxes could a piece of land like that ever pay back?"

"You said everybody wanted to know. You mean, they all asked him questions?"

"They *wanted* to. But the president of the council, he said this wasn't on the agenda, so they'd treat it like they would any other announcement. If this corporation wanted to donate land, they'd have to put the offer in writing, so the council would have time to study it before they made a decision."

"They could just say 'yes' on their own?"

"Sure. That's what I meant about packing the place. If the council decides on anything like that, they always tell the newspaper, and that sorry rag will print it. Word for word, no questions asked. So, if people want to, say, oppose whatever the council signed off on, they have to show up. And be serious about it."

"Sending a message? If the council doesn't change its mind, those people are going to get out the vote against them when they have to run again?"

"I guess so. But it's really just to show the flag. They don't all run for reelection at the same time, so knocking off one or two of them wouldn't give us a majority. But what people *can* do is recall any of them. Or all of them, if they put together a big enough voting bloc."

"Recall?"

"That's the only way to get some things done. You need a certain number of signatures to put something on the ballot. People say that you need *twice* that number, to keep signatures from being challenged and struck off."

"You can challenge them if they're not—what?—registered to vote?"

"Maybe. I don't know that much about it. But I'm going to find out."

"Dolly, if they give the land away, how could that help them? You said the guy wasn't even from around here, so it's not like he wants to be the next mayor or—"

"I said nobody recognized him, Dell. That's not the same thing. The way this village is set out, you could live here for years and pretty much no one would know. Know you by *face,* I mean."

"I need some sleep, honey."

"I do, too. I was in your chair because I was reading. I knew, once I hit our bed, I'd be out like a light."

I walked into our bedroom. It was all I could do—Dolly was ready to spend a half-hour on every sentence. Rascal gave me one of his looks on my way out.

By the time I got up, took a shower, and got dressed, I could see that if I wanted something to eat I was on my own.

Dolly was talking on her cell phone, two lines, telling one person to hold on, the other that she'd call them back, and sending out e-mails or texts using her tablet at the same time. She looked up just long enough to let me know she'd seen me.

Rascal didn't even go that far.

I never bring food into the basement, so I chewed on a piece of baguette I'd pulled off, and washed it down with some of Dolly's jungle juice. Taking my time about it—I had a lot to think about.

No invasion plan is risk-free.

An amateur never thinks about this, but even a professional knows you can't plan against random chance. Surprise always adds a player to the game—the best you can do is eliminate as much of that as possible.

There hadn't been any dogs at that log cabin Rhonda Jayne Johnson had driven to. They wouldn't have had to be outside for me to know that: anyone who knew enough to train no-bark night dogs—Dobermans are still the best for that—would leave them loose, and *any* dog will bark inside his own house if he picks up on a stranger approaching. *Just like Benton's house,* I thought.

The blue Audi made the usual car noises—its door gave off a solid thump when it was closed. Rhonda Jayne Johnson had hammered some kind of metal-on-metal door knocker, too. So even if she wasn't a stranger—and she couldn't be, not from the confidence she'd shown driving there—all those sounds wouldn't have been ignored by any dogs inside.

No fence. The windows hadn't been shielded with one-way glass; some didn't even have the curtains drawn. Maybe there was the kind of alarm system the owner could arm when he went out, but that didn't matter—when I invaded, I wanted him to be at home.

I hadn't gotten close enough to the house to see if it had security lights. It *felt* like it didn't—I'm not sure how to explain that, but I trusted it. That house's security was its location. It was probably listed on the tax rolls, but on an unnamed street—not the kind of place anyone would stumble across by accident.

I hadn't seen any signs like the ones we had nailed to one-by-two stakes at the beginning of our driveway.

NO TRESPASSING
BEWARE OF DOGS
PROSELYTIZING PROHIBITED

But even those house-to-house missionaries who were constantly canvassing like it was some kind of competition to see who could get the most doors slammed in their faces probably wouldn't visit a house they couldn't see from the road.

That didn't help me; I wasn't going to be knocking on the door.

I wasn't going to be smashing my way in, either—too much risk, in too many ways.

Real surveillance would take weeks. Did the guy inside have a wife or girlfriend? Roommates? A schedule he kept to? That and a hundred other things I'd want to know.

I didn't have so much time. What I did have was the certainty that he had to have some kind of Internet connection for what he did. A good one. He'd want to be off the grid for connecting to the *Undercurrents* server. Cable can be plenty fast around here, but all commercial cable goes through a shared pipe, so the speed would vary. Worse, no matter how much security you added, there was nothing to stop a cable company—or a DSL service—from data mining. Or some dummy could leave his laptop in his car. Not secure at either end.

But with all those trees, I couldn't see how he could be using his own satellite signal.

Wait! stabbed its way into my mind. Before I could blink, I was back to checking for an overlook.

I went upstairs, hand-signaled to Dolly that I'd be using the Subaru. She made a "Go ahead" gesture.

"Hey, Mr. Dell!"

"Franklin, didn't we make a deal about—"

"Oh, yeah. I forgot. 'Dell,' right?"

"Right. I came out here because I thought you could help me with something."

"Me? Sure. But I have to wait until I get off work. MaryLou's home—you want me to call her?"

"She can't help me, Franklin, not with this. I don't need something done, I need your knowledge."

"*My* knowledge?" The huge man couldn't decide between surprise and pleasure, so he crammed them both into those two words.

"Yes. You know those giant trees, the ones that grow on the back of our property?"

"The Douglas firs?"

"If that's what they are."

"If you mean those really tall ones, that's them. But they're not really fir trees—that's what Mr. Spyros taught me."

"Okay," I said quickly; I didn't want to learn everything Franklin knew about the damn things. "Good. Do they grow all around here?"

"Oh, sure, they do. There's no place near the coast that doesn't have them."

"How tall can they grow?"

"Two hundred feet, easy."

"Two hundred feet?"

"More," he assured me. "It just depends on how long they've been standing."

"And they could hold a lot of weight? Like, if a real heavy metal coil was wrapped around the branches, from the bottom up."

"That wouldn't be so much weight. But it wouldn't matter, anyway. A tree like that, it could hold a few hundred pounds like it was nothing."

"That's perfect, Franklin. I knew you'd be the one to ask."

"Mr. Spyros—"

"You already gave me everything I needed," I assured him.

Driving back, I remembered Franklin's saying Marylou would be at home.

Maybe that was just what he called his rented cottage, but I didn't think so. Not anymore. When I finished designing my invasion plan, I'd need the both of them, anyway.

No matter how many ways I drew the diagram, it ended up the same—one chance was all I was going to get.

Still, not all that difficult . . . *if* I'd had the time to scout the terrain, check on in-and-outs, watch for patrols. But the time just wasn't there. I could do the math: Something was in this for Rhonda Jayne Johnson. Something more than a regular client, even a rich one.

Okay, so what? I could get her to tell me, but I couldn't just walk away with whatever she said, even if I believed every word. And if I made her dead, there'd be no more leaks to Benton, so he'd know something had gone wrong.

That was the last thing I wanted. I didn't want Benton worried; I wanted him relaxed. The more sure of himself he was, the less danger he'd be to Dolly.

It all came down to the man in the log house. He'd founded *Undercurrents* a long time ago, built it from a little blog to the most trusted news source in the whole area. What would make him risk losing all his work had built?

That last e-mail from Dolly to *Undercurrents* had been enough for him to call the whore, so he had to know she was interested in anything that came in on whatever Benton was planning. But maybe he didn't know she *was* a whore. Had she told him a fairy tale about a potential scoop? One she wanted to do, all by herself? Her own investigation—maybe even big enough for a Pulitzer?

No matter how anyone had sized her up, *ambitious* would be somewhere in their assessment.

What could banish any journalistic doubts about *Undercurrents* better than achieving such recognition from an organization that had been so highly respected decades before the Internet ever existed?

He couldn't know she was leaking info to Benton—that would make her a traitor to his cause, and the stuff I got from the ghost showed that the CIF—I guess he'd see himself as "Editor-in-Chief"—wouldn't hesitate to purge members of his collective.

But I didn't want him to do that. A compromised organization always has cracks where seeds can be planted. If I could just convince the boss that there really was a story about Benton, a big one, maybe he'd be willing to help me with the planting . . . provided he got to harvest the crop.

If I wanted Franklin to come along on this, I'd have to get past MaryLou.

I wasn't worried about that. She'd have her own reasons to want to be in on it, too—lots of them. I knew one of those was to make sure I didn't get Franklin locked up, but that didn't bother me—my invasion plan would put him miles away when I moved in.

First, I had to modify some tools I had, and fabricate some others I didn't. I already had a night-work outfit, right down to the pull-off soles on the boots I'd be wearing. They were two sizes bigger than my feet—the weights I'd pressure-woven into the exposed outer rim would make the tracks look uniform.

Franklin would be walking behind me, so I added a thick backbone of fluorescent orange tape to my outfit. It wouldn't actually fluoresce until it was exposed to a mid-spectrum blue light—all Franklin had to do was tap the button on the flash-light I gave him to follow me. MaryLou would be on the perimeter. As soon as Franklin started back, she'd use a mini-strobe to guide him. In squid-ink darkness, a man can see a candle point of light at a thousand yards.

All that was probably overkill. It would be night, but not mineshaft-dark, and Franklin had a forester's sense of direction—he could probably have retraced our steps with his eyes closed.

The other tools were a necessity. I modified a woodsman's ax to give it a much wider cutting edge on one side, honed it *sharp,* then welded some extra iron to the other side. Kind of like a giant version of my tomahawk. I wrapped the long handle with the same plastic sheathing that covers wires—the metal head of the ax might conduct some electricity, but it wouldn't travel far.

In Franklin's hands, one swing would chop through anything covering the coaxial cable I knew had to be there . . . if I was right that the satellite receptor was as high off the ground as possible.

No point thinking that way—I *had* to be right.

The metal detector I built would guide us. Not the kind the treasure hunters used on beaches, or what the military used to detect land mines. This one used competing pulse waves to locate aboveground metal.

I knew any cable had to enter the house somehow, and *that* cable would be underground. But if we used a regular detector, we'd have a long line to trace, and we'd get a lot of false positives. An invasion has to move from where you start to where you finish without hesitation.

The pulse detector had its own disadvantages. A wrought-iron fence would confuse it. Even chain link would. But the back of that log house wasn't fenced. If there was any metal sitting waist-high in those tall trees, finding it wouldn't take more than a minute.

I already had the camouflage netting we'd need to pull over the truck. And we knew there was room to stash it less than a kilometer from the house. For Franklin and MaryLou, covering that distance was nothing, even if they had to move pretty fast.

The other tools I'd need, they didn't need to know about.

"One more time," I said.

"We got it the *last* five times you went over it," MaryLou snapped, showing her nerves a little.

"That's just Mr. . . . That's just Dell's way," Franklin said, as calm as if all I needed him for was taking out an opposing lineman. Or two. "He always goes over everything. Over and over. I've seen him do it even with Dolly."

I could feel MaryLou stiffen, then relax back into the same athlete's calm as Franklin's.

"Fire away," she said, softly enough so I'd not miss her message. She didn't much care what I was going to do. And she knew what I was capable of doing.

"You know the drop spot. You pull the truck in, we off-load the bike and pull the camo netting over. You wait there. When Franklin comes back, you pull off the netting and go. If I'm not where you'll be waiting inside two hours, just drive home."

"We could wait—"

"Any more than two hours means the thing went sour," I told them. "Dolly's going to be spending the night at Mack and Bridgette's, so she's alibied solid."

What I didn't tell them was the last message I'd left for the ghost:

|>If nothing from me in next 48, destroy any con-
nection. Then please send the message I stored to
my wife @ address you already have. Wherever you
go, my gratitude goes with you.<|

The address he had was one Dolly had set up years ago. She
didn't like doing it, but she went along when I told her that it
would be the last time she'd hear from me. It had never been
used; it only existed for that one purpose.

I can't remember exactly what the message said. Not without feeling the sadness I knew would hit her the second she
saw any e-mail flash at that address. But I know I told her that
if I hadn't shown how much I loved her in life, I'd find a way to
do it from wherever I ended up.

Dolly would erase the message, do a death-wipe on her hard
drive before she pulled it free. Then she'd go down to my basement and grab the machine I used to communicate with the
ghost. Both halves would go into the same canvas sack as the
hard drive. Then the little sledgehammer would take care of
the rest. The worthless tiny pieces would be dumped in the
ocean. Not from shore—Dolly had a good pal whose husband
was a fisherman, and she'd been out with them enough times
so it wouldn't be unusual for her to go again. Those boats cover
a lot of ocean. The little plastic pieces would be scattered over
fifty miles, coming and going.

Everything else could just stay as it was. There'd be no reason for Dolly to report me missing—nothing unusual for me to
be gone for months at a time, and there'd be no dead body to
kick off an investigation.

The law would need a warrant to search our house—*Dolly's*
house, they'd see when they checked the deed—and Swift's
threat to sue the cops for millions would probably be enough
to make them forget the idea.

I didn't carry any life insurance. Every dime of aboveground money was in Dolly's name. No motive.

And Dolly had a lot of friends who wouldn't like any intrusions into her life. Anyone who came around asking questions, they'd have a better chance of getting Rascal to talk.

"Ready?" I asked Franklin.

"We're *both* ready," MaryLou answered. Not speaking for Franklin, but making sure I understood she was just as much a part of whatever was coming as her man was.

Without saying another word, I jumped down from the truck and started moving. I could feel Franklin close behind— he wasn't making much more noise than I was, and I wasn't making any at all.

Nothing clumsy about the big man's movements. I didn't know his IQ, but his kinetic intelligence was probably off the charts.

You've got nothing to be grateful for, I remember thinking. *Everybody used you, one way or another. But if La Légion ever found one such as you . . .* We circled behind the house. No alarms went off that I could hear, and I knew that all those "home security" systems did was dial 911 when they were tripped, anyway. I couldn't see the local cops—if they even had any—going to "silent approach" mode . . . not in those night-black woods.

When we got to the highest trees, their tips were visible against the full moonlight, but none stood out—I couldn't see the cable I needed to be there, even with the night-vision goggles.

But the metal detector instantly scored a hit. I followed it until I was close enough to see the cable, standing stark against a tree trunk. Heavy-coiled stainless steel, it looked like.

I motioned Franklin forward, risked a quick flash to show him what I'd found, then stepped out of his way.

The big man came on fast. Even the rubber boots I'd told him to wear didn't seem to slow him down. He hadn't acted surprised when I'd said he'd need a pair of heavy rubber gloves, too.

He stepped back, flexed his torso to make sure of his purchase, and swung the ax. The solid *thunk!* of the blade sinking into wood was all I needed—anything between that blade and the tree was severed beyond repair.

I ripped the glow tape off the spine of my work outfit, and motioned for Franklin to return to the truck. He wouldn't have the tape to guide him, but I wasn't worried.

Or maybe I just put it out of my mind—I'd need to concentrate all I had on the next task.

O ne full circle to be sure.

The garage had room for three cars, but only one was there—an upscale sport-utility vehicle, maybe a Range Rover, in a dark shade of green. One light on in a side window, nothing else.

Knocking on the door would wake the whole house, and I didn't know who was in there.

I could blitz the window—this far from the road, no one would hear a scream. But you only do that when you want to paralyze the target—when your task is death, the target's panic would be your friend.

Not my job, not that night. So I probed for vulnerability, confident that the latex would keep my fingerprints off anything I touched. The first two windows moved so easily that I figured they were never locked. But maybe never lubricated, either. Still, a slow, careful lift would be better than broken glass.

More out of respect for my training than any real expectation, I gently turned the knob on the front door.

It wasn't locked.

That paused me for a second, but it kind of fit with everything else I'd seen, so I pushed in. Very gently. All the goggles picked out of the darkness was furniture. Some kind of parlor, not a living room. I made my way in the direction of an electric light's glow, following the maze down a side corridor.

At the end of the corridor, a partially open door threw a slice of light into the hall. I could hear a keyboard clicking. Whoever was in there wasn't watching TV—the clicking was almost frantic, as if they thought they could restore the cable connection if they tried hard enough.

I put the goggles into a side pocket with a silent Velcro closure, ran my gloved fingers over my balaclava to make sure it was in place, breathed in through my nose, let it out. The crossed-mesh plate would alter any sound I made. Okay.

I didn't much like using such a heavy-caliber pistol, especially a semi-auto, but I couldn't know what I'd be facing, and the Glock .40 with black-tip ammo would punch through pretty much anything at close range.

My left shoulder opened the door. I stepped inside with the movement, pistol up. A woman with a severe haircut was seated, facing a computer screen bigger than most TVs, her back to me. She didn't turn around—a combination of my silence and her concentration.

"Don't make any noise," I said softly.

She spasmed in her chair. Moved her hands to its arms and kept them there, as if to reassure me.

"Please turn around," I told her. "I just want to ask you a couple of questions, and then I'll be gone. There's nothing to be afraid of."

That last part isn't what I'd usually say—there's something

about those words that terrifies most people. But I could sense the woman would take them at face value.

She turned, not moving her hands from the chair's arms. Her rust-colored hair was cut just as severely in front—bangs almost to her eyebrows making as sharp a line as her just-past-collar-length had from behind.

"What do you want?" she asked, not raising her voice, projecting the calm people try for in high-stress situations. Not relaxed, just trying to use her body language and voice to tell me she wasn't a threat.

"Who else is here?"

"Here?" She seemed genuinely puzzled. "Nobody else is here. This is my . . . home."

"Please be sure," I said, raising the pistol just a couple of inches. "If I get surprised, you get dead."

"I *am* sure," she said, just this side of indignant. "This is my house. *Just* mine. Nobody lives here except me."

"All right," I said, keeping my voice level, telling her I accepted her answer. I believed she'd understood what I'd told her about surprises. She reminded me of someone who'd read a lot about what to do in certain situations, trying hard to follow a script she'd never really internalized.

"Rhonda Jayne Johnson" is all I said.

"*What?* You think *I'm* . . . ?"

"No. I know who she is. I know a lot more about her than her name. I don't know *your* name, and I don't want to know it. But I know something about Rhonda Jayne Johnson that you don't. Something you need to know."

"What?" She wasn't challenging me; whatever it was I had to say, she truly wanted to hear it.

"She's a traitor."

"A . . . traitor? Are you . . . ? Are you some kind of government agent or . . . ? I don't understand what you're saying."

"*Undercurrents,* that's you, yes?"

"That's right," she said, ready to defend her work against any opponent, but the pride in her voice was the tell. "You thought I'd be a man, is that it?"

"I didn't even have a guess," I lied. "But whoever put that operation together wasn't just skilled, they spent years and years investing in it. Not only money—although it had to have taken plenty of that—investing in its credibility. You're the most reliable news source for the whole coast, the one people *trust.*"

No response. So I poured a little more oil over the water I'd disturbed.

"It's not just that you don't take advertising—and I bet you get offers all the time. It's that you're all actually reporters, not shills who print press releases. You investigate, you check out who's doing what, and you could prove anything you put up online if anyone ever challenged it."

She didn't move her hands, but her eyes sought mine, as if to examine my soul. Good luck with that. All she'd see would be the greenish contact lenses with black iris centers. Empty ones.

"Rhonda Jayne Johnson works for you," I went on. "Or *with* you, I guess you'd probably say, since your paper is supposedly run by a collective.

"For all I know, that might even be true. Different people come and go, but not you, never you. You started this a long time ago.

"I know two things about you: you're a journalist that stepped in to fill a vacuum, and you knew that gaining the people's trust would be a long, hard road to walk even before you started.

"That's a life investment, all that. So I figured if you knew a member of your collective was leaking info to outsiders—info like the identity of folks who use your system to tip you off—you wouldn't let it slide. That would be against everything you stand for.

"Every time a tip comes in, you check it out. Double-source and fact-check. All the old-school stuff. You've built so much, why would you risk your credibility by trusting *anyone* blind?

"If people ever stop trusting that their tips will be kept confidential—off the record, or however you say it—you're done. The way you have it set up now, everyone for miles around is working for *Undercurrents,* right? They feel safe. Secure. That's what I came to tell you: everything you worked for, it's *all* in danger now."

"How do *you* know this?"

"Because I know that Rhonda Jayne Johnson has a relationship with a hedge-fund guy. I don't know what *his* game is, but it's got to be about money. Making a monster score."

"Relationship?"

"Enough of one for her to tell this guy the identity of some of your confidential sources. Enough of one for her to own ten grand's worth of shares in his fund."

"That's what you meant when you said . . . 'traitor'?"

"Yes. A traitor to everything *Undercurrents* stands for."

"She'd never . . ."

"Yeah, she would. She already has, like I just told you."

"And like I just *asked* you, why would you—whoever you are—why would you care about that?"

"All I want is your word that Rhonda Jayne Johnson gets kicked out. You've done that with other people before, although I don't know the reasons, so you can do it again. Just shut her out. That's all."

"No," she said, slowly getting to her feet. "No, it's not."

Without another word, she walked past me and out the door.

I followed her. Close enough to stop her if she tried to run, but not so close that she could whirl around and jump at me.

Two doors down, she turned left, hit a wall switch, and lit up what I guessed was the living room. I should have been suspicious of *any* switch she hit, but there was a kind of honesty to the way she was moving that reached out to me.

She sat down in an armchair that was covered with some brocaded material, gestured toward its mate, placed within a few feet of the one she'd picked. Between the two chairs was a brass stand, with an amber ashtray set into its top.

"You don't mind . . . ?" she said, taking a pack of cigarettes out of the padded vest she was wearing over a bright-red T-shirt. Then she interrupted herself with a semi-laugh. "That's cute, huh? I'm being polite to a man who walks into my house pointing a gun at me."

"I came to bring you something of value," I answered her, "something I thought you'd want to have. The pistol was just because I didn't know how many people would be here, and I wanted to be able to deliver my message without any interruptions."

"And your message was . . . ?"

"What I already told you."

"Fair enough. And the mask?"

"I'm a confidential source. From what I just told you, from what you know must be true. Because there'd be no other way *I* could know. The mask is more proof of that—I don't have any reason to trust that what I told you will *stay* confidential."

She lit a cigarette. Crossed her legs. Leaned back as she exhaled the first drag. A symmetrical face made her a good-looking woman by most standards, but there was nothing that stood out especially. I couldn't guess her age, but she was in good shape. She took another deep drag, pushing her breasts against the fabric of the red T-shirt hard enough so I could see she wasn't wearing a bra.

Wasn't being seductive, either. Just centering herself.

I waited.

"Rhonda Jayne Johnson," she finally said. "What you said wouldn't be so easy. . . . Well, it wouldn't be easy at all."

I waited.

"Finding this place, that wouldn't be easy, either. So what do you want to know?"

"I didn't come here to ask questions. I don't need any answers. I had a message to deliver, and I did that. I'm still here because it feels like you want to tell me something. If I'm wrong about that, I'll go. If not, I'll listen."

"I love her," the woman said, like she was saying it gets dark at night. "And she loves me."

"She betrayed you. Doesn't that change things?"

"Not . . . I don't know. I won't let her do that anymore. But I couldn't just kick her off the roster. That would hurt her terribly, and I . . . I don't know if I could do that."

"Why?"

"That's how we *met*. That was our first real *connection*. RJ is a journalist in her soul. Like me. If I cut her out of *Undercurrents,* it would be like punishing her for something she didn't do."

"*Didn't* do? Isn't leaking info about a confidential source as unethical as it gets for a journalist? People like you have gone to jail for refusing to do just that. All over the world. Some of them have been tortured. Some killed. I thought keeping anything they were told in confidence was something they were morally bound to do. A sacred oath."

"It *is*," she said. "But . . . look, what she did was wrong, I'm not arguing about that. She's never going to get a look at anything that comes in again. And she'll *learn* from this. There's no reason why she can't dig up stuff on her own. That's how she got . . . in with us. In the first place, I mean. The info she brought in, that was checked by people she never met. Never *will* meet. She *worked* her way in. Years of work. People make mistakes. . . ."

"You're making one, right now."

"Maybe I am. But that's my decision, not yours. She didn't 'betray' our newspaper; she screwed up."

"You said you love her?"

"I do," she said, her eyes steady on mine, cigarette smoke drifting from her hand.

"And she loves you?"

"Oh, yes."

"If you believe that, then it wasn't just *Undercurrents* she betrayed."

She lit a new smoke with the burning end of her first one, just before she stubbed that one out in the big amber dish. Then she closed her eyes, as if to show me that she'd listen, but she was done talking.

"*Undercurrents,* that's your baby. I get that. You're the boss; you call the shots. You say she didn't betray what you started, what you stand for, I guess that's your call. But once you opened that other door—that you love her, I mean—I see how she betrayed you, too. You, the person; not you, the paper."

"You're saying she has some kind of . . . relationship with whoever she disclosed the identity of that source to? Didn't you say she was making money from that, somehow? The same person who runs the hedge fund that she owns shares in? That doesn't mean—"

"She's a whore," I said, in the same tone I'd say, "The public library is just down the street."

"You have no right to judge her! You don't know—"

"I'm not judging her. I'm just telling you the truth. She's a whore, and she's been working you like a trick."

She sat bolt upright, slashes of red flaring across her cheekbones. "That's talk. Words. You know what I do. So let me ask *you*. Where's the proof?"

"You haven't even wondered how I knew who you were, and where to find you?"

"I did. And it scared me. But that's not what—"

"Yeah, it is. The people who hired me have some kind of computer department—they tried to explain it to me, but it sounded like they were speaking a foreign language. There's nothing they can't trace. Including Rhonda Jayne Johnson."

"The people who *hired* you told you . . . ?"

"Next time she drives her little blue Audi over here for a visit, ask her how much money her magic wand makes her."

"I don't understand what you're saying."

"I think that's probably true. So I'll spell it out. She's a working prostitute. Her game is 'white witch' magic. The customer says what he wants, and she turns herself into whatever that might be. Try 'Harness the Power.' Or 'Spoiled Brat.' Or 'Private School,'" I said—I wasn't going to give this one a URL she could check out in ten seconds. "The people who hired me, they said there's dozens of . . . roles she can play."

"Men?"

"You're like a rat in a cement box, aren't you? You're going to find a way out even if you have to work your teeth and claws down to bleeding nubs to make an opening you can slip through. But there *is* no way out of this.

"She's a whore. She does things for money. I don't have her little black book; they didn't give that to me, because all they wanted was to stop her from getting information out of *you*."

The cigarette was still burning slowly in her hand—the hand that never went near her mouth.

"You care about her?" I said, very softly.

"I told you," she answered, just as softly, but with no tone in her voice. "I love her."

"It's only your love that's keeping her alive."

"What?!?"

"She's a blackmailer. And a couple of her regulars talked way too much. That part's not a problem, but if she found out that the age—" I bit my tongue on that last word, knowing any journalist on her level would auto-complete "agency" on their own. "Look, I was supposed to just turn off the faucet. Kill her," I added, to take any ambiguity out of the room. "But when they found out she was connected to you, they got . . . twitchy."

"I—"

"They couldn't've known about you and her, or they would have told me. But they knew this: If any member of *Undercurrents* disappeared, you'd never rest until you found out the truth.

"Nobody wants *you* dead. It's not *you* who says she'll blow the whistle on her . . . clients. Not what you think. It's not like she'd tell their wives or something like that. The whistle *she'd* blow, she'd blow it loud enough for the other side to hear. That can't happen. They can't know if she'd really do it, but they aren't going to take a chance."

"I don't—"

"Yeah, you do. In another four, five weeks, the . . . the people who hired me won't have anything to worry about. Nothing she knows, nothing she overheard will mean a thing. She could 'blow the whistle' all she wanted; it'd be a sour note by then. But those blackmail threats make her look like a honey trap. So if she makes a move now, you'd both have to go. If she waits, *neither* of you do . . . if you play it straight."

"Meaning . . . ?"

"Meaning this: You keep quiet for, say, a couple of months,

just to be safe. Let everything go on as it is now, except don't let her in on anything any other member of your crew turns up. And don't let her know what *you* know. About her, I mean."

"And then?"

"And then you do what you want. You could confront her with what you know, and kick her out of your life. You could prove that you *saved* her life, too. And maybe, just maybe, that would be enough for her to see what true love is, I don't know."

"You want me to just go on—"

"I don't care what you do. If you tell her what I told you, she's dead. Her life, it's in your hands. Whatever choice you make, we'll know soon enough."

Her cigarette had burned down to her fingers all on its own, but if she felt the heat, she didn't show it.

I backed out of the room, then out of the house.

When I was close enough, I popped the flash.

By the time I got to the truck, the netting was off and the driver's door was standing open. MaryLou and Franklin were outside.

"Get behind the wheel," MaryLou said. "We'll push this down the road a little bit, so nobody in that house hears the motor start."

It would have taken too long to explain why that wasn't needed. I climbed behind the wheel, shifted into neutral, and keyed the ignition so the power steering would kick in.

The truck started rolling. I knew Franklin was a bull, and MaryLou had real power in her legs, but I almost looked at the speedometer—the damn truck had to be moving as fast as the two of them could run carrying a pillow.

One last shove and the truck was moving on its own. As it finally floated to a stop, MaryLou caught up to my open window.

"Move over," she said. "All the way over."

I did that, MaryLou was a half move behind me, and Franklin got behind the wheel. Neither of them was breathing hard. Franklin started the motor and drove without lights to the turn-off; then it was only a few minutes until we were all headed home.

"Did you get it done?" MaryLou asked.

She knew I must have had a real good reason for whatever I was up to, even if she didn't know what it was.

"Better than I hoped for," I told her. "Franklin really handled the hard work."

"We both pushed the truck—"

I quickly cut off Franklin's defense of MaryLou. "I know. I was talking about the tree."

"Oh."

"The only doubt I had was about you," MaryLou said, as sweet as ever.

"Me, too," I agreed. Then I finished pulling off the whole outfit, changed into the fresh one I had stashed behind the seat, and peeled the fake soles off the boots.

We hadn't gone ten miles before everything was as normal-looking as any cop could want. The fake soles had been reduced to little shreds of nylon with the tin snips I'd brought along. I kept them balled in my fist. If we got stopped for any reason, I'd just toss them if I could, and hand them to MaryLou if I couldn't. Once the cops found out who she was, they wouldn't be surprised to see her carrying a squeeze ball to keep that pitching hand exercised.

But nothing happened. Franklin wheeled into our drive-way, and I jumped off, figuring I'd grab a few hours of sleep before Dolly and Rascal showed up.

I was awake by the time I picked up Dolly's car on the monitor.

Nine-thirty in the morning—I guess Mack and Bridgette had stalled Dolly about as much as she was going to stand for. She and Rascal bounded in the back door like a pair of firefighters.

"You had breakfast?" were the first words out of my wife's mouth.

"Hours ago."

"Hmmm . . . ," she kind of hummed to herself, opening the refrigerator to pour herself some juice, then one of the cabinets to pull out a granola bar. I knew she wasn't hungry, just checking to make sure I'd really had breakfast.

That's my wife: she'd take my word that I was "working" for weeks at a time without raising an eyebrow, but when it came to things like making sure I kept up my nutrition, she was relentless.

"My girls—some of them—they'll be here in a half hour or so."

"Want me to . . . ?"

"Oh, Dell," she said, chuckling. "You do whatever you want to do. I know they'll drive you out of here on their own soon enough."

"They get to where they're all talking at the same time—it sounds like a wall of noise."

"To you, sure."

Meaning, "Not to me," I thought. But they were already starting to roll in. I didn't recognize the first three; that is, I'd seen them before, but I didn't know their names.

"Let's give the others a few minutes," Dolly told them, already bustling around, pasting charts back up on the cabinets, firing up her tablet, pointing at the coffeemaker to tell them they were on their own if they wanted any.

I didn't have anything to do, not yet. But that wasn't why I stayed in the kitchen. I was just being stubborn, showing Dolly that I *was* interested in whatever they were up to . . . and the white noise hadn't started yet.

There were seven girls inside before Dolly kicked it off.

"If the town accepts the offer of that strip of land," she said, pointing at the map with the thick pink ribbon standing out boldly, "it'd probably cost more to provide it with services— water, sewage, electricity—than they'd get back in taxes. But I asked around, and that isn't the game. See, unless the land is *used*—like, to put houses on it or something—the town doesn't have to put any of that in."

"So it's just a freebie? For real?" a girl with spiky hair and black eyeliner asked, her tone saying she didn't believe there was any such thing, anywhere.

"No!" Dolly told them. She reached into a net sack that was next to the sinks, took out three of those miniature tangerines— they're called something, but I didn't remember what—and started to juggle them. The girls watched, fascinated, as Dolly kept them spinning, as if they were doing the work themselves.

She talked right through the tangerine wheel. "We found out that TrustUs, LLC, is actually owned by PNW Upstream. That hedge fund up in Portland that Benton manages."

"So?" the little redhead with owl glasses asked.

"So the donation itself is worth money. How *much* money depends on how the town assessor 'values' the land."

"The town says it's worth a million bucks, they get a million-dollar tax credit for land they bought for—what?—five percent of that?" the beanpole said.

"Yep," Dolly answered, still spinning the tangerines.

"Where'd you learn to do that, Tontay?" one of the cheer-leader girls said.

"In the circus," Dolly said. "I used to be a high-wire walker."

"Wow!"

I closed my eyes, thinking of how Dolly had transformed from battlefield nurse to a new persona so perfectly that she never had to lie. If tending to the wounded in Darkville while staying neutral in whatever war was going on at the time wasn't a high-wire act, I didn't know what else you could call it.

"Could you teach us?" another cheerleader asked.

"To juggle, sure. But high-wire is another story—it takes years and years to work yourself up to that. Anyway, if you want to see a circus, all you have to do is come to the next council meeting," Dolly said, deftly catching all three of the baby tangerines in one small hand. "And that's what we're going to do."

I hadn't used the Glock, so disassembly was just a by-the-numbers routine, not a pre-disposal necessity.

All I could do was wait.

How long was up to me. I pulled up *Undercurrents.* They were continuing their investigation, but all they had to report was the same potential tax break Dolly had been talking about upstairs before. Their incoming letters weren't about anything close to home.

I realized it was Sunday. It usually doesn't make any difference to me, but today, it made me feel a little better, because I knew that Franklin would have gone to work even if he hadn't slept at all the night before.

Sometimes you can't track the enemy. All you can do is find the best spot to fire from, and wait for them to show up.

The headline wasn't in *Undercurrents.* It was the kind of big-deal thing that wouldn't interest them.

MAGNIFICENT GIFT TO PERMANENTLY DISPLAY LOCAL ART

The local newspaper made it front-page, with a separate foldout to explain. Architectural plans, computer-generated images of what the display would look like from all angles. They also showed three different pictures of Benton, one the usual head shot, one of him superimposed against something that looked like a flowing wall, and another of him standing before an audience.

A small audience—just the council, the County Attorney, and a few other people I didn't recognize.

One photo was captioned: *"What better way to represent our community's connection to the ocean than a wave?" George Benton says, as he demonstrates the unique features of his incredible act of philanthropy.*

The story explained in detail. An acrylic wall "the length of a football field" would be constructed as a "sandwich." It would have a flip-up slot running the length of its top for insertion of anything that could fit: photography, painting, poetry in some sections, small sculpture, glass-blown creations, even scale-model airplanes in another.

The sandwich would be made of varying thicknesses, so it could accommodate "all the art forms." There was even an "electronic slot" that would house tablets on which different blogs could be posted or a staged performance could run continuously. Benton was quoted:

If you look at the irregularity of the wall, you'll see it's really a sine wave, much as an oscilloscope would record sound. But, for our community, it becomes a "Sign Wave." A message to all tourists and visitors that our village is the artistic epicenter of the coast. And how much we value all those who contribute to it.

There it was. A potion of magic words. "Art" and "tourism" were the most sacred anyone in this town could ever speak.

"You saw the paper?" I said to Dolly.

"Of course I did. But . . . Well, so what, Dell? It's not going to hurt anyone, and the kids are really excited—it's all they're talking about.

"And now we know what he wanted that strip of land for, don't we? What if he *does* have an ulterior motive? Another tax break for his hedge fund—who cares? That's what it's like in this place. Everyone who donates *anything* gets his name on a plaque; part of the deal. I don't care if it's helping support the library, or buying some new chairs for the waiting room in the hospital; you put some money in, you get to put your name on it.

"And, believe me, Benton's name is going to be all *over* this 'Sign Wave' wall. Forever. You won't be able to look at one without looking at the other."

"So why tell you to not run around half-cocked?"

"Dell! Just stop it, now. Isn't it obvious? He's a supreme egotist. What's so strange about that? He just wanted to be the one to spring the big surprise himself. So, when *Undercurrents* ran that story about that useless strip of dirt being bought up, piece by piece, I guess he put two and two together and—"

"He saw the story in *Undercurrents,* right? So how did he know *you* had anything to do with it? They don't disclose their sources."

"I . . . I don't know. Maybe one of the girls bragged about the super-secret 'investigation' we were all doing."

"No, they didn't."

"How could you know that?"

"How could you *not,* Dolly? One of them talks about one

of your damn crusades, how long before *another* one finds out she's doing it? And then the girl with the loose mouth goes from insider to outsider in a half-second. Teenage girls—you really think any of them want to run that risk?"

"Well . . ."

"There's got to be more."

"More than huge tax breaks *and* an even bigger ego?"

"Why is this PNW Upstream group buying up tracts of land right around where you're going to build your dog park?"

"I don't know, but . . ."

I didn't say anything.

"You think I should drop *Undercurrents* another hint?"

"No, Dolly," I said, thinking to myself how desperately she had wanted to find her dream cottage by the ocean. Not for the cottage, not for the ocean . . . for a place where she could live in peace. "That's the last thing you should do."

"Then I won't, okay, honey?"

"Sure."

"Dell . . ."

"There was nothing to vote on," Dolly said when she got back from the "open meeting" of the council.

"Because it's not going to cost the taxpayers a dime?"

"That's the least of it. It's going to bring in business, sure. And this place is always going to be way in favor of anything that supports the arts. I saw people in the audience who do all of that. Poems and crafts and . . . you know. Just imagine, all their stuff, on *display*—if it *was* put to a vote, it'd be a landslide.

"And you know what? It *is* kind of fascinating. The project, I mean. Nobody ever heard of anything like it. It's going to be built with local labor, too. All Benton has is the design. Which he paid for himself. They're going to have to build a small cast-

ing plant just to create the acrylic sections, never mind transporting them and fitting them into place. That means even
more new jobs."

"Everybody wins, then?"

"Who loses?"

"I don't know."

That was the truth—I *didn't* know.

But what I did know was that, for whatever reason, Rhonda
Jayne Johnson was still part of *Undercurrents.* So the boss hadn't
talked to her. Or stabbed her. But I dismissed that last thought
as soon as it came up—whoever that severe-looking woman
was in her heart, she was a journalist in her bone marrow.

I was still thinking about that when Dolly came into the dark
kitchen where I'd been waiting for her to return from another
council meeting.

"We're never going to have our dog park," she said. Not raising her voice, but I could see the steam coming off her.

"Why?" is all I asked.

"You know what 'eminent domain' is, Dell?"

"When the government takes private property for some public purpose."

"Ah! You've been reading up on it?"

"No."

"I . . . Never mind. Listen to this: That strip of land, you
know, where they're going to build that 'Sign Wave' thing Benton promised? It's not wide enough to let people park their cars.
There's only space for a walkway. We're not getting any tourists
to come here just to drive by and see that wall at thirty miles
an hour. And we're not getting any ego strokes for the artists if
people can't *stroll* by and admire their work."

"So now they want to . . . ?"

"Build a bridge! A quaint little wooden bridge, but with a heavy steel skeleton for bracing."

"But if they can't park, what's the use?"

"The bridge isn't for cars, Dell. It's for people. The parking is on the other side."

"On parcels this PNW Upstream group owns?"

"Yes. But that's not the . . . the *all* of it. There has to be a road built to get *to* those parking spots."

"Even so . . ."

"Even so, *nothing*! If the town takes the land by eminent domain, it has to *pay* for it. Full market value—whatever that means. And, remember, they have to supply electricity to the strip, too. To light up that 'wave' at night."

"So the taxpayers . . . ?"

"That's what I thought, too. But Benton, he had all that covered. His group is going to build all kinds of special shops along that strip. Rent them out. Plus, they expect to make money from the parking. So this hedge fund, it's going to give us all that for free! Clear the land, build the bridge, and even pay the electricity bill. Pretty nice, huh?"

"What else?" I asked her, knowing there had to be more. If Dolly was this hot, it wasn't over losing land for a dog park. With this "fair market value" coming into the picture, her crew would come out way ahead. And land wasn't that scarce around here that they couldn't just buy some other parcel.

"The council says, after the land is cleared, and the bridge built, and the wall in place, and everything, then there's a way for the town to turn a big profit, too! The *town,* not the hedge fund. A 'convention center.' A big one, with hotel space attached, so people could come down to the coast to have their annual meetings and things like that.

"There's plenty to do here, and conventioneers, they always

have money to spend. We can't have a casino, not with the Tribe so close by, but it's not much of a drive if you want to gamble. And they were talking about bringing those MMA fights here. Big-name acts, too."

"And the hedge fund would own it?"

"No! We'd own it. The village, I mean. You know how much that would cost, just to get it built? Sixty-five million dollars!"

"Where would . . . ?"

"Municipal bonds." Dolly chopped off what I was trying to ask and got right to it. "It turns out that there isn't a single GO bond issued by this entire state."

"You're losing me, honey."

"Ah . . ." Dolly exhaled. Then she started brewing herself a cup of tea.

Even Rascal relaxed as Dolly sat down.

She threw him a rawhide chew, said some sweet things to the mutt, and laid it out for me.

"It works like this: a GO bond is a tax-free municipal bond, backed by the full faith and credit of whoever issues it . . . which means that the investors get paid back from government revenue. Fancy word for taxes. Oregon doesn't issue them, because this state doesn't have the credit rating of a deadbeat dad. But individual cities can issue them, usually only on a project-specific basis.

"Say they want to improve a road where it passes through the town. They can issue these bonds, but the full-faith-and-credit deal only applies to the revenues of an individual department, not the whole government. So, say ODOT—Oregon Department of Transportation—doesn't get enough revenue coming in from the new highway. Well, that's just too bad for the investors.

"And what *that* means is two things: one, taxes go up; two, the bonds have to pay a pretty high interest rate to attract investors. The smaller the municipality, the higher the rate . . . in both directions."

"The council can't just decide to raise taxes, right?"

"No, they can't. In fact, there's a state law that prohibits bonds from imposing too high a percentage of property taxes on any community. But there's one exception to that law. If the town *itself* votes for it, they *can* issue those bonds."

"Why would . . . ?"

"I already told you, Dell. People *want* this 'wall' thing. It doesn't matter what you call it—they want it *bad.* They don't see it costing *them* much of anything, not really. But, given the sixty-five million—and you know *everything* that gets built runs over budget; it's actually *expected* to—just to put the place up, the bonds may not sell all that easy.

"*That's* the joker in the deck! Amazingly enough, PNW Upstream is willing to build the whole thing—convention center, hotel, the golf-cart transport system so tourists can drive around for free, and not pollute the environment, of course. They'd run it, too."

"Damn! That's a bigger score than a thousand kilos of dope. All legal, too. Between the graft on the contract to build it—"

"With local labor." Dolly dripped scorn over the garbage dump. "An endless stream of revenue; all of it high-profit, *no-*risk . . . it's a beauty."

"Too late for *Undercurrents* to expose . . . ?"

"There's nothing *to* expose. So the hedge fund makes money—who cares? People are getting what they want, and it's not coming out of their own pockets."

"The taxes—"

"Like I said, they'll go up a little bit. Not nearly enough to start a tax revolt. Sure, *Undercurrents* could expose that this whole thing was a staged setup from the beginning, but there's no one really interested in that kind of news. It's the *result* people care about, and this result is one they *want*."

"No one's going to raise a stink?"

"Fait accompli," my wife said.

Some people get confused by logic—their emotions fog the mirror.

Olaf had taught me never to make that mistake, months before he spat out his last will and testament through the blood frothing his mouth.

"All true logic centers in mathematics. All else is nothing but perception. And emotion clouds perception, making the picture even more hazy."

"I don't get it," I told him.

"A *refusal* to understand is no different from volunteering to be stupid."

"I'm not—"

"Shall we see?" the icy man asked. He wasn't taunting me. Olaf didn't do things like that, amuse himself by mocking others. I'm not sure he did *anything* for amusement. He stood apart from the rest of us. Not physically; he was just on a different level inside his head. It was only because he could occupy that ground without judging the rest of us that I had ever gathered the courage to begin to speak with him. After that, he was my teacher.

Pressuring him to say "yes" or "no" was a bad move. Just a couple of weeks before, a Slavic thug who I knew from my legionnaire days was trying to get some players for the dice game he always set up whenever we made camp. He never changed his pitch: "Afraid to risk a little cash, pal? We're out here risking our damn *lives*, what's a few bucks?"

He hadn't been stupid enough to try that on Idrissa. The Senegalese warrior didn't always understand English perfectly. If he thought he was being called any kind of coward, his long, curved sword would flash and blood would spurt. Idrissa carried his weapon on a leather strap that he could cover if we were in sunlight, but he did his best work in the darkness.

But I guess the Slav thought Olaf's age and his Nordic skin made him a better target. Like I said, Olaf was very good with his "scribes." But if you didn't force his hand, you'd never know that.

Olaf's spikes were always out of view. And he never seemed to carry them in the same place.

Nobody mourned the Slav. It wasn't like La Légion—mercenary commanders never demanded explanations when they saw a dead body lying just past where we camped. We weren't "comrades in arms," we were hired guns. And we didn't bury our dead unless we were going to be in the same place for weeks—vultures are afraid of live humans, but they have more patience than any of us do.

"Yes," I said to Olaf's proposal.

"One plus one equals two?"

"Yes . . . ," I said, kind of wary. Olaf didn't mock, so there was something behind that simple question I knew I was missing.

"That would be true if it was, let us say, one rock plus one rock. That would be two rocks."

I didn't say anything.

"But rocks can range from pebbles to boulders. One man plus another man *could* be a force equal to five men. Or putting them together could result in the death of both—so *less* than one."

"But—"

"We are walking a trail when we pick up the enemy's spoor. If I toss you two grenades, what do you do with them? If you perceive them as weapons to be used against the enemy, you silently signal your gratitude. If you perceive them as duds, you know that *I* am your enemy."

"You wouldn't do that."

"Why?"

I was about to say, "Because you're my friend," but I could see that would be a wrong answer, so I said, "Because you'd have to carry those duds around with you. Extra weight. And for what? If you wanted to kill me, you could just do that."

Olaf nodded. "That is a logical conclusion. But it is *your* logical conclusion, based on *your* perceptions. Worse, it assumes I *share* your logic. Who would carry dud grenades in some insanely elaborate plot that had such a small chance of success? And the very real possibility of death if it failed?"

I shrugged.

"Then listen: an insanely elaborate plot would seem quite logical to an insane man."

"But you can't walk around assuming everyone you meet might be crazy."

"Why?" Olaf said. "Why must that be so? Is it some law of nature I don't know about? If it is logical to be suspicious of all strangers—and that *is* logical—why is it not logical to include the possibility of insanity in your assessment of others?"

I wasn't a kid anymore. I didn't have Patrice, and that hurt. But I wouldn't have needed him to teach me things I'd already learned. "Whether you get shot in the heart or you get your throat slit, you're just as dead."

"Yes. But there is a significant difference between the two."

"Dead is dead."

"So—no difference, then?"

"I don't see one."

"You could be shot in the heart from a half-mile away. But your throat could be slit only by someone who was able to get very close to you."

I nodded my head. What Olaf said was obviously true. But it

wasn't until he was dying that I realized that what he had been trying to tell me wasn't about logic at all.

I thought about that. All the different pieces of it.

People say things like "Why would a man with millions of dollars steal?" as if they were employing some form of dispassionate logic. But I knew better. Some people do things because they *need* to. A wealthy man might not need money . . . but he might need to steal.

So, yes, there was a mammoth pile of money in the whole scheme—not a guarantee, but certainly in potential. Still, whenever I went over the whole thing, it reminded me of Olaf's "insanely elaborate plot."

Posing as gay, a patron of the arts, a community activist for years. And *then* putting a lot of pieces together: bribes, graft, kickbacks. Why go to all that trouble for money when you already *had* money, especially when you risked *losing* money if some thread got pulled and the whole thing unraveled?

I let myself fall into those thoughts, releasing a carrier pigeon with a question I couldn't be sure would be delivered, much less that an answer would be returned to me.

It ran through my mind like a ribbon unrolling. *Why pay a prostitute when you could get all the women you want for free?*

And Olaf was there, watching. Logic inside the illogical. You pay a whore to *be* a whore. Not to use her body for your own pleasure, to use it for your own purpose.

Rhonda Jayne Johnson wasn't Benton's creation. She had probably been doing business for years before he found her. Maybe it took him a while to find another use for her than he originally intended.

Or maybe he didn't find that other use until she showed it

to him. A blackmailer threatens to expose secrets; a traitor sells them. It's not a long leap—blackmailers and traitors usually have the same motivation. They both gather information—the only difference would be the methods. If Rhonda Jayne Johnson had threatened to expose Benton, she would have investigated him much more deeply before she ever voiced a demand. She wouldn't have to know her client's endgame, only that piercing his disguise would ruin it.

Just wave the wand—that magic, expensive wand—and I can be whatever you want.

Blackmail is a dangerous game. Some will let you bleed them white, but others will see the end coming and tie a tourniquet into a noose. If suicide seems the only way out, homicide instantly becomes another option.

Selling information is a much more lucrative occupation. The opposite of extortion—the more you tell, the more valuable you become. That was why I'd let the half-completed "agency" slip out. And why I'd spelled out "honey trap" to make sure the founder of *Undercurrents* got the message.

Dolly's e-mail to *Undercurrents* had started a tiny little campfire. One that Benton thought he could extinguish by casually spitting on it. He didn't know Dolly, but he knew Rhonda Jayne Johnson. At least he thought he did.

I waited for Dolly to take off for one of her meetings.

I knew that she wouldn't be going alone, and that her crew would stop for coffee after it was over.

The time window was an easy three hours. I didn't need more than a few minutes . . . provided I could find Mack quick enough.

I didn't want to go to his house. Bridgette always contorted herself to stay out of any conversation if she thought it was business. I once told her that nothing I'd want to talk to her husband about would be about his clients, so confidentiality wasn't an issue.

"It is for me," Mack cut into what I was trying to explain. "I'm not putting Bridgette in a position where she'd think she had to do something."

I gave him a look, but kept my mouth shut.

"If you came over and said you wanted me to help you rob a bank, Bridgette would want to drive the getaway car," he told me, his tone of voice matching his eyes. "Even if I could stop her from coming along, she'd be frightened—frightened for me— while she was waiting. What kind of man puts his woman in fear?"

So I called his cell.

"You busy?"

"Working."

"I need a few minutes."

"I'm with Khaki," he said, making it clear he wanted who- ever was with him to hear him speak. "We're just hanging out. By the monument."

The monument was the slab standing inside a little hexago- nal building, open on all sides. On it was a brass plate with the names of local fishermen who had been lost at sea. Every year, more names were added.

"Fifteen minutes," I said.

Khaki saw me first—no surprise there; he was a scout in that army his mind had created. He was dressed in the trademark outfit that had given him his name.

"Major!" he said, getting to his feet and snapping a salute.

"As you were," I told him, returning the salute.

"Face was just telling me about the new HQ we're getting."

"At least twice the sleeping space," Mack added. "More privacy, too."

"You give Khaki the scouting assignment yet?"

Mack shook his head. That wasn't his role—only the leader of the unit got to call the shots.

"We need a little slice of land," I told Khaki. "Maybe an acre. Close to the bayfront, but not in the commercial district. Back off in the hills a bit. We don't want to rent, so look for a piece of land with 'For Sale' signs posted."

"Sir!" Khaki said, again getting to his feet. "Catch you later, Face," he said to Mack. He threw me a salute, then started his patrol.

"He's never going to drop that *A-Team* thing?"

"Why should he?" Mack said. "Khaki made me 'Face,' so you had to be 'Hannibal' for it to all fit together. He hasn't missed a day of his meds. He's going to stay delusional, but he's walking-around proof that schizophrenics aren't all dangerous lunatics."

"So he's like a guy carrying a sandwich board?"

Mack looked at me carefully, then made his decision. "He *is* a great ad for the program, sure. But he wouldn't be if he wasn't getting better all the time. There's a ceiling he'll hit, like I said. I don't expect Khaki to get a job—although I'm not saying that's impossible—but he'll never have to live in some 'mental hospital' again. He's integrating inside himself nicely—you couldn't find anyone around here who thinks he's a menace."

"Okay," I said, before Mack could launch into a speech about the whole mental-health system.

He went quiet, waiting.

"You have a private client. He's on a government contract, but not on a payroll. Did an audiovisual capture job for us, a while back," I said, careful not to mention the name of the video ninja.

"Uh-huh."

"We have another job for him."

"Not . . . ?"

"No. Pure surveillance. That work for you?"

"Lay it out," Mack said. "Then I'll know."

"You got it all, Conrad?" Mack said, tapping his temple to show the video ninja that covert operatives like us never write anything down.

The man with a never-leave-the-cellar complexion and an obsession Mack had been working with him to redirect just nodded.

He respected Mack. He even believed that we worked with a never-to-be-named government agency on special assignments, so we had cover IDs to account for our presence in the area. It made sense to him that this agency would have occasional use for his special skill set, and he'd be well paid for such work. Why not? It had happened before.

When Mack told me that an occasional "assignment" would go a long way toward moving Conrad into the daylight, I'd given him some cash and told him to pick the targets out of the phone book.

But the ninja would always be afraid of me, and I didn't have a cure for that. He could still feel the saw-toothed Tanto against his throat. My assurances that we were friends hadn't comforted him much, maybe because of the way I had delivered the message. We *must* be friends, I had reasoned for him—otherwise I would have made him dead.

"Photo only," the video ninja said, keeping his voice down

even though he was in his own house, proving he didn't need to write down instructions to memorize them. "As many as I can get. Color, black-and-white. No enhancement."

"Yes. And this is very important, Conrad; you have to make sure he doesn't see you."

"Nobody *ever* sees me," he said. Not boasting, just stating a fact.

Maybe that's what started him off, I thought. I kept that speculation to myself—Mack was the expert, not me. All I knew was that every man I soldiered with seemed to have a different reason to be wherever we were.

"Perfect," I told the video ninja. "You've got his address. He'll either be going out at night, or coming home late. Might stay in some nights, no way for us to be sure. So you have to decide: flat rate or per diem. Understand?"

"I . . ."

"Flat rate for this job is two thousand," I said, deliberately not using his name. "Per diem is five hundred a night."

"I still don't—"

"On flat rate, you get the photos the first night, you make two thousand for maybe a couple of hours' work. On per diem, it takes you one night, you lose fifteen hundred. But if it takes you ten tries, you make five thousand."

"I understand. But how would you know if . . . ?"

"We'll know, Conrad," I said, extra-soft, to make certain he got the message. A message from a man he'd videoed committing murder. A man who knew where he lived.

He took the flat rate.

Conrad must have gone right to work—it was less than forty-eight hours later when Mack called.

"I'll pick you up" is all he said.

I'd never understand why Conrad did his watching. He'd earned the "ninja" tag from me because he worked invisibly to his targets, and he was very good at what he did.

Better than good. Mack had pages and pages of photos, showing the man who called himself Roger—"Or you can call me 'Rod'; most of my friends do"—Mason from every angle imaginable. Full-face, profile, full-body (complete with reference scale running vertically at the side of the print), close-ups all the way down to a single eyebrow . . .

"He took way more than this," Mack said. "Saved everything to these"—handing over a trio of flash sticks. "They're all the same, but he converted to Windows, Mac, and Linux, just to be . . . professional."

"Here," I said, handing over some cash. "Tell him the agency pays a 'speed bonus.' Explain how that's just code for 'trustworthy.' That'll help, right?"

"A lot," Mack answered. "Conrad doesn't need the money. He'd do it for free. But no amount of money can buy the assurance that he's moving up in status. He's even shut down that back-channel Internet site where he used to post his . . . those videos he used to take."

H e was a good-looking man, this Roger Mason.

Longish chestnut-colored hair, dark-brown eyes, well put together but not body-spectacular. Thanks to Conrad's embedded reference scale, I could see he was about six one, maybe one eighty. No crow's feet, baggy eyes, or even a trace of a double chin. No reason a man in his middle thirties who worked out and ate right would need any kind of facial surgery.

But I didn't have time to waste on image-recognition matches. I suspected that, whoever this "partner" of Benton's was, he wouldn't have a Facebook page.

|>Eight images follow. ID not known.<|

I didn't wait for a response, but I was confident of one. If those images had appeared anywhere in cyber-space, the ghost could find them. The more governments insist on "clouded" data storage, the more vulnerable they make the data. As if they created this giant balloon, and couldn't imagine anyone would find it. Someone with a sharp little pin in his hand.

"You really don't care, do you, Dell? About any of it?"

"A dog park? A graft scheme? Crooked politicians?" I said, making the French gesture for *"Quelle différence?"*

"So it was just me. Me and my big mouth."

"There's no 'just' when it comes to you, Dolly."

"I didn't mean that! I meant . . . You know what I meant. Benton. If I hadn't mentioned his little 'half cocked' nonsense, you wouldn't have moved a muscle."

"That's true."

"But . . . now that it's over, you're not going to do anything more. Can you promise me that?"

"Mais oui!" I tried joking her out of the dark mood she'd been in for a few days.

Playing around didn't work, so I just lied: "I'm done, baby. Done with all of this."

When I snapped the machine together a few hours later, the ghost was waiting.

|<RN = Robert T. Fairmount. DOB = 1/4/1978. Released by Florida DoC 12/7/2002. Two priors: larceny-by-

```
trick, fraud. No wants, warrants, detainers. DL =
OR, Roger NMI Mason.>|
```

There could be a hundred variations on how they'd met, but the time line worked. By the time Benton had relocated here because he'd fallen in love with the coast life, he'd had years to put it all together. But he must have been passing as gay for quite a while—that was the kind of thing some people around here *would* check on.

I spent ten seconds wondering if this Robert T. Fairmount had specialized in victimizing homosexuals. Not likely. It takes years to work yourself into position, to build a cover ID. And if he'd invested that much time, he would have come into prison with a jacket that would make him a target.

He had to be a smooth worker—two separate felony convictions before he turned thirty, and they hadn't held him long on either one. He knew how to get paper, too: Roger No-Middle-Initial Mason had a valid Oregon driver's license, without a mark on it.

That didn't surprise me. I figured him for the kind of pro who wouldn't drink-and-drive, or even smoke weed before he took the wheel. If the cops took him, his prints would fall, and they'd know he wasn't who his license said he was.

Probably didn't take other kinds of risks, either. No playing around on the Internet, no side scams. So how hard could it have been to pose as Benton's "partner"?

What I didn't know was if it *was* a pose. Was he in for a piece of the score, or was he just getting paid?

No way Benton was paying him for piecework, I finally decided. It just wasn't logical. Didn't add up. Benton didn't mind paying for some things—Rhonda Jayne Johnson was proof of that. But trusting a professional scam artist wouldn't match up with anything I knew about him.

And then Olaf was talking to me. Not saying anything, just

making me replay the tapes. The two others who had run off and left Olaf to die and me to . . . Whatever happened to me, it wouldn't matter to them.

So—eight of us went in. Four died on the spot. Olaf dropped, and I stayed with him. The other two ran. Partnerships can dissolve as instantly as the first shot is fired.

I don't know what was in my mind when I finally made my own way back. I'm not an informant, and revenge would have made Olaf grimace in disgust.

As it turned out, there was no need to ponder the choices. Yes, I'd made it back. But I was the only one who had.

Why Benton's partner—the man Martin and Johnny had called "Roger"—moved to Oregon, I'd probably never know, but I could make a pretty good guess.

This state has got it all. The population ranges from fabulously rich to dirt-poor. Politically, it's as if geography made the decisions—the left side of the state leaned left, the right side leaned so far in the other direction that it left a kind of empty chasm along the dividing line.

Some people would cross the street to avoid the pollution of a man smoking a cigarette; others would leave a bag of meth as a tip in a bar. Some wanted to ban toy guns; some had arsenals that cost a lot more than their houses.

I don't know who makes up those statistics you see in newspapers, but whoever said Oregon had a low crime rate was basing it on reported convictions. That must be so: the sex killers who drive the paved corridor from Washington all the way through Oregon and down into California aren't out of business just because a few of them have been caught.

Not by "profilers" or some "multi-state task force." By informants, or a DNA hit when one of them was arrested on some other charge. Or by bragging on Facebook.

That kind, as soon as they were locked down for life, they always seemed to confess to a lot more kills. Or just drop heavy hints. They'd say they killed so many they couldn't remember them all.

There was no downside to that for them, and the cops treated them very nicely while they were "clearing" cases. The higher the body count, the more status. Celebrity status, I mean. An endless stream of letters, disturbed humans who'd set up a Web site for them, a market for their "art," TV interviews, marriage proposals . . . maybe even a book-and-movie deal, if they sold it hard enough.

Whatever Roger Mason had been looking for, he could find it here. His face was the right color, and he wasn't outrageously handsome, so he could blend wherever he needed to. Even the name he was working under was a con man's special: both names were too common to stand out. That Oregon driver's license meant he must have built a new ID kit before he came here. Probably had another couple put aside, just in case.

I was at no-choice roulette. But I couldn't do anything with guesses—even if a couple might be good enough to bet on, none were a sure thing.

And there was only one way to get both zeros removed before the croupier spun the wheel.

Rhonda Jayne Johnson wouldn't be the first whore to have switched gears when she found love, but that was one mystery that I'd never solve.

I didn't need to—whatever use she'd been to Benton was way past its sell-by date, but not her shares in his hedge fund.

Even if she didn't want the money, she wouldn't do anything that might make it seem she was a danger to him. Leaving her Web site intact wouldn't mean she was still working. And any hooker who worked off the Net would know all about minimizing risk. Today, pimps are for setting up Web sites.

Undercurrents got a lot of angry e-mails about the "power play" that had been engineered in our area, but there was nothing to dig into—corruption was no stranger to this part of the world, and no "background check" on Benton would find anything he'd so much as lied about, let alone any crimes he'd committed.

There were plenty of "comments" in support, too. Some called it an "everybody wins" deal, some said it was "business as usual." And some were outraged that this was taking public attention away from that disgusting logging road.

If any of those e-mails had gone into the CONFIDENTIAL bin at *Undercurrents,* the only thing that would have raised an eyebrow was a challenge to Benton's homosexual credentials. Around here, that would cause a stir. But he'd never actually *said* anything, just let people draw their own conclusions. For most, the fact that he'd never been married and lived with another man was enough.

And, really, so what? Being caught passing for gay in coastal Oregon might get you snubbed in some places, but it wouldn't bring out a lynch mob.

"**S**ummer's over."

"So what?" MaryLou said to me.

"I guess I thought you'd be going back to college."

"For what?" the big girl said. "There's no money in women's softball. The pro league is a joke, and Olympic Gold *might* get me a few minutes of attention—big deal."

"Remember when we went down to that college so you could score a yearbook?"

"Sure."

"Well, wasn't that woman supposed to be getting some kind of advanced degree, so she could coach?"

"Yeah. But she wasn't an athlete. She was all about 'monetizing.' You know, getting to be an agent, or a financial planner for some of the moneymakers who went pro."

"Couldn't you . . . ?"

"If it was representing females, they'd have to be real superstars to make any money. Males, I'd never get a shot. Anyway, that's not me. I'm not a negotiator."

No, you're not, I thought to myself. *It's not as if you tried to talk Cameron Taft out of using your little sister—you just shot him in the head.*

"Wouldn't a degree mean you could make more money, no matter what kind of job you wanted?"

"It would," MaryLou said, her tone telling me that she'd thought all this through. "And it wouldn't have to be a degree from a softball powerhouse. I know the game, inside out. There's no reason why I couldn't coach. High school, not college."

"You'd still—"

"I've only got the one more year left. I could finish that anywhere. Or I could take a year off, if I wanted."

"I guess that's right. But would they hold your scholarship . . . ?"

"They'd hold it for ten years, once they saw I could still bring it," the big girl said. Not bragging, stating a fact. A fact that didn't seem to make her all that happy.

"You could coach here," Mack said. "The high school would probably crawl through five miles of broken glass to get you."

"Here? After . . . after what happened?"

"Why not?" Dolly said, in her "How far do you want to take it?" voice.

"Yeah. Why not?" Franklin finally spoke.

"I thought we were here to talk about Bridgette's shop," MaryLou said.

Khaki was one hell of a scout.

The parcel of land Mack bought was slightly less than a half-acre, on a sloping, wooded hill. The owner couldn't wait to sell it: Mud slides are so common around here that insurance on the houses built on that hill is ridiculous. Plus, anyone fool enough to build there would have to walk up a hill to get to their own house.

The architectural plan Dolly got someone to do for her showed a tiny little house, with a "widow's walk" tower sticking out of the top. The whole place was six hundred square feet, so the tower would only take one person at a time—it looked like a long TV antenna growing out of the roof.

Bridgette was a jewelry designer. No shortage of those around here, but she'd built up a serious reputation already. Not just for her craftsmanship, but for the designing itself— there's nothing a woman likes better than hearing, "I never saw one like that!" about her necklace. Or earrings. Or bracelet . . . It didn't matter, because if Bridgette made it there never was going to be another one, ever. That's why she called the little shop One of One—everything she turned out was the ultra-max of "limited edition."

The little house would be more than spacious enough for working on her designs, and propane could provide all the power easily enough. If anyone wanted to make the trek, they could see whatever was on display. And going to all that trouble would only add to the cachet—that's what Dolly said.

Bridgette could also do a showing whenever she had enough

pieces ready—there was always empty storefront space, and a month's rent would be better than waiting for someone to actually open up a business in most of them.

"We could do it," Franklin said, more confidence vibrating in his voice than I'd ever heard. "A parcel that size, we'd have to cut a lot of timber, but it wouldn't go to waste. I know we couldn't get a truck up there, but there's a way to drag the wood out. You use chains, and make this kind of slide. Mr. Spyros showed me how to do it. We get a few jobs like that every year."

"A slab foundation," Mack said. "But it could be tricky, getting it all level."

"Not that much trouble," Franklin assured him.

MaryLou stood up and put her hand on Franklin's shoulder. Dolly was smiling with deep, true pleasure.

I was thinking about what kind of intel Conrad could pick up from that tower.

I figured on waiting a couple of months, so working on Bridgette's shop was perfect in a lot of ways.

Franklin could only work nights and weekends, but Mary-Lou was with me almost every day.

A couple of times, Mack walked up with a whole crowd of that "permanent homeless" crew of teenagers he watched over. Their leader, a redhead named Timmy, had already met me, and I recognized a few of his crew, so no tension there. And nobody asked MaryLou any questions, either because Mack had told them not to, or because the survival skills they'd been forced to develop had kicked in.

I guess half the town owed Dolly favors. People just showed up with their tools. There was an electrician, a plumber, four beefy guys with a sewage tank, Martin and Johnny harassing

Mack with questions about Bridgette's taste in plantings . . . they never stopped coming.

"She doesn't know about this?" Franklin asked Mack.

"Not a clue," he responded. "It's got to be a surprise."

"But . . . but what if she doesn't like it?"

MaryLou cracked him across the back of his head hard enough to cause brain damage in any of the awed teenagers. "She'll *love* it, you mope! When she sees what went into this, she'll get weak in the knees, I promise you."

Franklin blinked a couple of times. Not from MaryLou's slap—that probably hadn't even registered—but from the thinking I could *see* him doing.

You get the message yet? I thought to myself.

"Oh, *that's* the truth," Dolly backed up MaryLou. Whenever I was going someplace for the day, I would ask Dolly if she wanted me to bring her back anything. Her answer was always the same: "A surprise!"

I was sitting by myself on a big chunk of timber that would have to be cut a few more times before it could go down the hill, trying to work through all the possible outcomes before I moved.

"I wish I could do something like that," Franklin said, taking a seat next to me.

"You just *did* something like that," I told him, puzzled at the wistful note in his thunder-bass voice.

"I don't mean build something. I know I can do that, Mist—Dell. It's the . . . I don't know how to say it, exactly . . . the 'surprise' thing. Mack, he's so excited to be doing this, right? Because it's going to make Bridgette real happy."

"Sure . . ."

"See, making Bridgette happy, that makes *him* happy. If I could make MaryLou happy, it would make *me* happy. But I don't know anything I could do. Not like this, I mean," he said, swiveling his head to take in the whole scope of the work everyone had put in.

"Franklin . . . Uh, you're talking to the wrong man about this. You think *I* knew that women love surprises before Dolly told me? No. How would I? Me, I don't like surprises. So how could I . . . ?"

"Why don't you like surprises?"

The more I talk, the less I help, I thought to myself. How could I explain to Franklin that when I was his age there was no such thing as a *good* surprise?

"I'm not sure," I said, feeling my way. "I just don't. Never did."

"You think it's because you're a man?"

"That'd be the easy way out, Franklin. But I haven't known enough women to say they *all* like surprises. I know Dolly does, because she said so. A million times. But . . . ?"

"Like MaryLou just said to me, right?"

I just nodded. If Franklin was "retarded," I'd hate to meet a genius. I guess he just fell into the role because it was an easier one to play. Maybe he was slower to *get* things, but once he got them, they were locked down.

I remember Franklin vehemently saying that MaryLou just *couldn't* be gay. They went to the prom together. He loved her. Case closed.

I cursed myself for a fool, but I knew I owed the big man a try. "Franklin, you know what I think? I think *some* women love surprises, but you can't be sure about any of them unless they find a way to tell you they do."

"I know. I know now, anyway. But, see, Mack, he didn't only know his wife loved surprises, he even knew what kind of surprise she'd really like."

"Maybe you do, too," I said. "About MaryLou, I mean."

"Huh?"

"Well, you know you can build a house, right? Not by yourself, but with everyone pitching in to help. Like we're doing now."

"But how could I . . . ?"

"Franklin, whatever you're about to say is wrong. All those permits and code-compliance things, Dolly knows how to get them. Or get them *done,* anyway. You think Mack wouldn't help you? Or even that gang of kids he brought along?"

"But even if they did . . . I mean, even if I could get a terrific house, why do you think MaryLou would like that for a surprise, Dell?"

"I think she just *told* you she would, my friend."

I got up. Franklin stayed where he was. Probably had some thinking of his own to do.

"**I**'m scared of guns," Johnny said the next evening. "But Martin thinks we should have one, so we agreed . . . to ask you about it, I mean."

I didn't waste my time with any "Why me?" stuff. They weren't wrong, and we all knew it.

"I think it's probably a good idea," I said, picking my words carefully. "You live way out of town, and stupid people get stupid ideas."

"What stupid people?" Johnny demanded.

"There's no shortage of them," I said, catching Martin's nod out of the corner of my eye. "Especially with the coast becoming the meth capital of the country."

"We've never had any—"

"You asked me if I thought it was a good idea. I said it was. I don't want to argue with you, okay?"

"That's just the way Johnny talks," Martin said. "It sounds like he's starting an argument, but he's just making sure you understand before you go. We already agreed between us. That you'd know better than we would about this. And Dolly . . ."

His voice trailed off. I already figured this whole thing was my wife's idea. Not getting a gun, but settling a . . . disagreement between her two friends. Martin probably was dead-set on getting a firearm, and Johnny was probably not—it'd be just like Dolly to tell them to get some kind of independent arbiter. And nominate me for the job.

"You're talking about something for the house? For the store? To carry around?"

"Well, you're the expert," Johnny said, just short of waspish.

"You'll never need a gun for the store," I said. But even though Johnny was glad to hear that, he had to be himself, so:

"Why is that?"

"Because if someone wants to rob your store—during business hours, I mean, not some night-working burglar—the last thing you want to do is endanger your customers. It's just money. You can always get more money."

"And we never keep much cash in the shop, either," Martin said. "Most people pay by debit card, or a check. There's even an app if they want to—"

"Good," I cut in, thinking, *That's one down*. "Carrying a gun doesn't make any sense, either. Nobody's after you, nobody's going to pull a broad-daylight carjack, not around here. That's for idiots who go out looking for an old lady driving a Lincoln. They don't have a plan, they don't even know what to do with the car. Or a fool so wasted that he points a gun at someone because he doesn't have the money to get a cab ride home."

"True enough," Martin said. *Two down.*

"But for the house, yeah, it makes sense. To protect your*selves,* not any . . . not any *thing,* like a TV or whatever. And if you had a dog, you wouldn't need a gun to protect the house, anyway."

Before Martin could start off complaining that Johnny didn't like dogs, Johnny sliced in with: "*You've* got a dog. And I'll bet you're carrying a gun right this minute."

"The dog's not with me," I said, staying very calm. I don't like being baited, but I know how to spin when someone tries it. "That mutt's *never* with me unless Dolly is, too. Rascal's a great dog. He'd protect Dolly with his life, wouldn't even think about it. Rascal's not the problem; Dolly is."

"I don't under—"

"Come on!" I appealed to both of them. "You know Dolly. If someone broke into the house when I wasn't home, and Rascal went after them, Dolly'd jump right in to protect *him*."

They both laughed—they'd known Dolly a long time.

"We don't know anything about guns," Johnny finally said. "Could you show us . . . ?"

"I can show you how to use a self-defense weapon; that won't take more than a couple of hours. But stuff like making sure you have a clear field of fire, that you'd have to practice. Over and over. A shotgun is the best for what you need, but whichever one of you is holding it has to know that the other one is *behind* him before he pulls the trigger."

"A shotgun?" Martin said, clearly disappointed.

"Yes. You're both strong enough to handle a twelve-gauge. And with the right load, not only is it guaranteed to discourage anything that's on the wrong side of the weapon, it's the simplest and safest choice."

"You'll pick it out and . . . ?"

"I can't do that. You have to sign paper and go through some little background check—for a shotgun, they'll do it while you wait. You'd be the registered owner, so you'd have to make the buy."

"But we wouldn't know which one *to* buy," Martin said.

"You want a twelve-gauge, single-trigger side-by-side, one barrel full-choke, the other modified. There's a gun store not five miles from here. You've got the specs. Almost any brand will do. Ithaca, Remington . . . there's no real difference."

"Just like you said," Martin told me, a week later. He was holding a beautiful Parker 12-gauge out for inspection.

"That's not a new one."

"Oh, we understand," Johnny said. "It's really beautiful, isn't it?"

I had to admit it was, but: "You haven't fired it?"

"Noooo," Johnny answered. "We thought we'd wait for you to show us, and everything."

"Why are you doing all that?" Johnny asked, bending a little to the waspish side again.

Apparently, he wasn't crazy about my setting up the shotgun in a brace, then wiring the trigger with about a fifty-foot lead line, all before I broke the piece and loaded it.

"That isn't a new gun. Probably a hundred years old. And it's been updated quite a bit."

"Of course. We know it's an antique—a work of art, too. But that's no reason why it wouldn't work."

All I did was tell them to stand back. Then I pulled on the wire. Twice.

It didn't blow up, so I walked over, extracted the spent shells, and checked it over. Closely. Whoever had modified this thing meant to use it. I didn't want to ask how much they'd paid for this "collectible," or spoil their mood by explaining that every modification—and I could see a few of them—made it worth less to a collector, not more.

By the time the sun was setting, both of them were confident they could handle the kick—the extended buttplate of crosshatched rubber helped—and understood basic safety, like keeping the thing loaded but broke open, so all they'd have to do was snap it shut and be ready to go.

They'd be a little sore the next morning—went through a hundred rounds apiece—but nothing serious.

What *was* serious was the safety instructions I drilled into them until they were ready to chuck the whole thing. Well, almost ready.

And then I made them show me they could snap it closed, lift it to shoulder height, and fire twice before I was ready to leave the shotgun with them. The last ten times, I made them do it blindfolded.

"Really?" Johnny snapped at me.

"Someone breaks into your home in the middle of the night, you're gonna turn on the lights for them?"

"He's right," Martin said.

"I know. But I just don't . . ."

"What?"

"Never mind," Johnny sulked. But he let me put the black sleep mask over his eyes without any more bitching.

"Stay home this morning," Dolly said while we were eating breakfast.

Just me and Dolly.

And Rascal, who always scored his percentage.

I didn't ask any questions.

It was another hour or so later when we saw two cars pull up behind the house. Martin's hopped-up Mini Cooper, and some other one I didn't recognize.

"Could you come outside for a minute?" Martin asked me.

I got up, Dolly and Rascal right behind me.

The second car was a Peugeot 403. Had to be at least sixty years old. I knew that car; its engine was probably twice the size of my motorcycle's, but had to pull four times the weight. I'd driven a couple of them, years ago. A study in contradictions: it was small, but a real four-door sedan, and the back seat wasn't any less comfortable than the front. It had a four-speed manual, but the shift lever was on the column. And it had a sunroof that you cranked open by hand.

"You know what this is?" Martin asked me.

I told him I did. He didn't seem surprised—after all, I'd recognized the Facel Vega he was still "rebuilding" when I'd first seen the stripped body up on blocks years ago, and this *was* a French car. . . .

"Ever drive one?" he asked.

"A few times."

"Want to try it out?"

"Sure," I told him. Not to be polite—I really did want to see if it was anything like I'd remembered.

"The keys are in it," he said, opening the passenger door and climbing in. Dolly and Johnny went back to the house.

It fired right up. I slipped the lever into first, let out the soft, smooth clutch, and we were off.

Johnny didn't say a word as I reacquainted myself with that sharply accurate steering, tapped the brakes a few times to see how they held, even cranked open the sunroof. He didn't start to act nervous until we were going fifty or so, but when he saw me move the shift lever back up to neutral, then push forward and up to get into fourth, he let out a breath.

"It's perfect," I told him, as we were returning to the house.

"Well, it's kind of drab," he said, apologetically. "That's the original color, but you'd think a French vehicle would have more choices than gray or black. And it's got rust spots in a number of little places. But, mechanically, it's good as new."

"Sure feels like it."

"This one's a survivor," Martin told me. Meaning, not a restoration, just a well-maintained car that probably had outlived its owner. "We bought it from a lady whose husband kept it going all these years. For next to nothing. She seemed more concerned that it go to a good home than about getting a price—not that it would be worth much, anyway. This isn't exactly a collectible."

"I never got that collecting thing," I told him. "But keeping a good piece of machinery running, that makes sense."

By then we were back inside.

Johnny looked up from a cup of whatever Dolly had brewed for him. "You like it?" he asked me.

"It's a swell car."

"It's yours," Johnny said.

"What?"

"A little thank-you gift," he said, winking at me.

Smart move. "Thank-you gift for *what*?" was out of Dolly's mouth before his eyelid went back up. So she hadn't known what her two friends had been arguing over before she decided I'd be a good arbitrator.

"Dell helped us pick up some tools we needed." Johnny tried his best, but it wasn't going to fly. I could have told him that.

By the time the whole story was told, and retold, working backward, Dolly wasn't exactly overjoyed, but she was sort of okay with it.

Sort of. "I wouldn't expect *him* to say anything," she said, jerking her thumb in my direction, as if anyone didn't know who she meant. "But, Johnny, Martin . . . *you* didn't think I'd be interested?"

"They probably thought you'd be *too* interested," I said.

"We're all grown men," Johnny said. "We can make our own decisions." Another mistake. Well, he brought that one on himself.

Martin stepped in to protect his partner. "Do you really like the car, Dell?"

"It's a thing of beauty."

"Then it's settled," he said, getting up to make a run for it. "The papers are all in the glove box."

Naturally, they made out the bill of sale to Dolly. For five hundred dollars.

"I t's like having a better version of my motorcycle," I told my wife, half forcefully holding her on my lap.

"But . . ."

"Really, Dolly. It's no light catcher. No eye catcher, either— nothing to make it stand out. Anyone who sees it, they'd think it was one of those little sedans every company makes now— they pretty much all look alike.

"Plus, it's quiet, and I could probably go an easy couple of hundred miles without needing more gas. Your Subaru, every- one around here knows it. And I don't much like driving it, either. Ever since you had that special seat put in—"

"What?"

"Honey, I practically had to force it on you, didn't I?"

"You did. I would have been perfectly happy with—"

"The doctor said you were getting mid-back pain from that old fall you took, little girl. This one, it's set up for you . . .

just you. I have to make fifty different adjustments whenever I use it."

That wasn't much of an overstatement. The Corbeau was a beautiful piece of work, with exactly the right kind of support—it had both back and side bolstering, and the head-rest was positioned perfectly. It held Dolly in the right position even when she got a little enthusiastic behind the wheel, and it was as comfortable as an easy chair.

"That was awfully sweet of them, wasn't it?"

"I guess it was. But I don't think they expect us to start exchanging gifts."

"I'll make them something," my wife said, cutting her eyes at me in case I wanted to be stupid enough to argue with her.

I didn't.

"She's not . . . whatever she was." The severe woman's voice, burner cell to burner cell.

"We're together now. You understand?" she went on, in case I missed what she was really telling me.

"Yes," I said.

"Be *very* sure," she said. "Those shares, they've all been sold. Back to the fund, which still hasn't shown a profit."

"I *am* very sure," I told her.

I felt nothing.

Not in my mind, not in my body. My heartbeat was mea-sured and slow, my eyes were clear, and my hands without tremor.

Back to what I was trained to be. The zen of violence is to be calm, but never relaxed—to reach that state of being where you sense everything and feel nothing.

When this man of unknown motivations had warned my Dolly against "going around half cocked," he was already dying. He didn't know that. How could he? A man doesn't know he has prostate cancer until some test warns his doctor, and the biopsy comes back bad.

Not all biopsies come back bad. But all autopsies do.

I couldn't allow anyone to even so much as speculate that Dolly was connected to Benton's death. It had been months before he left town on one of those "business trips" he'd dutifully report to the IRS.

"No assassin allows the client to set a time limit." Olaf's voice. "Listen!" he whispered. "Logic must rule. If a client knows when and where the target will be killed, that client can have another man waiting . . . to clean up any loose ends.

"But even if the client is not planning to destroy *any* evidence that might surface later, even if the client is simply hiring a contractor, 'assassin' and 'impatient' are an inherent contradiction."

I wasn't going to risk my Peugeot being spotted.

Even if nobody paid it much attention, Los Angeles is a car culture, and every fool walks around with a cell-phone camera. The license plate alone could give away too much.

So I drove down to Sacramento and borrowed a generic Toyota from whoever left it on the street, then I switched its plates with another Toyota's a few miles south.

Why anyone would order a prostitute from a Web site was almost beyond my imagination. But I had learned there were people who trusted "The Internet" with unrestricted idolatry.

And centuries before there was an Internet, there were always those so certain they could turn any situation to their advantage that they never concerned themselves with risk.

For them, everything was a *sure* thing.

The other side of that coin had always been there, too: those who were only truly themselves when they took risks.

All idols—even reflections in a mirror—share one characteristic: they demand sacrifice.

No elaborate ruse was required. My cyber-ghost accessed the target's computer with the ease of an apex predator—at one with the environment that held both him and his food supply in eternal suspension.

The target was in Los Angeles for less than an hour before he ordered off the pull-down menu, methodically placing his checkmark under the choices offered under the "preferences" tab.

Very conventional choices, all well within his belief system. Countless young, blond, toned, do-whatever girls were within miles—perhaps even blocks—of his hotel.

They weren't all as young, or young-looking, as the target wanted. And they weren't all blondes. But they all had given up on whatever dreams brought them to this City of Seconds.

No more waiting to be "discovered" for these girls. Even the ones who looked twelve years old had already aged out. The porn industry likes to talk about its "shining stars," but never reveals that they all lose their light. And drop from the night sky.

What gets used will always get used *up*—the only variable is how long that takes.

The feeder stream that carried them in would eventually reverse itself—dreams travel much faster on the way down. At some point, they all exchange their never-happen fantasies for the always-would reality. Juggling pulled-pin grenades, promising themselves that they'd go back home as soon as they caught enough cash in one hand before the grenade exploded in the other.

If there was one acting skill they mastered, it was lying to themselves.

The doorman greeted me with a "Welcome back, sir."

He'd never seen me before, but I wasn't carrying any luggage, so he played it safe, assuming I'd checked in before his shift had started, gone out, and was just now returning. I confirmed that impression by walking up from the same side as drop-off cars would exit, waving a languid hand over my shoulder to dismiss whatever limo had dropped me off.

In the lobby, there was no security to bypass other than the quick eye-scan to see if the man in the gray alpaca suit and black silk shirt with designer sunglasses was important enough to warrant a personal greeting as he passed through the entrance to the elevators, casually holding up a room-key card.

Poseurs were far more common than the real thing, and sophisticated staff pride themselves on being able to tell the difference.

So the key card was enough to get me to the elevators, but not enough to merit that personal greeting. Even my gelled and spiked corn-silk-yellow hair and the prominent mole on my left cheek didn't merit a second glance.

This staff would never fail to recognize a genuine cinema star, and the town was supposedly full of major character actors. But they wouldn't need facial-recognition skills to pick out the real deal. One thing they knew for sure: no *truly* major player would ever be unaccompanied.

When he looked through the peephole in the door to his suite, the customer wasn't surprised to see me.

Not me, personally, just the package he'd been expecting. Well dressed, properly groomed, my face unsmiling but not threatening. I was just a man on business, perfectly in tune with the hotel's ambience.

The Web site had told him that the girl he ordered was "too fresh" to be allowed out unless there was a "chauffeur" sent to look the setup over first. The girl was just another variety of room service—higher-priced, sure, but still no more than a finger-snap away. The client had already placed his order, and paid through a cleared credit card. Tips were "welcome"— there was no need to spell out "in cash."

Anyone who used the "catering" Web site would be informed that the chauffeur's task would be to check the premises—not just the living room, the whole suite—to make certain the client was alone, then punch a button on a cell phone to summon the merchandise.

As soon as she arrived, the chauffeur would go downstairs and wait in the car until the client was fully satisfied. He'd paid for a three-hour "unit," but if he decided he wanted to extend, he knew how to contact the service provider without going near a phone.

The dead man ushered me inside.

As he closed the door, I shot him in the back of the head. The quieted round—a .22 short with some powder removed— passed soundlessly through the hand-turned barrel of the tiny pistol. He might have made some noise falling against the door if my grip on the back of his shirt collar hadn't prevented any such possibility.

I used that same collar to haul his body into the jet-nozzle bathtub, placing him so he was lying on his back. I removed his wallet—the kind you carry in the inside pocket of your jacket— his wafer-thin oversized watch, and some cash from his slacks.

Then I put another round into each eye, draped a paper stencil over his forehead, sprayed a burst of blue paint to create a ♀ symbol, pulled off the stencil, plastic-pocketed it with the little can of paint, and walked into the unused bedroom.

Two pieces of luggage. Both Tumi, each marked with "GBB" in red on a raised portion designed for such personalization. The gusseted black leather oversized attaché case would fit any airline's definition of "carry-on" and slide under any seat in First Class. No waiting in Baggage Claim for Mr. Benton. And no chance of the airline's sending checked luggage to some other destination.

The larger bag didn't interest me. I just wanted to make sure the carry-on had a portable computer of some kind.

It did. As well as one of those phones that allow connection to the Internet.

I knew the cops would call it an "execution-style" killing. And at least one of them would tip the press about the blue symbol on his face. That would start another round of gossip about the Manson Family giving birth to a second generation.

Even experienced investigators couldn't ignore the possibility of a group of psychos. L.A. was never short of cults, usually led by a mind as dream-killed as an aged-out porn star.

Crazy people could be clever enough to think that taking the dead man's wallet would delay an ID.

Of course, it wouldn't—he would have paid for the room by credit card. But I wanted the cops to have every possible excuse to do a forensic examination of his laptop.

The corridor was soundless.

I knew its thick carpeting would mask footsteps, or even a service cart, so I scanned carefully with an extendable dentist's mirror before I stepped out, checking that the "Do Not Disturb" placard was still in place over the doorknob in the same motion.

The security camera wasn't an issue—a quick spritz of fog-colored paint had made any kind of ID impossible, even if someone was watching in real time. Not much chance of that—this wasn't a casino.

I walked up three flights of stairs, checked the elevator buttons, hit an unlit one with a latex-covered knuckle, and took an empty car down to the first floor.

The same doorman greeted my exit as sincerely as a mortician's grief. I kept walking for a few blocks until I was satisfied nobody was interested.

I was in the right neighborhood for a leisurely walk.

And dressed for my surroundings. To any watcher, it would appear as if the limo had dropped me off in front of one of the buildings, and I wanted to grab a smoke before I entered my studio's headquarters, or my agent's offices. The slabby cell phone shielded my face as I . . .

Anyone taking a look would fill in that blank themselves, depending on who they were. Or thought they were.

Turning the corner brought me to the verge of another world, a world I needed to look over until I could stabilize pattern recognition. By the time I retrieved the car from the parking garage, I was wearing orange-lensed HD sunglasses, a banana-yellow tank top, and an L.A. Clippers adjustable ball cap. I carried the alpaca jacket, silk shirt, and tie in one hand, rolled together.

I paid the cashier on the way out. If she noticed anything, it would have been a man with a black eye patch and a white sweatshirt with "13 ½" silk-screened in red across the chest.

Two blocks later, the eye patch and sweatshirt were under the front seat.

The drive to Sacramento took me deep into the darkness I needed.

I pulled off the road, checked the undisturbed little markers I'd left, and got to work. The Walmart box cutters made short work of the alpaca suit and every other item I'd been wearing— I'd brought a half-dozen with me so I wouldn't have to spend time changing blades.

The torn strips went into a hole I'd already trenched out, along with the shoes and socks I'd worn into the hotel.

Then I coated it all with what *légionnaires* dryly called *"flambé"* in places where they spread it over humans like jam on toast. It burned perfectly, but didn't send up smoke. I refilled the hole, tamped it down with my hands, and stirred until it was indistinguishable from any of the surrounding dirt.

I removed the barrel of the little pistol, pressed one end tightly against a cube of steel, then emptied the vial of acid into it. When the hissing stopped, I used a sculptor's hammer to turn it into a shapeless lump.

That lump flew out the passenger-side window as I drove toward the Oregon border, where I left the "borrowed" car in an empty garage.

By the time I returned to our cottage, I was back to where I'd started.

But I'd learned a lot since then. More than enough for me to revisit the man I'd once been all the time.

My hands were clean. There was no back-trail.

Just one more tile was needed to turn the whole mosaic into a single black slab.

I made four passes in my little Peugeot before I was certain. Leaving some lights on didn't tell me the house was occupied, but the figure moving around on the second floor was perfectly backlit.

Only one way to make certain I could rewrite the ending originally plotted by another.

I parked the Peugeot in the dark part of the huge yard. Then I walked to the front door and pushed the pale-pink illuminated button with my silk-wrapped thumb before I returned the pocket square to the lapel of my charcoal suit jacket.

That jacket was a masterpiece. It not only held my flat semi-auto without showing, it had room in the sleeves for those foam-cushioned wraps people with tennis elbow wear—the kind that looked like a honeycomb of little protective pads. Mine were different. Scalpel-cutting into each pad to extract the foam and insert precut pieces of lead had taken a long time. Elbow strikes rely on bone to cut flesh; now one from me would break any bone it hit.

Sixty seconds was running in my head. If he didn't come to the door by . . .

The door opened. It was the man I'd hoped for—the man in Conrad's photo array. Even if he had company, they'd never be able to tell the police any more than what time the doorbell had sounded.

"Mr. Fairmount? Please excuse me for using that name, but

Mr. Benton said it would be the only way to assure you that I was working for him. My *bona fides,* if you will, sir."

He was looking at a man dressed in an expensive suit, but not some mere "driver." Not with my faint French accent and use of his real name. Before he could process everything, I said: "Please, come with me, sir. I have a car waiting to bring you to Mr. Benton. He said to tell you that a meeting was necessary, because a *very* large sum had just been introduced by a new player and a . . . demonstration would be required to close."

"What's that supposed to . . . ?"

"Sir, I know only what I was told. And I have repeated that to you."

"I'll have to—"

"Sir, my instructions are to take you to Mr. Benton."

"And if I don't give a damn about your 'instructions'?"

"I understand. Mr. Benton said if you did not accompany me without delay, I was to leave without you. I cannot call him, because he specified that no cell phones were permitted—I am to report only in person."

I turned as if to go, but his hand was on my shoulder before I could take a single step.

"George has made some strange moves, but this is . . . weird, even for him," the dead man probed.

I didn't take the bait. He hadn't tried to jump out, so he didn't know his door wouldn't open. Besides, a true con man always tries to *work* a mark, not overpower him, and this guy was as true as they come.

"He did not share any information with me, sir. My job is simply to—"

"Yeah, I know," he cut me off, switching to a more conde-scending tone, inviting me to prove I was no mere hired hand by telling him something—*anything*—to show I was an insider.

That one didn't work, either.

"This car, it's not . . ."

That bait I took. "Mr. Benton wanted to be certain no atten-tion would be attracted, sir."

"Well . . . how far are we going, anyway?"

I glanced at the odometer, making sure he saw me do it. "Perhaps another dozen kilometers, sir."

He stiffened a little at "kilometers," but recovered instantly. He wouldn't get himself mixed up with dope, and he knew Benton wouldn't, either, and I was *some* kind of Mediterra-nean, so . . .

We drove in silence for a few minutes. I don't know what he was thinking, just my own thoughts: *He's no muscleman, but panic does strange things to people. I don't want to leave any pieces of him in this car, but if he . . .*

"What the hell is this?" he asked, looking at the long-abandoned Thai restaurant just off a two-lane stretch of asphalt.

"Everyone is inside, sir. We enter from the back," I told him, pushing the switch to allow his door to open.

Once he got out of the car, I walked next to him, on his left. He probably never heard the wraith's whisper of the black steel baton as it dropped out of my sleeve and whipped behind his head. Sounds carry a long distance outdoors, and a knife won't stop a man from screaming . . . or leaving some DNA around, either.

Fractured skull, unconscious. He was done, but I wasn't. I planted the spike deep behind his ear, kicked it all the way home, and left it in place while I went back to the car and opened the trunk.

Wrapping him in the sheets of roofer's plastic didn't take

long. I carried his body back to the trunk, which was already triple-lined with more of the same stuff.

Then I drove off to wait for the sun.

W hen I rolled up to the job site, Franklin was waiting.

I didn't know exactly what job he was working on, but I knew it was on a hill that was wooded on one side and clear on the other.

I wasn't halfway out of the Peugeot when he came charging down to where I parked. "Do you need any . . . ?"

"Just for you to stay in place, Franklin. You're still using the tree chipper on this job, right?"

"Yep. We've got a big one, a Bandit. They cost a lot, but Mr. Spyros said, for what they charge to rent those things, buying one was going to pay for itself pretty quick. And he was right. It'll probably take another couple of weeks to finish everything, like I told you."

"You've been running it every day?"

"Every day."

"Nobody's complained?"

"Somebody came by, but he was more curious than anything. When he got out of his truck, Mr. Spyros talked to him."

"So he won't be back?"

"Mr. . . . ? Oh, you mean the guy in the truck?" Franklin snorted—kind of like a bull does when it's pawing the ground. "Nah. Not a chance."

"Okay, Franklin. We went over this, right?"

"Yes, sir!"

I caught his eyes—there was a hint of merriment in them that I'd never seen before. More confident on his home turf? For Franklin, working with Spyros *was* home. Maybe that was it. But I could almost feel MaryLou standing there. Standing *with* him.

"Okay. Now I'm going to drive my car partway up, right into that canopy you made. It's perfect."

"It wasn't so hard. All I did was—"

"Not hard for *you,* maybe. I know I couldn't do it. Hell, I don't think a whole crew could do it, not in the time you had."

"Well . . ."

"You left my chain saw in there?"

"Sure!"

"All right. You go back to that tree-chipper thing, fire it up, and start pushing timber through it. When you see me coming, I'll have something over my shoulder. That's your cue to turn around and walk back over to the canopy where my car is. You've got work to do in that area, too, right?"

"Oh yeah. And plenty of it. Mr. Spyros left me in—"

"Great. Now, remember, your job is to keep anyone from walking past you. Nothing else. Don't look back—I'll be down here pretty soon."

"I'd never tell—"

"I know that, Franklin. That's because we're friends. *True* friends. You wouldn't take a chance on getting me in trouble. Well, that goes both ways—*you* can't get in trouble over something you never knew anything about, understand?"

"Yes" is all the big man said. A lot more soberly this time.

By the time I shoulder-carried the plastic shroud up the hill, Franklin was sitting off to one side of the machine. It really was reducing trees to little chips, but making less of a holy-hell racket than I expected.

Unrolling the shroud took only one long pull. I put a slab of plywood on another piece of the plastic, then dragged the body over on top of it. The chain saw dismembered Fairmount like he was a thick, dead branch.

When I ran the saw's blade all the way through his throat, I had a brief image of those heads on stakes that Dolly and I had planted. After MaryLou's trial ended the way it had.

Tossing different pieces of him into the chipper was even easier. The plywood went last, after I flipped it over to make sure nothing had soaked through to the wrapping I'd carried him in. Then I tossed in the trio of five-gallon plastic jugs full of alcohol. The chipper treated them as it did everything else entering its maw.

I took one last look at the growing pile of chips. Even if there were microscopic pieces of human remains in there, they didn't worry me—who'd ever look?

I turned my back on the whole thing, and started down the hill.

"I've got to go put all this someplace," I told Franklin, holding the rolled-up black plastic in one hand and the chain saw in the other.

"I've been thinking," he said. "Sometimes that chipper leaves kind of a mess. Mr. Spyros says, if that happens, just pour some gasoline over everything on the canvas tarp we use to catch it all. Then trench all around it and set the chips on fire. It's what we call a 'controlled burn.' You think that might be a good idea?"

"It's a perfect idea," I told him. "I wish I'd thought of it."

About an hour later, it was finished.

Everything I needed was in the trunk of my car: A jug that looked like the ones they use to refill water coolers was actually glass, filled with high-concentrate sulfuric acid. And the deep stoneware pot looked like something you'd plant flowers in.

There was a lot of the black plastic, but once I rolled it all up tightly, it was easy for the chain saw to reduce it to small chunks, almost filling the stoneware pot. Then I put on thick goggles and heavy rubber gloves, and poured in the acid.

I was patient about it—a little bit at a time, very careful to guard against a splash.

Once all the plastic pieces were part of the acid, it turned an ugly brownish color for a few minutes, then started to clear as it ate into the pot itself.

I used the wedge I had kicked under the pot to stick a long pry bar into place, and all my strength to pour it out, a little at a time. I could have used Franklin's muscles on this part, but I didn't want him to know what I was fouling the soil with, and I couldn't let him help without safety gear.

A sledgehammer cracked the pot into shards. I shoveled those into a hole Franklin had already dug about ten yards away, then refilled it with the mound of dirt he'd left right next to it.

He never asked why I wanted him to do any of this. Maybe MaryLou had told him what I was capable of, maybe he sensed it—I don't know. But he knew that I had done some of those things to protect MaryLou once, and that alone would have been enough for Franklin.

A man who always pays his debts drifted into my head. Olaf had been a genius. Franklin couldn't come close to Olaf in some ways. But in one way—one critical way—they were brothers.

Dolly was waiting for me.

"Took your new car for another test drive, Dell?"

"That's about right. I'll probably need to add some more candlepower up front; those headlights don't exactly peel paint."

"Uh-huh."

"Leave it, Dolly," I said.

She gave me a look I couldn't read, but I was too tired to try and decipher it. All I wanted was to cover myself with alcohol, then shower it off and get some sleep.

Anyway, that's all I thought I wanted, until Dolly stepped into the shower, just to be sure I did a good job.

VANISHED!

The headline in the local newspaper. George Benton, well-known philanthropist and community activist, hadn't been seen for weeks. I guess the L.A. cops were still working his laptop for leads, and I'd been told their department wasn't lenient about leaks. Not anymore, anyway.

A police "welfare check" of Benton's house revealed no sign of Roger Mason. Turned out that he hadn't been seen for a while, either.

No sign of foul play.

Nothing in *Undercurrents* except a lot of e-mails ranging from gay-rights activists to self-appointed "profilers," all larded with gross speculation. Some said they had demanded that the FBI investigate, but had been rebuffed.

The local police—all of them, from Village PD to the Sheriff's Office, to the County Patrol, even the Tribal Police—collaborated on a letter saying that both parties were adults, no one had the authority to report them as "missing," and their premises had been gone over thoroughly "by the best forensics teams from all departments" without finding so much as a strand of the wrong color hair.

And, no, a DNA analysis had not been performed, because

there was nothing to test. Nothing had been disturbed, nothing stolen. They issued a combined public statement: there was nothing to do unless some "indication of criminality" emerged.

Either the L.A. detectives had contacted the locals and told them to keep the killing quiet, or maybe they figured small-town cops would only impede their investigation. Equal possibilities— either one served each group's interests.

It didn't stop people on Facebook from "calling for" action— like reporting "sightings" to a page they set up for that. Over a thousand in the first week.

"Nobody gives a damn," Dolly told me almost a month later.

"Everyone's still getting what they want, even if it might take a little longer. The bond issue passed easily, so they'll have their precious Sign Wall, and that convention center will be going up when all the land is cleared.

"And all of us who owned that land where we wanted to build a dog park? We'll end up with enough money to buy a much better parcel, one already zoned, with a nearby road and everything."

I just shrugged my shoulders—none of this had anything to do with me.

Maybe that fooled Dolly. If it didn't, I'd never know.

Rascal yawned.

There are times when logic can become your enemy.

I can still remember banishing pain from my thoughts as I slogged through a blood-lusting jungle, one leg useless from the metal fragments implanted by a land mine, its weight on a crutch I had fashioned from a hacked-off tree limb.

Logic pounded at my mind, demanding entrance. It wanted to tell me how lucky I'd been, how the soldiers moving ahead of me on that tracking trail had not. But it had other messages as well, and any computation of odds would have reduced my will to keep moving.

If I could just keep moving, I'd find safety. No other thought could enter my mind. My sole focus was on that . . . dream? . . . fantasy? No! It was ahead of me, that place of safety.

For Dolly, our little cottage was that place.

A place of true peace Dolly had longed for ever since she left Médecins Sans Frontières. Or maybe since she had walked away from whatever was in her past to enter one battle zone after another. As with me, it was down to two choices. Polar opposites, no middle ground.

Keep moving or die.

When I'd first learned of Dolly's dream, it took me full circle.

All the time I was working to make it come true, I never gave a moment's thought to the cold logic I had blocked from my mind as I slogged through that jungle so many years ago.

When I found the place Dolly so desperately longed for, only then did I realize the truth: she would not have shared her dream with me unless she was willing to share its coming true with me as well.

That knowledge came slowly. As I moved toward the little cottage, all I knew was that it was worth my life to find it for Dolly. Not the cottage, that place of peace.

When I found it, when Dolly became *my* Dolly, I'd taken lives to keep it so.

Within that peaceful zone, Dolly found a way to keep doing her work. Rescuing, that was her work. Her choice.

Killing, that had been my work.

Luc had taken on a debt when he called me "son." I had taken on a debt when I'd put Patrice's lifeless body on my shoulder and carried him all the way back to base. Had I been allowed, I would have taken him home. But I wouldn't have known how to find his home, and I couldn't have answered any of the questions that would have been asked along the way.

Olaf paid the only debt he still acknowledged in his last moments of life. It cost him some pain, but I would not disrespect his sense of honor by taking that pain away.

Die for Dolly? I would do that with pride. Kill for her? I had done that. But I was no storybook knight in armor. How much of what I had done, what I was always ready to do, was nothing more than my unwillingness to live without her?

That I would never know.

"Can we, Dell? Really?"

I kissed her forehead.

It was much too early for Thanksgiving. The holiday, I mean. For what we shared that day, there would never be a date marked on a calendar.

The kitchen table was just the right size for all of us.

Martin and Johnny.

Mack and Bridgette.

MaryLou and Franklin.

Dolly and me.

Rascal even shared his food with Minnie. Probably because the mutt couldn't possibly eat everything that kept getting tossed into his washtub of a dinner bowl.

Dolly loved them all. But when Franklin didn't seem aware of the tears tracking across his cheekbones, she gave Mack a "Stay out of this!" look. Me, she didn't even bother—I knew her a lot better than he ever would.

MaryLou stood up, leaned over, and whispered something about flowers in the giant's ear. They were outside for quite a while. When they came back in, Franklin handed Dolly a bouquet he had picked from her garden.

"I hope you—" he had started, when Dolly said, "Oh, they're perfect!" and pulled his head down to plant a kiss on both cheeks. "That's exactly what this table is missing." Then she wheeled on Johnny and Martin, like *they* should have thought of it themselves.

They all loved Dolly.

I don't guess I loved anyone but her.

But I could feel Luc and Patrice, hovering. So maybe I really *was* back to myself. Not what I was turned into. Not what I'd made a living doing. Into what I was meant to be, truly.

Andrew Vachss is a lawyer who represents children and youths exclusively. His many works include the Burke, Cross, and Aftershock series, numerous stand-alone novels, and three collections of short stories. His works have been translated into twenty languages and have appeared in *Parade, Antaeus, Esquire, Playboy,* and *The New York Times,* among other publications.

The dedicated Web site for Andrew Vachss and his work is www.vachss.com.

A NOTE ON THE TYPE

The text of this book was composed in Melior, a typeface designed by Hermann Zapf and issued in 1952. Born in Nuremberg, Germany, in 1918, Zapf has been a strong influence in printing since 1939. Melior, like Times Roman (another popular twentieth-century typeface), was created specifically for use in newspaper composition. With this functional end in mind, Zapf nonetheless chose to base the proportions of his letterforms on those of the golden section. The result is a typeface of unusual strength and surpassing subtlety.

Typeset by Scribe, Philadelphia, Pennsylvania

Printed and bound by Berryville Graphics, Berryville, Virginia

Designed by Betty Lew